THE CURSE OF THE VAMPIRE

KARL ALEXANDER

PINNACLE BOOKS **NEW YORK**

ACKNOWLEDGMENTS

I'd like to thank the peole of Transylvania for their hospitality. May their traditions and legends endure. I'd also like to thank Mike Hamilburg—a legend in his own right.

THE CURSE OF THE VAMPIRE

Copyright © 1982 by Karl Alexander

An original Pinnacle Books edition, published for the first time anywhere.

First printing, December 1982

ISBN: 0-523-41874-4

Cover Illustration by John Solie

Printed in the United States of America

PINNACLE BOOKS, INC.
1430 Broadway
New York, New York 10018

THE CURSE OF THE
VAMPIRE

For Laura

Prologue

In a village outside Risnov in the Fagaras Mountains of Transylvania, a large, thick man staggered out of a warm tavern and shut the door behind him, stilling the accordion music and the laughter. While he paused to get his bearings, his red-rimmed eyes watered at the sudden chill and his breath came out in funnels of vapor. Then he started forward but after two steps, lurched back against the white stucco. He cursed, emitted a great belch and tasted the sweet plum brandy he'd been drinking since mid-afternoon. Now the moon was high over Mount Timpa; long shadows fell across the village and the valley beyond. The man heard wind in the pines and shivered despite his bulk. His flat nose already hurt with cold.

"Primavara," he muttered with disgust and pulled up his threadbare wool jacket so it covered his balding head. Spring. Once again he launched himself forward, his heavy feet crunching on patches of ice. *How can they call it spring when there is still snow on the ground? When the air is so frigid your skin is brittle? Custom. They always have and they always will,* he supposed. *Yes, it is customary.*

He scowled. Speaking of tradition, he remembered

that tomorrow, April 23, was St. George's Day. Since his given name was Gheorghe, he would have to pick some flowers and tie them on the arch above his gate as a sign that he was serving drinks to all visitors. *At least I can get drunk again,* he thought, climbing into his pony cart and sprawling onto the seat. His mare lifted her head and automatically started for home, hooves clopping on the ancient cobblestones. The man gazed up past the high-pitched roofs at the black sky and saw the stars spin. Spring. He hated it. Years ago in April his wife had taken their life savings and left him for a Gypsy. True, he still had his pigs and his pension, but that was small consolation. He was certain that the villagers knew the whole story and mocked him behind his back. He wished he could leave. He did not want to see spring blooming full on the mountainside once more, reminding him of joys—of sons and daughters—that he did not possess. Why didn't he leave, then? Certainly, it wasn't the state. Official policy encouraged malcontents to emigrate to the west. He frowned and closed his eyes, letting his head loll on the wood. He knew. For centuries his ancestors had lived and died here. Like it or not, he was part of that heritage, and when he strayed too far from the mountains, the valleys, invisible ties brought him back. *Ghosts of the past keep me here,* he thought, *waiting for me to join their legends.*

Then he slept and did not see the sleek, dark brown Dacia sedan ease out of the shadows and follow his cart down the narrow, twisting alleyway. The mare turned onto a dirt lane and left the village proper behind, trotting past great stands of beech and alder that canopied the roadway. After four kilometers, she swung alongside a fence woven from wattle and then stopped by an old wooden gate.

Beyond was a neatly-kept yard and a pleasant house with a new shingled roof instead of the traditional thatch. Dried peppers and onions hung from the eaves, rustling in the wind.

The mare whinnied softly and pawed at the ground, waking the man who pulled himself upright, swayed, then pitched off the cart onto the road. He groaned, slowly got to his feet and brushed the half-frozen mud off his front. When he felt steady enough, he shuffled to the gate, leaned against it and reached for the latch. Suddenly, he stopped and blinked. Something was different.

Wrong.

He stepped back and stared, momentarily confused. As long as he could remember, the carvings on the gate had been representations of horses, chiseled there by some ancestor who foolishly believed that the symbols would protect his house and land. Now the carvings seemed changed. *Am I that drunk or has someone actually done it?* He moved closer, bent down and peered at the gate, fascinated. With a finger, he traced one of the symbols and frowned. A feeling of dread came over him. The horse had been altered into some hideous creature he had never seen before. It wasn't like the carving of the dragon in the village church or any other representation of evil. It had a vaguely human form, only the teeth were exaggerated and the hands resembled claws. Had some cruel neighbor done a caricature of him? No, the carving was too horrible and grotesque. Only who? . . .

A car door clicked shut.

Quickly, the man straightened up, whirled around and stared down the lane, but could see nothing except the black outlines of the trees against the sky. He studied the darkness for a long time, then shrugged and was about to turn away when he heard footfalls moving up the lane. The mare snorted nervously, her ears turning back toward the sound.

"*Cine e venite?*" the man shouted.

There was no response.

"*Cine e venite?*" he cried, his voice thin and fearful now.

As if answering, the footfalls quickened, sounding like the padding of a large cat. The breeze stilled, and the night seemed heavy, the air, pregnant with malevolence. *I must get inside*, the man thought, rapidly losing control of himself.

He turned back to the gate and fumbled at the latch, but his hands were numb with cold and shaking so badly that he couldn't open it. Never had he been so terrified. *The hunting rifle*, he thought, trying to compose himself. *The weapon my grandfather gave me when I was a boy. It's leaning in the corner of the back room next to the fireplace.* He listened again. The footfalls were much closer now, moving even faster, and he knew definitely that someone— something—was coming for him. Moaning, he clawed at the latch, then jerked on the gate. Fear tingled up and down the back of his neck. Finally, the gate opened. He flung it back against the fence and ran for the house, his squat body crossing the yard with remarkable speed. Then he jumped the steps and crashed through the door. He slammed it behind him, dropped the bolt and leaned against it, his chest heaving. After a moment, he felt safer. Bolder. He crept to the window, kneeled on the bench that lined the room and peered outside. Nothing moved; the night was still. *It must be a joke*, he thought. *Of course. The villagers who laugh behind my back are out there. Tomorrow the same ones will be in here drinking my brandy, winking at each other,*

*and telling stories about St. George protecting us
from evil. Bah!*

Suddenly, his mare neighed with alarm, and the
shrillness cut through him, making him weak and
sick. He saw her rear against the harness, then break
into a run and disappear up the lane, the empty cart
careening behind her. A form flitted across the yard,
dancing toward the house. For a second, the man
wondered if he were hallucinating, but the apparition did not vanish. It was real. Panicked, the man
ran into the back room, unable to stop himself from
whimpering. His only thought was the rifle in the
corner, so he didn't bother to turn on the light.
Halfway across the room, his shins hit something
hard and sharp. There was a crash and an explosion
of blue sparks. He fell and rolled, grunting in agony,
his eyes brimming with tears. He had run into the
table that held the television, and now his most
prized possession lay shattered on the floor. It didn't
matter. The rifle. He gritted his teeth, ignored his
pain and got up. He stumbled to the wall, groped
for the ancient weapon and finally found it. When
his trembling hands closed around the cold metal,
he felt relieved and no longer helpless. He released
the safety and cautiously started back for the front
room, his shoes crunching on the shards of glass
from the television. He scowled. *They will pay for
this. The bastards!*

In the doorway, he hesitated, hearing muffled
thumps outside. Still, he went on into the front
room, then gasped, seeing the door buckle as something slammed against it again and again. The heavy
wooden bolt bent and cracked. Snarling noises came
from beyond the door—flat, alien growls that did
not sound human. Astonished, the man backed away,
too frightened to call out. He raised the rifle, aimed

at the door, and waited until the thing on the other side hit it again. Then he fired.

The rifle blew up in his hands.

He screamed, dropped the weapon and staggered back, his hands over his face. Blood streamed between his fingers; he couldn't see. Frantic, he wiped his eyes clear, but the blood kept flowing, and he didn't know if he had been blinded or not. He fell to his knees, crying softly. Then he realized that the thumping had stopped. He held his breath and listened.

Silence.

He exhaled in a hiss and sagged. He was still safe in his house. Alive. Maybe the thing had given up and gone away. Maybe his one shot had miraculously killed the creature despite the rifle exploding in his hands.

Suddenly, he heard glass tinkling at the other end of the house. He moaned and shook his head. No, he was not safe. The thing was coming in the window.

"*Doamne, nu!*" he sobbed, crawling forward, feeling for the rifle. *If only I could see! Please, God, let me see!* When he found the weapon, he scrambled to his feet and brandished it like a club. He heard clattering and grunting in the other room and imagined that the creature had gone berserk and was smashing the fine plates and pottery that adorned the walls. It didn't matter. Nothing mattered except he had to get away. Heart pounding, he scurried to where he thought the door was, only banged into the wall instead, the bench cutting into his bruised shins. The pain was incredible. He hissed low, stopped and forced himself to mentally picture the room. When he thought he had his bearings, he felt his way along the wall and prayed that he was heading toward the door.

There.

His hand touched the bolt, but before he could lift it off, he heard clacking and felt a presence. A hideous warmth. Screaming, he shrank back, wildly swinging the rifle butt in a circle. Suddenly, it was jerked out of his hands and thrown through the window. He heard it break the glass and thud on the ground outside. He couldn't move. He was frozen in that final moment and saw the past with amazing clarity.

Teeth sank into his throat. Something razor sharp tore at his thick girth. As his life slipped away, he remembered wondering about the pain of death while he watched someone else die long ago. Now he knew; it was awful. He supposed he deserved it.

Across the lane high in a beech tree, a cuckoo bird woke up and burst into song.

One

Melanie Ross opened her green eyes, sleepily raised up and noticed the pink glow behind the window curtains of her bedroom. Sunrise. A glance at the clock on the bedside table told her that she still had fifteen minutes before the punctual desk clerk gave her the usual wake-up call, so she flopped back on the huge, canopied bed, determined to think it through. Three weeks earlier, she had flown into Romania from Los Angeles to act in a film and had felt strange ever since. When not working, she sequestered herself in this lavish suite on the top floor of Brasov's finest, the Carpati Hotel, and wondered why. She wasn't ill; the job was going smoothly; there were no problems at home. What was wrong? *I'm protecting myself from something, only I haven't a clue to what it is. I don't have any reason to feel that way, either.*

After all, she'd always wanted to see the country where her grandparents had lived. That was why she accepted the role in the first place. Yet, she hadn't ventured out and explored, even though everyone said the Romanians were charming and ingratiating. She sighed. Maybe that was it. She'd always had a mysterious quality, which made people look twice and think that she was extraordinarily beautiful. And when she was in a quiet, private mood, she didn't want to be stared at, talked to, or disturbed. But for three weeks? She shook her head. No. She wasn't afraid of people. Something else was going on with her. There was an inner voice she heard; a theme of joy and sadness; of caution.

She closed her eyes and let her mind drift farther. *It's not just a voice—it's an entire symphony, and I don't understand it at all. Nothing has changed with me. I love John dearly just as I always have. I adore the boys. I miss my home surrounded by oaks and pines in the Santa Monica Mountains. Still, I'm enjoying my work and doing a good job. I've got that light touch again, which is my best style, even though I could never be a "serious" actress. Everything seems ideal. Too ideal, if you ask me. Am I being pampered to death? Battered by Romanian hospitality? I never did like being treated with kid gloves despite what comes with the occupation. Is that it? Or am I merely losing my mind?*

The telephone rang sharply.

Melanie jumped, then quickly rolled over and answered before it could jangle again. She heard the familiar voice of the desk clerk telling her that the time was seven o'clock. As usual, she asked to have coffee and rolls sent up, thanked him profusely and hung up. Then she lay back and bit her lip in frustration. Damn the telephone! Why did it have to interrupt her?

Suddenly, she sat up, snapped her fingers and laughed with excitement. Sometimes if you can't beat modern technology, you can join it. She grabbed the phone, dialed the international operator and gave the lady her home number. While she waited, she glanced at the clock and made a quick calculation. It was just past nine, the evening before, in California. John would already have the boys in bed and would be relaxing in front of the fireplace, watching television or maybe in his studio, working on a new drawing.

"Hello?"

"John, it's me!" She closed her eyes, imagining she was with him. She could see his broad, content face, his thick torso, his sandy-colored hair with streaks of gray, his big hands with the long fingers of a born artist. Briefly, she recalled their five years together and how far they had come. She knew him well now and he seemed so strong compared to then. She had nurtured his self-confidence like a rare flower. Now it was on the verge of blossoming, and she was proud that she had given him such sustenance. "How are you?"

"I'm doing okay. I've got everything under control and I'm working even though it's slow, but—hey— it's great to hear from you! What's happening?"

"Oh, nothing." She blushed and didn't know what to say right away. "I just felt like calling."

"Honey, you're in Romania!"

A pause.

"Is anything wrong?" he asked, suddenly anxious.

"I don't know that anything's right or wrong, I just—I guess I miss you, that's all."

"I miss you, too."

Another pause.

"Melanie, we've been getting your postcards. What's it really like over there, anyway?"

"I honestly don't know." She laughed sheepishly. "I haven't seen anything yet."

"Come on, sweetheart," he said. "You didn't go over there to crawl inside yourself, you know?"

"I know." She nodded. *This is stupid. He really*

understands me and vice versa. We shouldn't be
this far apart. She sat up very straight. "John?"

"What?"

"Why don't you come over here and we can see
this country together?"

"What about the boys?"

"Bring them with you. They're not learning a
damned thing in that school, anyway."

"You know, that's not a bad idea."

"Of course it isn't! It's a great idea. Okay?"

"See you next week."

"I love you, John," she whispered.

"Me, too."

"*La revedere.*"

"Hey! What's that mean?"

"I'm not sure." She laughed. "But they say it
around here all the time."

After she hung up, she bounded out of bed, stood
on her toes, stretched and felt good. He was coming.
They could take long walks in the park across the
street from the hotel; she could talk to him, and he
would understand even if she didn't. He was coming. They could meander along the narrow streets of
old Brasov hand-in-hand; they wouldn't have to say
anything if they didn't want to. He was coming.
They could just be together, and the music inside her
would become pure melody again. Sweet. Familiar.

She took a quick shower, dressed in jeans, boots,
and a dark-blue sweater, then went to the vanity.
After brushing out her long, dark hair, she inspected
her face critically. On location every morning, the
make-up artist was fond of admiring her and saying
in his broken English that it would be a crime against
God and nature to touch her face with his inferior
cosmetics. She chuckled, wondering if the man were
sincere or just wanted to avoid work. Nevertheless,

she didn't think it was a crime, so she rouged her lips, lined her eyes, and added color to her alabaster complexion.

Satisfied, she went into the suite's living room, where she was greeted with a tray of coffee and rolls, a bouquet of fresh flowers, and the morning edition of *Drum nou* even though she couldn't read a word of Romanian.

Had she been able to, on page three she would've found a rather cryptic account of a grisly murder near a village outside Risnov.

* * *

A half-hour later, Melanie left the hotel in the back of a Zil limousine provided by the production company. While the driver rattled on about association football, she nodded politely and stared out the window. Brasov amazed her. Ancient white buildings with steep, red-tile roofs coexisted with new soviet-style high rises that resembled stacked ice cream sandwiches. Pristine gothic spires and belching smokestacks. The city was crazy—a haphazard mixture of the twentieth century and the Middle Ages. She grinned and for a brief moment felt a kinship with it.

They left Brasov behind and climbed into the mountains, heading south for the resort town of Poiana Brasov, a winter sports center, where the film was shooting. Overhead, Melanie saw a cable car sparkling in the sun, making its first trip of the day to the top of Mount Timpa. The operator waved at them. She waved back, then gazed at the serrated peaks in the distance, still dark and shrouded with fog. The trees. So green and fresh. They were everywhere. *This land is spectacular,* she thought. *It's so lush and beautiful that there has to be something savage at the heart of it. Maybe that's why I'm . . . afraid?*

Just the other side of Mount Timpa, Melanie saw a car on the shoulder of the road with its hood up. A thin man wearing a turtleneck shirt and a leather jacket was hunched over the engine, appearing confused, his blond hair waving in the breeze. He turned toward them, but hesitated when he saw the black limousine. The driver sped right on past, but Melanie leaned forward in her seat.

"Petre, please go back. That man needs help."

"That man is a stranger."

"No." She shook her head vehemently. "I know him from some place."

"As you wish, Mrs. Ross, but it is against my better judgment." He made a U-turn, accelerated back to the disabled car and turned around again.

Melanie wondered why she was acting impulsively, then shook off the apprehension. She pressed a button and the tinted window hissed open. "Can we help?"

The man turned, saw her and made a slight, formal bow. "*Buna dimineata*," he said in a soft, lilting accent.

"I'm sorry. My Romanian is terrible."

He shrugged, a charming smile spreading across his face. "If you speak English here, you are considered sophisticated."

She laughed. "If they only knew, right?"

He chuckled and nodded, then gestured helplessly at his car. "I do not know what happened."

"It won't run?"

"All it does is click like a dying insect."

"We're going as far as Poiana Brasov." She swung the door open.

The man nodded, climbed into the limousine,

eased into the seat and sighed, appreciating the luxury. Petre drove away and once again they were cruising down the highway. An awkward silence. Melanie had second thoughts about giving this man a ride. Finally, they passed a waterfall at the head of a serene valley.

"It is beautiful, no?"

She nodded, glanced at him and quickly looked away. He was a stranger, yet on the back seat they were as close as lovers, and she could smell his heavily-minted breath. She frowned and felt naked. There were no barriers between them—just three feet of heavy, clumsy space. She shifted on the seat, uncomfortable. He seemed familiar.

"Transylvania," he said wistfully. "Everytime I see it, I am captivated."

"You're not from here?" She asked courteously, trying to place him.

"I live in Bucharest now."

"You're working on the film, aren't you?"

"I'm operating the second camera." He smiled nervously. "My name is Mihail Popescu. We met briefly three weeks ago at the start of production."

"Oh, yes."

"I suppose you can say that because of the zoom lens, I have seen a lot of you, but you have seen nothing of me."

His comment was supposed to be humorous, but Melanie didn't see it that way. She considered the remark downright chilling and shuddered. Then she started to protest, but saw that he was looking out the window and took the chance to study him. Blond hair, blue eyes, around thirty-five, pleasant to look at, but not handsome. His face was wrinkled like a jigsaw puzzle. At certain angles, it seemed bent, its tanned features belying an inner despair.

She finally recognized him and scowled. *Yes, of course! He isn't just operating second camera. Between takes, he's the one who's been staring at me all the time!*

Invariably, he would be on the periphery, partially hidden, and when she turned in his direction, he would always look away. She felt stripped bare. *The voyeur syndrome. I suppose I should be flattered. After all, isn't it a compliment?* She shook her head with disgust, moved farther away from him and looked out the window. She couldn't tolerate strangers who took with their eyes. They had no respect for her rights or privacy; worse than that, she always felt they were trying to steal her soul.

"Did you grow up in Romania?" he asked.

"No."

He shrugged and twitched. "You look Romanian."

"I was born and raised in Southern California," she stated coldly. "And ever since I got here, you've been watching me, haven't you?"

Startled, he tensed and paled, his eyes showing fear, then remorse, then embarrassment. "It is not what you think, believe me."

Surprised by the admission, she looked at him.

"You must understand that I meant nothing—" He groped for the right word.

"Carnal?" she suggested drily.

"No, no, I meant nothing at all. It's just that you seemed familiar to me. I thought maybe we had grown up together, but I was afraid to ask."

"I don't think so," she said, her tone softer.

Clearly disappointed, he went on, "When I was a small child, I used to see a girl in church who looked exactly like you. We used to steal smiles from each other during Mass. The one time I got enough courage to go to her house and introduce myself, she wasn't there. I found out her family had gone to America."

"I'm sorry."

"So am I. I'm sorry for that and I'm sorry for offending you. I remain innocent." He turned away and stared out the window.

She raised her eyebrows, glanced at him, then laid her head back on the seat and relaxed. *He could've just denied it. He didn't have to say anything, but I'm glad he did. It's reassuring. It makes me feel better, and I like that.* She smiled, now comfortable in this man's presence. Romania no longer seemed such a beguiling, forbidding place. How could it be when a stranger turned out to be a perfect gentleman? If there were something savage at the heart of this land, certainly it hadn't affected the people she'd met. Suddenly, she realized she felt like her old self again and was completely at ease. The sense of well-being made her grin foolishly.

She did not wonder why.

*   *   *

His car totally forgotten, Mihail Popescu twisted on the seat, agonized, certain that he had made a complete fool out of himself. He couldn't bring himself to look at her again, so he closed his eyes, but that was frustrating, too. He saw her in his mind as he saw her often through the lens. At wide angle, she was standing near a ski run, appearing alone and in need of someone. She seemed frail, yet winsome. Zoom in. Despite the ski clothes, her figure was curvaceous and sensual, and he imagined her nude. Magically, the lens pulled her closer, filling the frame with her head and shoulders. God, she was lovely. Her dark hair, back-lit and sparkling. Bright eyes that were almost asiatic. High cheekbones and a wide mouth with full lips. She was perfect. Except for? the light. Today he would have the assistant put gauze over the lens, which would soften the highlights around her face and give her an ethereal quality. He would even dare to ask the director of photography if they could put up a silk and make the light softer still. A true princess, Melanie Ross deserved to be photographed with such subtleties.

He remembered where he was and groaned under his breath. How could he think about lighting this woman when he had just alienated her forever? He glanced quickly at her and knew that she would haunt him. She was even more beautiful in reality than she was through a camera, and that was why he had been unable to stop staring at her. He grimaced. There were no doubts in his mind. This woman had him. *Mei Doamne!* What was he going to do? If he told her how he felt and she rejected him, then she would complain and the production company would replace him His wife would learn of the incident, and he would be subject to further humiliation. Worst of all, he would never see Melanie Ross again—except, say—in the pages of *Le Monde* or *Paris Match*. The alternative was for him to be as mute as a tree. That was the safe, intelligent thing to do. But what about his feelings? He had never been so captivated by a woman before! He could not stop himself from desiring her Must he take a chance? If he did, he knew that he would jeopardize his career and marriage. True, they might be mediocre, but they were better than nothing. He released a troubled sigh. Weren't they?

Much to his surprise, she spoke to him then, and her voice was pleasant, even gentle. She asked him about his career in cinema, and briefly he described his carefree years at the film institute and then his long apprenticeship, first as a loader, next as an assistant, and now as an operator. Yes, of course he wanted to be a director of photography. They were extraordinary, talented men, head and shoulders above the herd. Which brought him to the subject of his dreams—those elusive, distant images, usually expressed in brief moments of inexplicable behavior. Such as a pick-up football game with the boys in the neighborhood and visions of one-hundred thousand people chanting his name. Such as a gracious conversation with a buxom secretary at the studio—polishing his *savoir faire*, while seducing her with his eyes. Well, suddenly Mihail Popescu's Venus Urania was right beside him—the most unattainable, alluring dream of all. How should he proceed? He thought in terms of his career and blushed. As a technician who flirts with secretaries? Or as a director of photography worthy of a beautiful film actress?

"Everyone wants to be a director of photography."

"Either that or a rock 'n' roll star," she commented ironically.

He did not understand, and there was another awkward silence.

"Have you been enjoying your stay in Romania?" he asked haltingly, finding it difficult to make conversation, chagrined that his charm had deserted him.

She laughed and turned toward him. "Frankly, no."

He groaned with shock, threw up his hands and knew he was overreacting, but could not control himself. "Why not? Is it the film? The crew?"

"No, none of that ever bothers me." She thought, then shrugged. "I guess I just miss my family."

"Your mother and father?"

"My husband and kids."

"Oh." It was just as he feared; she was married. There was no hope. Here, he was—so close to her, it was maddening. Crestfallen, he looked down at his hands.

"Hopefully, they'll join me soon, and the four of us can act like tourists."

"Yes," he said with forced enthusiasm. "Especially in Transylvania."

"I'm looking forward to it."

And then he found himself leaning forward, hands spread, eagerly asking her, "In the meantime if you like, I would be happy to show you our countryside."

She turned away and gazed out her window, considering his offer, but he did not see. Slumped in the seat, he had his hand over his eyes and was moaning softly, not quite believing what he'd just said. How could he have asked? He felt like a buffoon. When he glanced up, though, he was astonished, for he saw her nod slowly, while still looking off.

"Yes," she said. "I think I'd like that. How about next Sunday?"

*   *   *

The week went quickly for Melanie. The role she was playing—an American lady who had come to Romania in search of her real father and gotten involved with terrorists—did not require heavy concentration. She could ease in and out of character at will, and already the director was calling her performance superb. Although being relaxed helped, she knew that her work was going well because she wasn't taking it seriously. Her mind was elsewhere.

On Sunday morning, she was up early, looking

forward to the day. She dressed comfortably in her usual jeans and boots, then chose a loose pastel blouse since the weather looked warm outside. The silk felt cool against her skin, and she liked the way her breasts hung free inside. At the vanity, she dabbed White Shoulders on the nape of her neck, while thinking that the outing in the countryside was really a sensible thing to do. When John and the boys got here, she would already know what was worth seeing and what wasn't. That way she could act as a guide for them. Besides, Mihail Popescu had agreed to take her to the town where her grandparents lived. She blushed, then grinned with excitement. Perhaps she was being a little self-indulgent, but she couldn't remember the last time she'd done something for herself. Usually, she was involved with business or motherhood. Usually, she gave her free time to John and his work, offering encouragement, criticism, and solace. Usually she ignored her own whims of fancy, figuring that if she were happy being a wellspring for her family, she needn't change.

She frowned, suddenly afraid of herself—afraid of those amorphous, innermost feelings she could not identify.

Regardless, she left her suite, walked down the staid hall furnished in abstract gothic and went into the elevator. As the door closed, she felt a sharp twinge of remorse and gulped. *What am I doing going out with a strange man I thought was a voyeur? Jesus. What am I doing going out at all? I've been happily married for five years!* Her ears burned, and she decided to cancel. She'd go back upstairs, call the desk and leave a message for him, saying that she was awfully sorry, but something had come up and she couldn't make it. Only when the elevator doors slid open, she saw that he was there in the lobby, waiting, nervously smoking a cigarette, and delighted to see her. There was no way out. Disgusted with herself, she crossed the large room and greeted him coldly. Confused, he asked if she weren't feeling well, and she replied that she was fine. He nodded once, accepting her indifference as natural and then escorted her out of the hotel, his hand pressed into the small of her back. He talked and gestured exuberantly, very much the typical European male proud to have such a pretty female companion. She found herself smiling and no longer angry. Then she sighed, figuring that she might as well enjoy herself. What harm could come from an excursion into the country?

They took Route 73, the road that led to the medieval town of Bran (now a commune), even though that wasn't their destination. Just to make conversation, she asked him about his car. He smiled and said that it hadn't been a problem at all. Since the production company owned it, they had taken care of the towing and repair costs. "Automobiles are very expensive in Romania. I have been saving up for one for years. At home, I have a bicycle."

Then he was quiet, and she gazed out at the hills—carpeted by evergreens and occasional stands of beech and alder. The sunlight was misty, sometimes creating a mirror effect so that she could not see the land distinctly at all. Only colors. Light greens, dark greens, shades of black beyond the haze.

The highway was not a broad, modern swath like the one to Poiana Brasov. Instead, it snaked its way up the mountains and into patches of fog, twisting back on itself in a series of tight switchbacks. They went through arched tunnels; they crossed stone bridges of Romanesque design that spanned deep gorges; they skirted cliffs, where the road was bordered by low stone walls. Eventually, they came out of the mountains, and through a veil of mist Melanie saw a forested valley far below, dotted with small farms. At the near end nestled against more mountains was a town. The scene resembled a Renaissance landscape, and she hoped the image would stay fresh forever.

Still climbing, they swung around a steep curve. Suddenly, Mihail swore softly and had to brake hard. The road was blocked by a flock of some three-hundred sheep. A shepherd wearing the traditional brown cloak and a wide-brimmed black hat had led them up a mountain slope from the valley. Holding his staff with both hands, he stood at the roadside and gazed impassively at Melanie, his broad face a mystery of wrinkles. She thought he gave her a nod of acknowledgment, but wasn't certain. She could have imagined it. Actually, she could be imagining the entire scene, for the shepherd and his flock seemed out of time.

"Have we stumbled onto a pageant of some kind?"

"What do you mean?" he asked.

"Well?" She laughed ebulliently. "This is the new Romania?"

"Some things have not changed in these mountains for a thousand years. Probably they will never change," he explained. "In the village, there will be a celebration. They have wished the shepherd good luck."

"Go on," she said, fascinated.

"Every spring the farmers place their sheep in the care of one shepherd and he takes them to the highland pastures." He gestured. "Over that ridge there."

"How do you know all this?"

"You said your grandparents were from here."

"Yes."

"Well, you aren't the only one who has—as you say—his roots in these mountains."

When the last of the sheep had crossed and the shepherd waved them past, Mihail drove onward. After negotiating another mile of switchbacks and curves, he stopped, then carefully turned left onto a narrow access road that was so steep he had to drive in first gear.

They wound through a dense forest of spruce and fir and some five-hundred feet up, crested the ridge and started down the other side. Melanie was awestruck. Below her on a shelf of rock with a commanding view of the valley, the town, and the mountains beyond was an ancient castle that rose up like a giant, graystone fist. Semi-circular, it had turrets and towers on either end; spires and a profusion of high-pitched red roofs were in between. The national flag and a tourist ministry pennant fluttered from the highest tower, the *donjon*.

"God," she exclaimed. "Where are we, anyway?"

He smiled. "In Romania, they say that from modern technology to the Middle Ages is but a few miles of mountain road." The road descended into thick groves of trees, where there was little sunlight, then emerged on a meadow. A half-mile away was the castle, magnificent against the sky. After crossing the meadow, they came to an ancient stone gatehouse and wall. In Romanian and other languages, a sign read:

Welcome to the Vladimir Castle
and Feudal Art Museum, Admission
10 Lei
Courtesy of O.N.T.

Where the wall had crumbled, a high fence topped with razor wire had been erected; and in place of the old wooden portcullis was an electric, chain-link gate.

They stopped by the gatehouse and waited. From inside a radio played light classical music. Finally, an elderly caretaker wearing remnants of a World War II uniform shuffled out and approached the car. Mihail paid him the fee. He pressed a button; the gate swung open; he waved them through with a gesture of disinterest.

They parked in the bailey—now a graveled lot—strolled through well-kept gardens of tulips and roses bordered by blossoming cherry trees, then entered the keep. In the rotunda, they were greeted by a tape recording that droned local history and a mildly pleasant guide who added, while admiring Melanie's breasts, that the castle was finished over seven-hundred years ago. Mihail informed the young man that they didn't need his services since he, himself, was already familiar with the place.

He led her along a stone corridor rich in brightly colored carpets that opened onto vast, cold rooms. At first, she was disappointed. The usual glass display cases with objets d'art were everywhere plus the standard suits of armor and arrangements of weaponry, roped off from curious hands. Quiet again, Mihail seemed distracted. Melanie wondered if he were bored and began hurrying past things with only a quick glance or a casual, muted remark. Yet, she was always aware of the official green arrows reminding her where she could and could not go.

After an hour of such exploration, they came to a huge, circular room lit by shafts of colored light, where the sun shone through stained-glass windows. The effect was magical, and Melanie paused in the doorway, delighted. Since they'd trekked up and down so many stairs, she wasn't sure what level they were on, but she guessed they were inside one of the turrets.

"The crown room," he said. "I'm told that the princes retreated here to meditate."

"In such a large space?"

"They did not have small minds."

She laughed. "I guess not." She pointed to a massive oak table and chairs across the room under a shaft of amber light. "Now *that's* a beautiful sight."

"Would you like to sit there for a while?"

"How can we? It's roped off."

He moved the barrier to one side and led her into the room. "It isn't any longer."

"Won't they throw us out if they see us in here?" She whispered, following him across the stone floor.

"Bureaucrats are lazy," he said disdainfully, helping her into a chair. "But should they come this way, believe me, we will hear them before they see us."

Then he sat at the head of the table, produced a flask from his coat pocket and poured them portions of plum brandy, using the silver wine glasses that were part of the table display. He raised his glass. "Forgive me for being so bold." He toasted her. "To Melanie Ross, a princess."

Laughing with surprise, she managed to nod and say, "You're forgiven!" Then she returned the salute and tried the liquor. It was too sweet, but had a musty quality giving it character and age. She tasted it again, smiling at him over her glass, noticing that the light made him appear removed. His features were softened. Indistinct. *How curious,* she thought. *I know he's at the same table with me, but it's like he isn't here. If I didn't know, I'd think I was watching an old movie on TV.*

"You like it?" he asked, meaning the brandy.

"Not bad."

"We call it *tuica*."

"*Tuica?*"

He nodded. "In the village it will be overflowing." He chuckled, then gazed at her. "By the way, I am very happy that you've come with me today."

"I'm enjoying it."

"But you are disappointed by the Vladimir castle."

"This room is marvelous."

"And the rest of it?"

She sighed. "Honestly, it's like a cross between the Smithsonian and Disney World."

His brittle laughter echoed off the stone like scattering pebbles. "It is the communists. They try to make a castle into a museum. Everything is either roped off or locked up." He shook his head with disgust. "All they know are green arrows and red stop signs."

"I wonder what it was like before?"

He stared off, contemplating. Then he turned back to her and leaned forward, his eyes sparkling. "I cannot snap my fingers and make it as it was, but there are places in this castle that haven't changed. The communists don't even know they exist."

"How is that possible?"

He smiled knowingly. "I'll show you."

With a toss of his head, he led her out of the crown room and back down the main corridor. They heard giggles and hoots, went around a turn and encountered a group of children coming the other way. Mihail waited until they had passed, looked in all directions, them pulled Melanie into another room. They hurried across it to an archway, which

opened into a narrow, curving passageway that went
back the other way. Having lost her sense of direction, Melanie looked up and saw that the angle of
the light coming in the high windows was the same
as it had been when she was at the table. That
meant that they were on the same side of the castle—
the one over the cliff. Wait a minute! It suddenly
occurred to her that they could be between the
walls of the turret.

The passageway dead-ended at a wooden door,
which was locked and had a stop sign, now yel-
lowed with age, stapled to it. Mihail took a knife
out of his pocket, jimmied the lock with ease and
pushed on the wood. As if released from below, a
sudden gust of wind caught the door and slammed
it back against the stone wall. The dull thud echoed.
Melanie jumped back, turned and looked behind
her.

"They'll hear us!" she whispered, afraid.

"No, they won't."

She stepped forward, looked, and saw steps that
curved down into darkness. She hesitated.

"Come on," he urged. "Where is your sense of
adventure?"

"After you," she replied.

He shrugged, turned, and casually started down
the steps. She watched him for a moment, then
followed, reasoning that since they were already
off-limits, what difference did it make how far they
went? Besides, Mihail certainly seemed to know
where he was going. As she went down, she counted
the steps. There were sixty of them, and at the
bottom it was so dark she couldn't see her hand in
front of her face. She brushed against damp stone,
recoiled and suddenly was seized with terror. She
rushed forward and collided with Mihail who had

been waiting for her. Gasping, she swore softly. He patted her shoulder reassuringly, then took her arm. They crossed a dirt floor to a door, which he opened.

Sunlight streamed in, and she had to shield her eyes from the glare. Then she blinked and saw that they were in a tiny walled courtyard, dead from years of neglect. In each corner there was a shallow alcove, which seemed purposeless. She looked skyward. The walls went straight up for a hundred feet and the only windows were tiny slits at the top for ventilation. You couldn't see into the courtyard, and, except for a patch of sky, you couldn't see out. *As a matter of fact,* she thought, *this whole place seems purposeless. No wonder it's never used.* Mihail took her arm again and started across the courtyard, but she pulled away, then faced him, hands on her hips.

"Did you used to work here? Is that why you know your way around so well?"

Before replying, he read her face, silently asking for trust. Finally, he said, "I was born here."

"You're joking."

"No. My family used to live in this castle and my ancestors ruled the land. I am a descendant from royalty."

She thought for a moment. "You're a prince, then."

"I suppose I would have been," he said modestly. "But when the communists came to power, they threw us out and made the castle a tourist attraction. I'm surprised they haven't built one of your McDonald's by the front gate."

She laughed with appreciation.

"I love this place." He touched the stone wall where it was warm from the sun. "I come here often." He went to the alcove diagonally across from them, bent down and began counting the stones from the ground up.

Melanie turned in a circle, looked up and shrugged. "I don't understand. What did they use this place for? Was it a cloister?"

"Of sorts."

"What do you mean?"

"Prisoners," he said, straightening up. "They used to exercise prisoners in here."

"Oh." She turned and saw that he had removed a stone from an inside wall of the alcove. "What are you doing?"

"Don't you want to see the dungeon?"

"The dungeon?"

He reached into the hole where the stone had been and pulled a latch. The entire wall swung open without a sound, revealing more steps that led down into the bowels of the castle. Astonished, Melanie shrank back, but her eyes remained fixed on the obscure opening. A dim light emanated from below, which struck her as being strange. Fascinated, she moved closer.

Mihail ran his hand over the stone face of the door. "This was a necessary precaution," he explained impassively. "If invaders were fortunate enough to take the castle, they had the nasty habit of releasing the prisoners so they could butcher their former masters. Aside from winning battles, one way to discourage that practice was to hide the dungeon." He paused and gestured at the entrance. "Shall we?"

"I'm not sure that I want to go down there."

"Why not?" His eyes glittered, challenging her. "You've come this far."

"Really, Mihail. I'm serious."

"*C'est la vie.*" He moved to close the door.

"Wait!" She put her hand to her mouth and continued peering down into the opening. Was that wind or was she hearing voices again? She nodded slowly and glanced at Mihail, then hesitated once more. "Is it safe?"

"Absolutely."

"All right."

He started down the steps. She took a deep breath and followed, muttering about the perils of her curious nature. A dozen steps down, the passageway twisted claustrophobically, and she scowled, wishing for the clarity of a straight flight of stairs. Medieval architects must've worshiped snakes, she mused, as the steps spiraled again. Halfway down the air turned moist and stagnant; the stone walls were wet and slick with fungus. *Snakes?* Moaning, she reached out and grabbed Mihail's coat. She trembled.

He turned. "Would you like to go back?"

"Just get me off these damned steps!"

When they reached the bottom, they came to a door with an iron grate in it. They went through it and suddenly were in a long, cavernous room that had been hacked out of stone centuries before. An explosion of bats stirred up a chalky dust. Melanie shrieked and cowered and held her hands over her head. Mihail remained motionless and calm. Coughing, she finally straighened up, but kept her arms over her head. She just stood there and stared. When the dust settled, she could make out a pit that had traces of lime on the sides. To her left was a wooden wheel used to stretch people. Beyond were two rows of catacombs, where the doomed had awaited torture, death, or perhaps nothing at all. Now, the doors to the cells were open. Mercifully so. In places, the floor was littered with great piles of guano, and Melanie could hear the bats crying, their wings flapping as they settled against the ceiling once again. She shuddered.

"Are you all right?"

She nodded bravely and lowered her hands, having regained her composure. "You might have warned me."

"I'm sorry. I forgot about them. I guess they never bother me."

She looked behind her and discovered where the light was coming from. Vertical slits had been chiseled through the wall to the outside. *The condemned have to breathe, too,* she thought. Then she frowned with puzzlement and moved toward the wall. *What outside?* She wanted to look out one of the slits, but they were impossibly high. Instead, she listened and heard a distant, steady roar that she didn't recognize right away. Eventually, it came to her. The sound was a river flowing through a gorge far below, which meant that the dungeon was *inside* the cliff, with the castle a good fifty feet above it!

That discovery made her feel more confident and adventurous, so she went over to the musty catacombs, pausing to look into the cells and wonder. She was awed by the past of this sorrowful, ancient place. *How many poor souls have been locked up in these holes, listening to others being tortured? Did the screams of agony drive them mad? My God, the futility, the despair, the wretchedness. What could anyone do to deserve such a fate? And how could anyone see this and not be ashamed for the human race? How many have groveled here? How many have been broken here, left to die without a shred of grace or dignity?* Filled with sadness, she began crying. She turned. "Why did you bring me here?" she demanded. "Why?"

There was no answer.

She stopped, listened, then looked in all directions. "Mihail?" She waited. Nothing. "Mihail!"

He was gone.

Intense fear came over her; her skin tingled; she grew cold. Panicked, she ran out of the catacombs, but stumbled and almost fell into the lime pit. For an instant, she gazed down and saw a partially disintegrated skull facing up at her. Heart pounding, she scrambled to her feet and hurried toward the door.

Suddenly, a large bat brushed her face and briefly hung there, flapping its wings. She could feel its velvetlike fur and thought the creature was caught in her hair. Screaming, she frantically pawed at it. When the bat flew away, she fainted onto the dank stone. Glistening in the dim light, a tiny drop of blood formed on her hairline, where the creature had sliced her with its razor-sharp teeth.

She had felt nothing and did not know that she had been bitten.

Two

Mihail was halfway up the steps when he heard her cries. At first, he was puzzled because he thought she had been right behind him. Hadn't they left together? Then he spun around and dashed back down to the dungeon, taking the steps two at a time. He paused in the doorway, saw that she lay crumpled on the floor, and was filled with dread.

"Melanie!"

He raced across the dungeon and disturbed the bats again, but paid them no heed. *Mei Doamne!* Was she dead? "Please, God," he whispered, "don't let her be dead! Please make her be all right! She has done nothing! Please! I will give up my soul for her." Reaching her, he knelt down, grasped her by the shoulders and shook her until she regained consciousness. Her eyes fluttered, then focused on him. Briefly, they showed utter terror before her expression went blank.

"Are you all right?"

He helped her to her feet, and, after taking several deep breaths, she seemed to be fine.

"What happened? I thought you were right behind me!"

She held out her hand and checked to see if it

were shaking. It was steady and she nodded with relief. Then she looked at him and apologized for being so timid. Shamefaced, she explained that a bat had gotten caught in her hair and she must have just fainted. She was okay now. Still, he insisted upon examining her, but could find nothing wrong. "I am sorry. I am so sorry," he said, while taking off his coat. He placed it around her shoulders.

"Let's go now, please, Mihail."

"Of course. Forgive me for bringing you here. I am so sorry. I feel so stupid."

They started up the steps. She tried to go too fast, slipped on the mossy stone and had to grab his hand for support. He helped her recover, and they continued on. When they reached the top of the passageway, he noticed—to his pleasant surprise— that she was still holding his hand. Her flesh was warm against his and her hand fit neatly inside his. He felt as though it belonged there and pulled away reluctantly only so he could close the secret door to the dungeon steps.

They left the castle, drove back over the ridge and continued southwest on Highway 73, dropping down into the valley. Neither spoke. She seemed lost in thought, which was fine with him, for he wouldn't have known what to say. He felt terrible about the incident in the dungeon. Yes, it did mean that she was vulnerable, but he hadn't wanted to find out that way. He would make it up to her. If only she could understand how he felt about her. Perhaps he could show her by making her happy. He suddenly remembered last week when he had been so forlorn, so unsure of himself in the presence of this beautiful woman. Today he was different and so was she. Was it the castle that had infused him with confidence? Or the strange occurrence in the dungeon?

He wasn't sure, but no longer was he nervous about what she would say or do; no longer was he worried about the outcome. There was a sense of inevitability in the air. Still, thank God no harm had come to her. He would have felt eternally guilty.

They crested another hill and below them, about a kilometer off the highway, was the town of Vladimir. Mihail smiled and shuddered with pleasure. The view never failed to impress him. It was like stepping into a landscape by Monet. The town was set back against a mountain, surrounded by lush trees and (so the old ones believed) protected by a river. Wisps of smoke rose from chimneys, indicating roasting food and good company.

Mihail and Melanie crossed an arched stone bridge and entered the burg, the car rattling on the cobblestones. Indeed, there was a celebration. As they inched along the narrow streets, they saw flags and bunting hanging from the balconies. They encountered knots of revelers dressed in traditional peasant garb, ambling along. Mihail was careful to stop for them, and, as the car idled, a young man stuck a wineskin of *tuica* in the window. Mihail took it, drank, passed it back, nodded thanks and drove on, expecting nothing less. This was the day of "Shepherd's Custom," and strangers were welcome here. He grinned. Only he wasn't really a stranger. Even though he had left the castle as a baby and had been raised and educated in Bucharest, he still felt an affinity for the people and the land of his ancestors. He had merely gone away and become a highly skilled professional in order to survive in the new Romania. These were still his people. And as always, on a warm spring day their generosity was overflowing.

They parked in the town square, which had been

taken over by the celebrants. Along the sidewalks and amidst the colonnades the women of Vladimir cooked sausages and prepared *sarmale*, the traditional stuffed cabbages and pork wrapped in grape leaves. Occasionally, the sharp odors of venison broiling on oak coals mingled with the gentler smells. Tables abounded with vegetables and salads. Someone handed Melanie a bottle of wine.

At one end of the square on the steps of the People's Council building, a Gypsy band played, the musicians wearing threadbare black suits and no shoes. A group of men danced a hora, while others clapped along. Mihail pivoted, his arms spread, taking in the festive sights as if the world were his. "It is wonderful," he cried and could not remember when he had been so happy. "Truly wonderful."

Delighted, Melanie rushed forward to get a closer view of the dancers, but Mihail restrained her, bowing courteously, eyes sparkling. "My dear lady, in Romania you don't stride at times like these. You saunter."

She laughed then took a long drink of wine. The band shifted into a more contemporary tune, and a gargantuan man who had drunk a considerable amount of *tuica* approached Melanie, said something to her and waited for a response.

She turned to Mihail. "What did he say?"

"He complimented you on your beauty."

She blushed and looked down. When she remembered the Romanian phrase for thank you, she said to the man, *"Multumesc."*

He said something else to her, his sweating face kind, but intense.

Once again, she turned to Mihail, eyebrows raised.

"He just asked for your hand in marriage."

Melanie was speechless. The man exploded with laughter, adorned her with a headdress of flowers, then pulled her out into the square and began dancing.

Mihail watched them, chuckling at the ineptitude of the heavy peasant. Later, in the evening when the music was slower and more romantic, he would dance with Melanie Ross. He could already feel her next to him. She would be so close he could smell her perfume. The thought made his knees weak. Suddenly, he felt a presence and slowly turned. An old man was behind him frowning suspiciously. He returned the old man's stare, then snorted with disgust and moved off to find a place to eat. The encounter was unsettling because he did not know why the old man had looked at him that way.

*   *   *

Breathless, Melanie refused a dozen offers for the next dance and ran laughing from the square, quite giddy, quite free. *So this is where my grandparents were from. I can see why they loved it and hated to leave. Now I understand why their eyes always sparkled when they reminisced.* She strolled along the perimeter of the square, half-looking for Mihail, but not anxiously so. She was ecstatic just to be by herself in a crowd where no one thought she was anything more or less than a welcome stranger. She paused and gazed past the dancers at a statue, surrounded by an oval garden of flowers and small trees. She smiled. A stone likeness in the midst of a celebration. The image was joyful and slightly religious. Intrigued, she headed for the statue, but ran into Mihail.

He laughed. "We've got to stop meeting like this."

"Oh!" she said. "There you are."

"Are you hungry?"

Reminded of all the delicious smells, her mouth watered, and she nodded eagerly. He took her down a side street lined with buildings now completely in shade. At a large table under an awning, they found two places and dined on *sarmale*, sausages, and corn, washing it down with wine and then *tuica*. Melanie found herself chattering about how marvelous everything tasted until she realized that she was slightly tipsy and everyone else at the table was listening to her politely, not understanding one word of her English. She blushed, then fell silent. Mihail, meanwhile, had gotten into an argument with a party member about collective farming.

When the sun had dropped below the tree line and streaks of golden light shone across the town, Melanie left the table and went to the statue in the square. She saw a tall, graceful figure carved from black granite. It was a woman who stood there, with hair that flowed over her shoulders into the outlines of a loose garment. The woman stared straight ahead, yet had her arms outstretched and her hands turned skyward. The pose was one of heroism, then supplication. Melanie gazed at the sculpture, wondering what it was about.

"It was erected in nineteen-thirteen," said Mihail, appearing by her side.

"Who is it?"

"Veronica Preda," he replied, then translated the legend etched into the pedestal base. "She was a heroine who lived from thirteen thirty-eight to thirteen sixty-four. She saved the villagers from a massacre by warning them of a band of Szeklers who were about to raid the village. Later, she was accused of practicing witchcraft and was burned at the stake."

"How strange."

"Not really. You see, Romanian history is full of ironies, many of them cruel. They say that if she hadn't been a witch, she never would've known the Szeklers were coming."

"But why kill her?"

He shrugged. "Witchcraft was evil, wasn't it?"

She frowned and looked up at the statue again, feeling the same empathy that she had earlier in the dungeon. *You poor lady. You poor, dumb creature. If only you'd kept your mouth shut. You were ... twenty-six. My age.* She shuddered. *What a horrible thought—to die at twenty-six against your will, thinking that there must be so much more you will never experience. Veronica Preda, my heart goes out to you. You saved them and they condemned you.*

But Melanie didn't want to feel sad right now. She was having such a good time. So she insisted that they have more *tuica* in the twilight haze. And when the colored lights shone over the square, she danced with Mihail under the moon and stars. Soft in his arms, she closed her eyes and let her head fall back. The music. A cool breeze. Sweet.

Now they were dancing on the other side of the square in the shadows of the colonnades behind the statue, where the lovers were. He put both arms around her and held her close. Feeling warm and comfortable, she placed her head on his chest. They twirled. She looked up at him and smiled.

He kissed her.

How nice, she thought at first. How romantic. What a perfect way to end an evening. She'd forgotten. The kiss grew more intense, and she found herself responding without hesitation. Suddenly, his hands fumbled under her blouse, coming up quick and hot against her breasts. She pushed away and slapped him hard.

"No!" she said, shaking her head. "You have no right to do that!"

*   *   *

For a moment, Mihail just stood there and watched her briskly walk across the town square. His face burned where she had struck him, and he could not believe what he had just done. How could he have behaved like a dirty teen-aged boy? How could he have lost control? This woman had made him a madman! Then he was following her, mouthing apologies, but she did not turn around. He caught up to her at the car. She climbed inside and slammed the door. He shrugged for the benefit of anyone who was interested, then got in, too, and they drove off toward Brasov. He had to hold the steering wheel tightly to keep his hands from shaking.

"I-I am sorry for being a pig," he whispered. "If it means anything, I have never done that before."

She did not respond.

As the car climbed out of the valley into the mountains, his embarrassment subsided. The feel, the taste of the kiss lingered, and he could think of nothing else. The moment had had such passion and bliss; he hadn't known that he could be aroused so intensely. True, he had been violently rejected, but for a few seconds, she had desired him. She had accepted him. He had felt her melt against him, her mouth sweet and liquid. That was enough to make him ecstatic. And there would be other times. He just knew.

Near Mount Timpa, they encountered a storm. At first, the rain was gentle, but soon was coming down in sheets making it hard to see the road. Mihail slowed down and strained to see. Lightning struck, and in the blue flash he saw trees bent by the wind and rain. Then thunder rolled by, the shock buffeting the car. He heard Melanie breathe in sharply and glanced at her. The next electric flash was very close, and her eyes widened with terror. Strangely, he was calm now and drove mechanically; yet, he was amazed by the lightning, which kept hitting all around them; he had never seen it like that before. Perhaps it was a sign, he thought. A message from the Fagaras Mountains. . . . The intensity of the storm. The danger. The sudden violence. A gentle rain, even. This, he felt, was how it would be between them. He wondered if she was listening, if she knew what was going on. Pray God, she must.

At the Carpati, Mihail let her out of the car and whispered good night. She nodded formally for the sake of appearances, politely thanked him for the day, and went into the hotel. He watched her leave, then had to laugh, for in the distance there was one last flash of lightning and roll of thunder.

For Mihail Popescu, a good Romanian, the Transylvanian weather had played a coda.

* * *

On location the next day, Melanie avoided Mihail. She didn't catch him staring at her, either, although she did notice that it was taking longer than usual for the second camera to set up. For the first time in her career, she complained. The director listened patiently, then—much to her horror—told her not very tactfully that *she* was to blame for the delays. Surely Mrs. Ross must have her reasons, he said in essence, but as a director he was certain that if she stopped vamping to the camera, her close-ups would be more in character and they could move on.

Shocked, Melanie went through the rest of the day in a fog. She couldn't believe what the director had told her and found herself blushing constantly. *Am I so transparent that others can see feelings inside me I haven't identified yet?* Her lips still tingled. *Why did that man have to kiss me? Do I want him to do it again?* She scowled and shook her head. *Perish the thought.*

After they were finished shooting, Melanie hurried to her limousine, settled back in the seat and tried to relax. As she was driven to the hotel, she stared out the window at the trees and let her mind just drift. *I was petulant today. I had no reason to complain. One of the first things I learned about this crazy business was never let your personal life affect your work. Well, I've done it now.* She nodded. *Maybe I'm finally taking myself too seriously. Maybe it's finally catching up with me because I never really paid any dues. Acting. It's not a game any more. I can't laugh. I have no perspective. Jesus. I don't have any reason to be shitty to anyone! A suite in the best hotel in Eastern Europe. A limousine at my disposal. The star treatment when I'm no star. Maybe that's it. After all, what normal person ever heard of fresh flowers with your morning coffee or black caviar at lunch?* She sighed. *And now a goddamned Romanian camera operator stirs me up inside. At least I was strong enough to say no to that.* She looked out the window and frowned.

Then why can't I put him out of my mind?

Back at the hotel, she stopped at the desk for her key, and the clerk gave her a message which said, "Please call. Love, John." She carefully folded the piece of paper around her key so she wouldn't forget, then headed for the elevator. *Forget? What's*

*happening to me? How could I possibly forget to
call home?*

Once in her suite, she rushed for the telephone,
but suddenly stopped and checked the time. In California, it was eighty-thirty in the morning, and John
would have taken the boys to school.

She went into the bathroom, stood under a hot
shower, and tried to think it through. Granted, she'd
had an extremely good time with Mihail on Sunday,
but so what? What was one day? How could anyone
appear less than intriguing with props like a castle
and a town celebration? In reality, the man was
ordinary, despite his charm. Besides, she had only
desired him for a fleeting moment. The fascination
would pass. If she pursued it, then she would lose
her integrity. If she allowed anything to develop,
then she would live to regret it. Pure and simple,
her future, her well being lay with John and the
boys. She had sacrificed for them and they had
done the same for her. There was no higher form of
commitment.

Suddenly, she began crying. She couldn't help it.
Strong, sensuous images of Mihail Popescu stayed
in her mind, and she couldn't shake them. The
harder she tried, the more vivid the images became.

She took dinner in her room and cried all the way
through that, too—frustrated that she couldn't control her thought processes. Baffled, she felt manipulated by an unseen force that was going to make her
do things she did not want to do. Disconnected and
horrified, she knew she was powerless to stop what
the immediate future held in store. The events, whatever they were, seemed hopelessly predestined.

At ten-thirty her time—when she figured John
would be home having lunch—she went to the telephone like an automaton and placed the call.

"Hello?" He sounded comfortable and happy.

"John, it's me."

"Hey, you got my message. Great! I had a feeling you'd call about now. Listen, I just wanted to tell you that I got our visas and made reservations." He paused, chuckling. "God, Romanians are weird! They all sound like Bela Lugosi doing Count Dracula. Are they that way over there, too?"

"You get used to it."

"Well, anyway, we have to change planes in Rome, but we should get into Bucharest Friday afternoon. Can you meet us?"

"John—"

"I gotta tell you, honey, the boys are really looking forward to this."

"John—" She started to choke up.

"Melanie, what's wrong?"

"No matter what happens, I love you very much, okay? You must understand that."

"Me too, but what's the matter?"

"I don't want you to come, John."

A long pause. Static clicked and rattled and buzzed over 7,000 miles of line and cable.

"I don't understand," he said flatly.

"I just don't want you to come!" Then her voice broke and she had to put her hand over the mouthpiece so he wouldn't hear her crying.

"What's wrong?"

"Nothing," she managed to reply.

"*Nothing?* Melanie, what the hell's going on?"

She tried to tell him then, but she couldn't because she didn't understand, either. She could not explain what she didn't know. Instead, she grasped for words and phrases—anything to fill the void. "It's not right, John," she whispered. "It's not a good time. I'm not well."

"What's the matter with you?" He asked, suddenly full of concern.

"I don't know."

"Jesus. Have you seen a doctor?"

"I'm going to."

"Promise me you will."

"I will."

"You'll call me and let me know what he says?"

"Yes."

"Listen, if I could get someone to look after the boys and come on over, I'd take care of you."

"No. You've got your work, and I'm almost finished here."

"Well . . . shit." He sounded disappointed. Deflated. "I'll be thinking about you, honey. Please take care of yourself."

"I will. I love you."

After she hung up, she collapsed onto the bed, sobbing. She cried until the grief had left her empty and then just lay there, staring at the canopy over her bed. She had never committed an act of treachery before; she hadn't known herself capable.

An hour passed and she began feeling restless. She crossed and recrossed her legs, rolled over several times, chewed on her hair. Warmth enveloped her body, but her mind was blank. She reached for the telephone again, this time to call the desk and discreetly ask for some information.

* * *

Depressed, Mihail sat in his room, flipping through a copy of the *American Cinematographer*, which he'd already read a half-dozen times. Since Romanian television signed off at 10:30 P.M., and it was too late to go out, there was nothing else to do. All evening long he had been looking for something other than Melanie Ross to occupy his thoughts. Visions of her tormented him and made him morose. Unlike the day before when he was certain that she desired him, now he was convinced that she wanted nothing to do with him. He frowned— helpless on an emotional roller coaster.

With a sigh, he supposed he should just go to bed, but for the past month he hadn't been sleeping well. Maybe it was those pills the doctor in Timisoara had given him for the migraine headaches. Except lately he had been forgetting to take them. He cursed his intermittent lapses of memory. Ever since he had become infatuated with Melanie Ross, he hadn't been able to remember the simplest tasks. Like telephoning his wife, for example. Why, just this evening she had called him to complain that he was always gone and didn't care for her any more. He shook his head and felt guilty, realizing that she was absolutely right, no matter how vehemently he might deny her charges. He stared off, his jaw slack, muttering under his breath, "What am I going to do about my marriage? Regardless of what happens, it will never be the same."

He felt a dull throb behind his temples. Still talking to himself, he got up from his chair, went into the bathroom and got the pills. While searching for a glass, he noticed the bottle of Kentucky bourbon given him by the American director because the first three weeks' dailies had been so good. He had forgotten to try it. Setting the pills down on the dresser, he held up the bottle and attempted futilely to pronounce "Kentucky." Failing that, he shrugged, uncapped the liquor, poured a glassful and took a large swallow.

"*Mei Doamne!*" he gasped. "This stuff they call bourbon certainly has none of the subtleties of, say, a fine Moldavian wine." Still, it made him feel warm, and lately, he had been so cold. He took another drink.

Knocking.

He spun around and stared at the door, frowning and blinking. Who could that be? It was almost midnight. Was there an emergency of some kind? He unlocked the door and opened it.

Melanie Ross stood before him, looking distraught and not at all beautiful. Her hair was stringy and messy. She pushed it to the sides, revealing her tear-stained face. Astonished, he stepped back. She came into the room and closed the door, her eyes intense, never leaving his face.

"Would you—would you like a drink?" He asked awkwardly.

"No." She took a deep breath. "I'd like to know what it is you've done to me."

Puzzled, he grinned weakly and didn't know what to say. What could she possibly mean? Except for his crude attempts in the town square, he had been a model of decorum! No one had shared his thoughts, and certainly she couldn't read his mind. Yet she was here in his room. He couldn't believe it. With a trembling hand, he poured himself more whiskey and drank it in one gulp because he imagined that was how an American male would act in a similar situation. The liquor burned, and his eyes watered. "I have done nothing to you."

She gestured at herself. "Then why am I like *this?*"

"Quite honestly, I don't know."

"You have poisoned me."

"That is absurd!"

"You've used some psychological, hypnotic trick, haven't you?"

His eyes were wide. "I don't understand what you're talking about."

"Mihail Popescu, I don't want to have a damned thing to do with you," she cried. "But I can't stop thinking about you!"

He spread his hands. "And you say that is my fault?"

"Yes," she replied forcefully.

"But why?"

"Because this has never happened to me before!"

Bewildered, he shrugged, then said innocently, "I-I apologize for being myself. No matter what you think, I have no mystical powers. I have no hold over you. I would not want it to be that way between us."

"But I love my husband," she hissed.

"I am sorry for you."

"You won't admit it, then?"

"I have nothing to confess."

"Very well." Her eyes narrowed and she put her hands on her hips. "Then let me warn you. I'm stronger than you. I won't succumb." She turned to leave.

"Please, wait!" He caught her shoulder. She spun around to slap him, but suddenly stopped in mid-swing and studied him, her lips parted, chest rising and falling with her breathing. Then she stepped into his arms and kissed him, emitting soft moans of release. Astonished, he thanked God for his good fortune and returned the kiss, while imagining his mind was inside hers. He was tired of being detached. So tired. He held her tighter. Closer. He couldn't breathe. It didn't matter.

Gasping, she pushed away, and he assumed that he had been rejected once again. He started to reach for the whiskey, but stopped when he saw her take off her clothes, put them on the chair, then turn to him. Head bowed, she stood motionless like an offering. He gazed at her, comparing the reality of her body to his expectations. Her breasts, her curves, the willowy lines—nothing surprised him except for the skin. It was so remarkably white that for a moment he thought she was an apparition. With fumbling hands, he hurried to undress, afraid that she would change her mind.

She didn't.

Trancelike, she came to him. They embraced and kissed again, both shuddering at the touch of flesh against flesh. Their bodies fit well together; in such a familiar way that he was surprised it was their first time. He thought vaguely that he must have made love to her in his dreams, and was embarrassed that he did not remember.

Later, they lay next to each other on the bed, but were not touching. She was rolled into a ball, whereas he was stretched out on his back, hands beneath his head, looking at the ceiling. Thoroughly pleased, he sighed and could not stop smiling. The experience had left him humble. Eternally grateful. He was surprised that he felt no guilt. Only peace and a oneness with all things.

He played the scene back in his mind, relishing the sensations, the memory. Actually, he was amazed that it had happened in the first place, then awestruck that it had been so perfect, so . . . celestial. With his wife, Ioana, sex was mechanical, even dull. Over the years, he had accepted that as reality, always slightly disappointed that it had never been more. Yet, like it or not, they were two ordinary people with an average life. He had never considered infidelity before, not wanting others to discover that he was commonplace.

Just then he realized that he would never be ordinary again. Melanie Ross, an exotically beautiful American film actress, had come to him. She was beside him now, peaceful and content. Minutes ago, she had been moving underneath him, her fingernails in his back, calling his name. If he were good enough for her, then he was good enough for anyone. For anything. No longer need he suppress his charm for fear of offending a superior. No longer need he be meek and mild. No longer need he accept obscurity, mediocrity, the average, the usual, the humdrum. He half-rose, his eyes widening as the implications registered in his mind. *Mei Doamne!* He didn't have to laugh at his dreams any more! He had just surpassed his wildest fantasy! He fell back on the bed, grinning. The world was finally changing for him. His star was on the rise. Before Melanie Ross, he had been blind to his own potential. No longer. *Finis.*

Wait a minute! If he was good enough for her, then he was good enough for America, too! He had always wanted to escape to that distant land of plenty, but had never had the courage to take a chance. He had chosen to bide his time here in Romania rather than pursue impossible dreams; but that was not to say he was leading a safe existence with predictable outcomes. For example, he had no guarantee that he would become a director of photography despite his talent and knowledge. Why should he worry about it, then? Why not go to America, work there and become famous? Expatriate European filmmakers have a certain mystique— they are loved and worshiped! The enormity of such an idea made his gasp, except his thoughts were coming too fast and furious. He frowned and shook his head, chastising himself for grandiose, romantic

visions. Better he should attend to this ghostlike
queen on the bed next to him than entertain notions
of instant fame in the opulent West.

"Melanie, *mei amora?*" he whispered.

"Yes?"

"Thank you." He caressed her flank. "Thank you
for making me something special."

She turned over, read his face, then nodded once.
He reached for her, and she slid into his arms.

*   *   *

When Melanie left Mihail's room, she felt used
and dirty. Burning with shame, she took the elevator up to her suite and walked in just in time to
answer the desk clerk's wake-up call. Then she went
into the bathroom and showered, washing her body
obsessively. She scrubbed until her skin glowed red
and hurt to the touch. In places, she made herself
raw.

Later, when she was dressed and at her vanity,
she took one look at her ravaged face and turned
away. *The makeup man will earn his money today,*
she told herself. *If he can stand to look at me.* Filled
with self-loathing, she went into the living room for
her usual breakfast, but just the sight of the steaming coffee and hot rolls on the tray made her stomach churn. She left the suite, walking briskly, even
though there was no real hurry. In the elevator, she
realized that she was trying to leave herself behind.
*If only it were possible. If only I could discard my
used body. If only I could be worthy again. If only
my flesh were innocent.* She sighed. *I hope I feel
better tomorrow. Time heals all wounds, I suppose.
And, if I were destined to have an affair, better to
get it over and done with. Now I can put it behind
me, hurry up and finish this movie and then go*

home. I've heard that every married person gets curious and sleeps with someone else, so I guess I'm normal. Except for me the first time is going to be the only time.

But it wasn't.

Although she never talked to him or hardly even looked at him, Melanie was compelled to keep the late night rendezvous with Mihail. She needed him to touch her, to fill her. In her presence, he seemed transformed. There was an aura about him, a power she did not comprehend because others were not affected by it. She was convinced that he had brainwashed her. Unfortunately, she could think of no clues. She even searched his room on one occasion, but found nothing secretive other than a copy of *An Immigrant's Guide to the United States*.

Remorse settled over her like a dull ache; she became used to it and welcomed it as a way to cloak her sullied character. She felt dead inside and rarely smiled. Sometimes at work when she had to deliver speeches with a moral bent, she wondered how she could do it since she was so totally deficient in spirit. Yet, her readings were always strong and full of conviction. If nothing else, she knew then that she really was a good actress. That was no small or easy irony.

Melanie sleepwalked through the rest of the film, and everyone thought her performance was brilliant. She didn't know and she didn't care. Her only show of genuine emotion was at the end of the principal photography when she was so grateful she could finally go home, she kissed everyone good-bye. Except Mihail. Her nightmare was over.

She took a plane from Bucharest to Vienna, where she bought cuckoo clocks for the boys and a new quartz watch for John. Then she boarded a direct flight to Los Angeles and settled back into the plush first-class seat, provided with a tray of *hors d'oeuvres* and a bottle of champagne that for once was not Romanian. After two glasses, Europe was behind her, and the hardness that she had built up in such a short period of time dissolved. Thankful that no one was seated next to her, she turned her face to the window and sobbed.

She prayed that her life would not change; she hoped that John would still have the same feelings for her, even though she did not deserve his love. How long would it be before she could forget, she wondered. Years? Once again, the guilt washed over her, making her tense. She shuddered. What insidious things would that do to her? To her family? Still crying, she shook her head in frustration, her face twisted and agonized. *What could have possessed me?*

She fell back into the seat, searching for an answer, as she had done so often in the recent past. Suddenly, she groaned, realizing that if she had to do it all over again, she still would have had an affair with Mihail Popescu.

*   *   *

Los Angeles International Airport.

John Ross stood inside the Pan American Airlines terminal and watched a steady rainfall through the windows. His boys, Mark, four, and Todd, three, were on either side of him, holding his hands and asking him questions about the storm he could not answer. He knew nothing about weather—least of all why it would rain in the middle of May. Yes, he could draw the best airplanes in the whole world, though, and some day he'd paint some on the walls of their room. They looked up at him and grinned mischievously.

As it always did, the approaching whine of jet engines took him back to Tan Son Nut airport during the fall of Saigon. He was a frightened nineteen-year-old marine then, waiting for evacuation, when an NVA rocket attack hit the terminal. Miraculously, he survived, although the incident still made him nervous. Needless to say, he did not like airports. They made him uncomfortable.

Pleasanter memories were about school and becoming an artist. During that time, he had met, loved, and married Melanie. His life was secure now. Finally. Before, he had been an orphan, a state of being he wouldn't wish on anyone. He automatically squeezed the small, soft hands of his sons, fiercely proud that despite his own problems and insecurities he had already given them more than he had ever had. And he would continue to do so.

The loudspeaker announced the arrival of the flight from Vienna. He grinned. Melanie—home safe and sound. Beautiful. Actually, he had done all right since she'd been gone. The house was together and the kids were fine. No major illnesses or injuries. Tiberon, the old white cat with the gray tail was fat and happy, too. Melanie had owned Tiberon since she was a teen-ager, and John was always afraid that the cat would die when she was away. Not this time. He'd even managed to finish another series of drawings for a show in the fall.

A *small* show. He grimaced. A *small* show for a man with a *small* reputation. Maybe someday that would be different. Except now it was of no importance. None whatsoever. Melanie was home, thank God, so why should he even dredge it up? He nodded vehemently, tried to shake himself loose, but couldn't. Ever since she had told him she wasn't well and that he and the kids shouldn't come to Romania, he had been worried and unable to relax. Something had happened to her over there—something she hadn't discussed on the phone. He was a patient and generous man, though. He would wait until she told him and hope that everything would be all right.

When she came into the terminal, after passing through customs, he could tell that she was drained and tired. His heart went out to her instantly. They embraced and kissed, while Mark and Todd clung to their mother's legs.

"I'm really glad to see you," she whispered, then kissed him again.

He smiled and was immensely relieved. It was obvious she still loved him. Nothing had changed. Why had he been so paranoid? So worried? Her body felt the same against him. There was no reticence about her whatsoever. "Let's go home. You look like you could use some rest."

She nodded, then began chatting to the boys as they walked toward the baggage concourse.

Later—after the boys had been put to bed—John built a fire upstairs in the den, where they liked to share moments alone. The room had a small deck with a view of the mountains and the trees, and sometimes they just took in the serenity and did not need to have any conversation. He straightened up, looked around, saw that the room was dusty, then realized he hadn't used the space since Melanie had been gone. He smiled sheepishly. There hadn't been any reason to.

She entered the den, carrying a bottle of wine and two glasses, looking refreshed, having showered and changed. He wondered why she hadn't just put on her robe, but made nothing of it. He knew that it took awhile for two people to get familiar if they had been separated, no matter how intimate they had been before. She poured them wine. They sat close together on the old sofa and stared into the fire. The oak log burned sedately, whereas the pine underneath crackled and hissed.

"Nice," she said.

"Takes you back," he commented quietly.

She dropped her head back on the sofa, closed her eyes and smiled. "Good times."

He looked at her, while tracing the outline of her face with his finger. Her beauty never failed to amaze him. Sometimes he was even humbled by it, although he was wise enough to never take it as more than appearance. The real Melanie was much more difficult to fathom. But how could he describe what can't be seen? Qualities such as intelligence? Sensitivity? Talent? He often wished he could paint her, but everytime she offered to sit for a portrait, he declined, saying he wasn't good enough yet. Still, he wondered how he would approach it. He shook his head slightly. He didn't know. Forcing a smile, he stroked her hair. "Missed you."

"Missed you, too."

"Tough job?"

"Not really. Could've been a hell of a lot worse." Her voice grew tense. "But I wouldn't want to go through it again."

"Well, it's over. You can stay home for a while and get loose."

She smiled again. "Definitely." A pause. "When can I see your new stuff?"

"Tomorrow."

"I'll bet it's good."

"I don't know. I guess I think something's missing."

"Why?"

"There usually is, isn't there?"

She reached out and found his hand. "Don't."

Rather than argue with her, he rolled his head back and forth on the sofa and said nothing. Now was not a good time for that discussion. She always insisted that his work was much better than he thought it was. In his opinion, he had always created what was expected and accepted—never anything startling or fresh. Ever since art school, he had done pen and ink drawings of houses and rooms. The works were lavish, meticulous, yet impressionistic. Some considered them very chic and representative of the 1980s. As a result, he had a small, obscure following—enough for a critic to say, "Oh, yes, I've seen his work," if his name happened to come up during conversation.

Except the houses and rooms he drew were always empty. Try as he might, he couldn't bring himself to put people into his work and make it look as though they belonged there. The block was doubly frustrating because he knew that until he broke through, his art would never be great or even very good. He assumed his problem stemmed from a deep-seated lack of self-worth—the very same set of emotions that stopped him from painting Melanie. But he didn't want to think of that right now. Why ruin the evening before it had a chance?

The cat came into the room and sniffed the air, its tail twitching at half-mast. Glancing up, John thought it would saunter over to the sofa, give him a look of disdain, then jump into Melanie's lap and settle down for the duration. Instead, it yowled once, turned, and trotted off.

"C'mere, Tiberon," she said, without opening her eyes.

"He left."

"He's got a new friend?"

"Not that I know of."

"Has he been strange lately?"

"He's always been strange."

She nodded and drifted off into a different place. It was a familiar enough gesture, but seemed uncharacteristic to him because they hadn't seen each other in six weeks.

"You never called and told me what the doctor said."

"I didn't see a doctor."

"You said you weren't well."

She turned and looked at him. There was concern and anguish in her eyes. "You didn't worry, I hope."

"I assumed you were okay because the next time we talked, you didn't say anything, but, hell, yes, I've been worried."

"John." Her voice trembled. "I'm sorry. I'll make it up to you, I promise!"

"Hey, it's okay, so don't make a big deal out of it. I just love you and I want to make sure you're all right."

"I'm fine," she insisted, sounding almost frightened. "Really!"

"You're sure?"

She nodded anxiously, then tried to make light of it. "A few days around here and I'll be the same old bitchy me you were so glad to get rid of six weeks ago."

"Never."

She kissed him, then, full and with fervor, and he was aroused quickly. When they broke apart, he studied her, silently asking if the time was right. She gazed back, gulped and nodded once. They both stood and began undressing. She seemed nervous.

They'd done this a thousand times. What the hell would she nervous about, he wondered. He tossed pillows from the sofa onto the floor in front of the fireplace, then knelt on them and waited for her. When she came to him and he touched her, he was surprised because she was trembling. But his own desire was so intense that he didn't think to stop and ask her what was wrong. Instead, he rolled her down onto the pillows and pushed inside her.

"Hello again," he whispered.

"Hello yourself."

*   *   *

Melanie had slid partially off the pillows after they were finished. Now she basked in the warmth of the fire and John's love, not thinking. Her skin tingled pleasantly; she felt perfect. *My life is going to be normal again, thank God.*

John had been surprised that she had made love to him with such passion. She hadn't expected it, either, but now it made sense. She wanted to forget Mihail Popescu forever; she wanted to eradicate the fascination she'd had for him. Passionate sex with John seemed like a way to cleanse herself. *Yes, I am purged.*

When she turned to kiss John again, she saw that he had fallen asleep. She gazed at him, smiling softly, happy to be a part of this man's life. Never again did she want the terror, the compulsion of an infidelity. *Never again.*

Suddenly, she felt a twinge of sickness. Thinking that she'd had too much wine, she rolled onto her back and waited for the sensation to pass.

It didn't.

Instead, she became dizzy and waves of nausea overcame her. Moaning, she rolled into a ball, but the discomfort would not pass. She couldn't stand it. Sweating now, she scrambled up, ran across the room, opened the glass door and went out onto the deck. She grasped the railing and leaned over, expecting to vomit. Nothing happened. Except she got used to the nausea. Curiously, it did not go away, and she just stood there in the moist chill, shuddering on the edge of the sensation. After a while, it seemed natural—like a regularly twitching muscle, a tic or a heartbeat, even. Then she began pacing restlessly, the wood creaking under her feet, her nude body white against the black sky. In vain, she looked for a moon, but couldn't see even a sliver. She wished for the moon right now—it was cold and awesome, shining so that one could explore the darkness in one's soul. She loved the moon.

Just as she hated herself.

She stood and gasped at the revelation. Was it true? She resumed pacing, shrugging nervously. She supposed that there was much to hate about herself. She had deceived John and violated his trust by sleeping with another man. She didn't have the courage to tell him what she had done, either, and she knew that such an admission was unlikely but not because she was afraid of upsetting him. Rather, she didn't want to inconvenience herself. That was it, wasn't it? And there were other examples of her despicable nature, too. She didn't spend enough time with her children. She—

Gnashing her teeth now, Melanie nodded as she moved mechanically back and forth. *I suppose I don't really have any moral fiber. I lie and cheat and then carry on like I'm such a respectable, good, loving, caring woman. Face it, I am a hypocrite! The only reason I've had an easy time with my life is that people think I'm beautiful. Well, I'm not. Deep down I've always been disgusting and evil.* She dug her fingernails into her thighs and slowly pulled upward, lacerating her flesh. Blood ran down her legs. Next, she clawed her sides, her breasts, and finally, her face. She relished the pain and stretched her arms out to the night. *I deserve all the darkness in the sky, for I am dead in spirit.*

Grief welled up inside her and she began crying, yet was vaguely detached from the outburst. (Was she enjoying it?) She turned slowly to go inside. She planned to tell John how terrible she was, and maybe he'd have the good sense to take the children and leave her.

Just before she reached the door, she saw her dim reflection in the glass. She stopped in her tracks and gasped, then shrank back, certain that she had just hallucinated.

It was not her likeness.

Mouth agape, she peered at the glass pane. She had expected to see scratches and blood, but where was her long, dark hair, her green eyes, her fair complexion? Instead, she was seeing the faint outline of a hunched, crablike figure. Had John sketched something on the glass? No. It moved. Something was behind her. Filled with dread, she spun around, expecting to find a creature looming over her.

Nothing.

She turned back. The reflection was still there. And when she moved, it moved. Moaning with horror, she ran into the bathroom. She flipped on the light, stared into the mirror over the vanity and did not see herself. Something else looked back at her with eyes like open sores. The face—if one could call it that—was grotesque. Melanie remembered a mole on her right cheek; it had become a forest of mushroom growths. She had always feared that her nose was too long; now it was gnarled. She had always disliked facial hair; she was covered with great patches. She had always worried that her mouth was too large; well now, frozen in a leer, it might as well have been a shark's.

She stepped back so she could see more. All of her features were horribly exaggerated—especially those she had always been self-conscious of. She moaned, and the sound came out a growl. Then she covered her face with her hands and sank to her knees, heart pounding. *My God. I am twisted and ugly. What has happened to me?* She glanced into the mirror again and saw the same monstrous creature. The conclusion was inescapable. She had become the image, the personification of her own fear and loathing.

She screamed.

Three

The sound awakened John. He bolted up from the pillows on the floor, eyes blinking. Still groggy from sleep, he didn't know where he was or what had disturbed him. Then he saw the dim coals of the fire and remembered. Melanie. He almost smiled, but when he saw that she wasn't beside him, frowned instead. Suddenly, he heard another scream and then breaking glass. As he scrambled to his feet, she rushed into the room like she was on fire. Her nude body was lined with scratches and her hands were bloody.

"Jesus," he hissed, gaping at her. "Jesus Christ."

She went around the room in catlike strides, teeth gnashing, hands flexing like nervous claws. Her eyes were wild and her matted hair resembled bent straw. The scratches on her flesh were starting to form welts.

"Melanie, what's happened?"

She turned toward him, her arms spread, her face twisted. "Don't you have eyes?" she answered in a voice that was hoarse and broken. "Can't you see what has become of me?"

"You've cut yourself," he said, trying to remain calm. "I'll get the first-aid kit downstairs."

"Cut myself! I haven't cut myself! Can't you see?"

He backed away from her, astonished that he was doing so. Except for her wounds, distraught face, and disheveled hair, she looked the same as always. Yet he felt an alien presence and began shaking with fear. "Please," he whispered, "tell me what's happened. Tell me what's wrong." He put his hand on her shoulder.

With a snarl, she slapped it away. The force of her blow spun him around, and he was amazed at her strength. For a moment, he thought his hand was broken. He flexed it while staring at her, not knowing what to say or do. Then she began babbling and grunting and pacing around him in a semi-circle.

"Melanie?" he asked, bewildered.

She didn't answer. The fear returned, and he edged across the room toward the telephone. He didn't know who to call, but he had to talk to someone. Apparently, she had gone mad.

Just as he started to dial, she broke and ran from the room. He froze and stared after her, then slammed down the telephone and hurried to get dressed. He heard the front door close and cursed low. "She can't go out like that. Something terrible will happen to her!"

As he fumbled with his shoes, he heard the familiar sound of her Volkswagen convertible starting, and he knew he was too late. Barefooted, he ran downstairs and out of the house, shouting her name, but the only response was the whine of tires in the distance. He looked down the dark country road and saw her taillights swing around a curve and disappear.

*   *   *

Hunched over the wheel, Melanie drove as fast as

the road would allow, sliding through the mountain turns. She squirmed on the seat and enjoyed the recklessness, realizing that now she felt good and relished the ugliness that overwhelmed her. She did not yearn for her old self.

When she came to Malibu Canyon Road, she automatically turned toward the Pacific Ocean, not knowing where she was going. Or caring. *If it matters, I suppose I am pursuing the air,* she thought, *and it is cooler toward the beach. I love the cold and the moon. I love hate for that is what I have become. I am strong; I am evil; I am indestructible, like a relentless north wind.*

She headed south on the Pacific Coast Highway, following her impulses. Aware of the traffic, she drove normally, only because she did not want to be detained by something as insignificant as a highway patrol officer.

Eventually, she found herself in a residential neighborhood. Fog blanketed the area, diffusing the lights and giving her a sense of security. She could move as a shadowy figure, a force of darkness. She could do *anything.*

When she spotted a solitary man walking casually along a mist-shrouded street, she grinned. A plaything, an object. She drove past the man, parked a block ahead, got out of her car and waited behind a large mulberry tree, listening for his footsteps. A breeze picked up, swirling the fog and raising goosebumps on her skin. She shuddered with pleasure. In the distance she heard laughter and a stereo playing rock music; then a fog horn belched low. The incongruity made her smile. She nodded to herself. She would remind these gentle folk that the fog and the night were not to be taken lightly. She would bring back fear. She would become a purveyor of horror.

As she watched the man stroll past, she emitted a quick grunt, causing him to glance in her direction. But he saw nothing, for she was hiding behind the tree, clacking her tongue, enjoying the tiny seed of fright that she must have planted inside the man. Sure enough, when she peeked around the tree, she saw that he had quickened his stride. Then she trotted after him, her feet whisking on the sidewalk. When she knew he would sense her presence, she grunted again, then quickly jumped behind another tree. This time the man stopped and spun around apprehensively. He saw nothing because she wanted it that way. She imagined that uneasiness was causing the back of his neck to tingle. When she heard him resume walking, she followed on the other side of the trees, making no sound. Then she leaped high and touched a tree branch, rustling the leaves. He turned again, and she allowed him a fleeting glimpse of her before darting behind a tree. She heard his breath catch. A silence. She knew he would be confused and wondering if he were seeing things. After that his fear would blossom. Nervous sweat would roll down his flanks. Flight was inevitable.

When he started running, she chuckled triumphantly. Her feet light and sure, she cut across the sidewalk behind him, hurdled a low hedge and raced through several front yards until she was certain she was ahead of him once more. Then she waited behind a giant pyracantha, let him run past, then jumped out onto the sidewalk and growled. He whirled around, emitting short, terrified screams. She rushed toward him. Trying to run backward, he stumbled and fell, holding his hands above his head for protection. She crouched over him, surprised with herself, for now that the game was over, she had no idea what to do next. *Logic has no meaning. The moment is now. Do anything.*

Kill him.

Then she noticed that the man had stopped whimpering and was staring at her body, bewildered. She frowned, realizing that she was nude, and he did not see her as a grotesque creature. Annoyed, she growled and loomed over him. His terror returned.

"Please, no! Please!" He crawled away from her.

She let him scramble to his feet, but before he could escape, she danced in front of him, slashed his face open with her fingernails, then knocked him to the ground. He screamed in pain, held his face and rolled on the wet grass under a tree. She watched him with total detachment now, no longer interested in his fear or pain. Of course, she could kill him, but she was tired of this puling specimen of humanity. He wasn't worth any more of her time and energy. Let him pass. Let him live forever with the nightmares she had provided for his wretched soul.

The man got to his feet and ran away, shouting for help, occasionally looking over his shoulder to make sure she wasn't following. With a sigh, she turned and sauntered back toward her car, face lifted high, eyes half-closed, enjoying the mist that glistened on her naked body. *If only others could see me as I really am. If only they could appreciate my twisted form and distorted face.* She got into her car, started it, swung around in a U-turn and drove off, lost in thought. As she went north along the highway, she became convinced that specific victims awaited her. *Those are the ones I shall seek out and destroy. And it matters not where they are or how hard they are to find. I have the power of*

*the supernatural. When the time is right, I will kill
them and relish their pain.*

*   *   *

Later, Melanie found herself on a turn-out just off
the Mulholland Highway. A predawn gray lit the
sky, and she was cold and shivering. Her teeth chattered. Every time she moved, her skin stung pain-
fully. The lacerations frightened her; she didn't know
how she had gotten them. Worse yet, she didn't
know how she had ended up in her car, somewhere
in the Santa Monica Mountains at four-thirty in the
morning.

Naked.

Her smooth flesh streaked with dirt and blood.
Her usually placid face tear-stained and haggard.
Her long hair matted and tangled. What had *happened?* She could remember feeling nauseous the
night before, then pacing the deck and admiring the
moon, but the rest of the night was a blank. She
strained to recall what she had done and where she
had gone. Nonsensical images flashed through her
mind. She was in a bathroom for a long time. (When?)
She was smashing the mirror with her fists. (Why?)
She was driving like a madwoman. (Where?) She
was . . .

Nothing.

Except she had a feeling she had been on the
brink of something horrible. She put her face in her
hands and wept. *What has become of me? If I can't
remember the immediate past, then I must have gone
insane!* She continued sobbing, her voice hoarse
now, her body shaking badly. She could not recall
ever feeling so alone, devastated, and frightened.

She heard a car traveling very fast on the curves,
craned around and caught a glimpse of a dark-green

station wagon rocketing by. "John?" she whispered tentatively.

Suddenly, the car stopped, screeched backward, then bounced over the shoulder of the road onto the turn-out.

"John!" She was out of the Volkswagen, running toward the other car, safe at last. Although, she didn't have the presence of mind to ask herself if she were free of the demon that had possessed her and washed her memory clean. If she had, she might have concluded, *How can I be free of myself?*

*   *   *

Sliding the station wagon to a dusty stop, John could only think how grateful he was that she was all right. He threw the car into Park, leaped out, and gently collected her in his arms. They held each other tightly, and he could feel her trembling, her spasms as she sobbed. Whispering reassurances, he stroked her hair and back. Privately, he hoped he would never have to go through another night like this one, but was filled with dread that the experience would become commonplace. He placed his jacket around her shoulders and led her to the station wagon. He saw no reason to speak right now. Her nightmare would keep.

Later, after he had phoned the police and told them that his wife, Melanie, was fine, he made coffee and waited for her to finish showering and dressing. When she came downstairs, he took her out onto the verandah. She managed to smile and say good morning to Mark and Todd who were playing in the dirt beneath their new swing set. They just waved back. To them, nothing unusual had occurred, and, John thought—observing the scene—thank God for the sleep and innocence that protects small children.

They sat down on redwood lounge chairs in sunlight dappled by pines and elms, and he poured them coffee. From afar they must look like an advertisement for life in the country, John mused. How ironic.

He studied the haunted look in her eyes. He had seen it before in the faces of men who had spent too much time in combat; prolonged exposure to death had shaved their veneer of rationality too thin, leaving them permanently distracted, always waiting for the next horror. Chronic drug addicts had that look, too, and now it was on Melanie's face.

"Did you take something?" he asked gently. "Was that it?"

Her eyes flitted back and forth as she considered the question, wondering if she could just say, yes. Then it would be over, and she wouldn't have to have this anguished conversation.

"Did you, Melanie?"

"No." She tasted her coffee, but had to set the cup down quickly so she wouldn't drop it.

Puzzled, he sat back, not sure what to say. If only she had an excuse so he could dismiss his worst fears. If only she would offer a defense so he wouldn't think she might be mentally ill. "Then I don't understand."

"I don't either, John."

"You're not making it any easier."

"I'm sorry."

He leaned forward hesitantly, trying to find the right words. Finally, he just shook his head and stared off. "You acted like an animal."

She nodded and twisted her shirt.

"And then you ran off."

"Yes."

"Where did you go?"

"I don't know."

For a moment, he wondered if she were telling the truth, then sighed heavily and let it pass. "You kept asking me if I had eyes."

"Eyes?"

"If I could see what had become of you."

"Yes," she said, uncertain.

"Just what *had* become of you?"

She glanced down and shook her head. "I don't recall."

"You must remember something!"

She looked at him with sad, frightened eyes. "If I did, don't you think I'd tell you?"

"What the hell are we going to do, then? What if it happens again?"

*　　*　　*

"It's a dream," the corpulent psychiatrist said with finality. "A very vivid dream, that's all."

"You don't understand," Melanie replied, frustrated.

"I've been listening to you for almost an hour. Believe me, I do understand."

Surprised, Melanie glanced at her watch, assuming that she'd only been talking for a little while, but the man was right. It had been almost an hour. She couldn't believe it, though. After she and John agreed that therapy might help solve her problem, she had decided that no matter how ashamed she was or how bizarre her story might be, she would withhold nothing from the psychiatrist. The doctor came heavily recommended and if anyone could unravel her troubled psyche, surely it was him. So she had poured out her soul to him, sobbing frequently, and now he was telling her that she had only been dreaming? Her ears burned with embarrassment.

"Then why don't I remember everything that happened?"

"Memory lapses are common with even the most convincing of dreams."

"But, Doctor, my husband found me in my car in the middle of the mountains somewhere!"

"I believe the term is sleepwalking," he said tersely, then lit a cigarette.

She sat back and shook her head in disbelief. "You're kidding."

"Melanie—you don't mind if I call you Melanie, do you?" He didn't wait for an answer. "I never joke regarding emotional disorders."

"You don't believe me, then!" She exclaimed, her face hot.

"Of course I believe you." He spread his hands. "Why would you lie to me?"

"I did *not* have a dream!" She paused in midthought. Confused, she didn't know how to say it. "I *changed*, I—"

"The word is transmogrification and it cannot happen. It's fiction. The province of phantasmagoric novels, nothing more. In the Middle Ages, people used such superstitions as a convenient way in which to explain diseases like leprosy, rabies, even the plague."

"What are you suggesting?"

"That you're doing precisely the same thing only your condition is mental instead of physical."

"Doctor!"

"Wait a minute, wait a minute." He held up his hand; a diamond ring flashed. "I'm also well aware that you're extremely frustrated right now, but if

you don't listen to me, it's only going to get worse."
He leaned forward. "Now. How long have you been
an actress?"

"For nine years," she said, befuddled by the new
line of questioning.

"And you're . . ."

"Twenty-six."

He smiled, his jowls crinkling. "So you started
acting as a way to overcome traditional feelings of
adolescent alienation. You thought that if you were
center stage, you would be accepted. Am I correct?"

"No," she replied. "My parents were broke and
someone offered me a job."

He frowned with annoyance. "I'm sure it wasn't
quite that simple."

"Does everything have to be complicated?"

"You're avoiding me." His eyes locked on hers.
"Let's talk about your parents."

And so she innocently told him that her childhood had been full of love despite her father's chronic
unemployment. He had been trained as an English
teacher, but when he came out of school there was a
glut on the market. Since he had no skills other
than language, his career was a succession of odd
jobs. He refused to let his wife work, believing his
child's upbringing was more important. Tragically,
her parents had been killed in an automobile accident while she was on location several years ago.
She cried everytime she thought about it.

Like now.

When she pulled herself together, he looked up
from his notes and continued. "Did it ever occur to
you that you've been unhappy and under a great
deal of stress since then?"

"Since they died?"

"No. Since you had to go to work to support your parents."

"That wasn't the way it happened!" But she did wonder about it, now that the seed was planted.

He glanced at his watch and shook his head impatiently. "I'm sorry, I've got to let you go, Melanie, but I think I can help you. Why don't you come in day after tomorrow?"

She left his office, knowing full well she would not keep her next appointment. As she climbed into her car for the trip home, she realized the doctor wasn't going to probe further. She supposed that she should be angry; instead, she felt condemned and frightened. No one was going to help her. John would if he could, but he was as bewildered as she. Then again, maybe the psychiatrist was right in saying she had a common emotional disorder. But how was that possible? She had studied mental illness briefly in acting school and nothing she had ever read even came close to describing her experience. Except classic examples of schizophrenia. She shuddered as she accelerated up the freeway ramp. *What if I really am going insane and the doctor can't see it? What if I am on the brink right now and my mind is so fouled up that when I am crazy, I don't remember it?* Her grip tightened on the steering wheel, her knuckles going white. *What if I am changing into a psychotic killer?*

* * *

Ever since Melanie had gone berserk four days ago, John had been unable to work. Just this morning he had finally given up trying and had driven over to Zuma to think it out. Since it was cold, the beach was deserted and peaceful. Gulls squawked as they circled and kingfishers darted in and out of the waves, hunting for sand crabs. The perennial hard core surfers clad in wet suits drifted just past the breakers, drinking beer housed in a floating ice chest. Their laughter floated across the water, and John smiled, recalling his tenure as one of the bow-legged golden boys; it had lasted all of four months— between high school and the Marine Corps.

He strolled aimlessly, head down, large hands stuffed into the pockets of his paint-splattered levis. Maybe the psychiatrist would have some answers. And if Melanie didn't have a mental illness, then they'd get her cured and resume their life together. They'd already agonized too much, afraid it would happen again. And it had rubbed off on the boys, too— they must think their parents were real space cadets. Yeah, he was glad she was seeing the psychiatrist. Then he frowned and kicked at a half-buried bottle cap, realizing that his confidence was artificial. What if the psychiatrist couldn't help her? What if there was no precedent for her condition? Maybe there wasn't a cure for her form of madness. Maybe she'd get worse.

He lifted his head, scowled at the horizon and nodded. That was the real worry. The next time it happened he feared she'd go completely over the edge. And what would he do then? Institutionalize her? That was the dilemma. That was why he hadn't been able to work. That was why he was walking along the beach, absorbed with the problem. He needed a plan. There was too much at stake for him to be unprepared. Ever since he met Melanie, his life had taken quantum leaps for the better, despite his lack of success. From a starving art student without discipline, he had developed into a mature craftsman. In addition, he had become a good father who embraced the responsibility of children, something he had never believed he could do. But most of all, his love for Melanie had grown to the point where he would sacrifice himself for her. He cherished that love because it meant *them*, forever. And nothing in his life had ever made as much sense. So, if her sanity was threatened, then he was threatened. There would be no running away, either. No matter how bad things might become, he would see her through this tormented time.

So resolved, he strolled along more relaxed, but wondered exactly *how* he would help her. He was no trained professional—all he had were love and courage, two abstract emotions devoid of scientific expertise. The inner workings of the mind were a mystery to him.

The beach ended at an outcropping of huge black rocks; waves broke over them, sending spray high in the air. John scrambled through the rocks, stepping over an occasional tidepool, resisting a feeling of helplessness. He stopped himself as he vaulted down the outcropping and headed toward the next stretch of sand, realizing he did know something about mental processes. He recalled his fascination with Carl Jung and the hours he had spent immersed in the man's theories about psychology as related to human creativity. Duality had been the key word, and the person who could bring his conscious and unconscious minds into harmony was deemed self-fulfilled. So how did that help Melanie? Since she could not remember her bizarre behavior, John figured, that must mean that it stemmed from her unconscious mind. According to Jung, the unconscious mind had two dimensions. One was suppressed personal experiences. The other was that fountainhead of all human history, archetypes of the collective unconscious, passed down from generation to generation. One dimension influencing the other, John guessed, must be the ultimate in creativity or artistic expression. And that kind of mental process must result in Jung's self-fulfilled person. Therefore, if he could get Melanie to recognize the archetype that was possessing her, then that comprehension might give her the power to resist it. But how? He didn't even know how to hypnotize a person. He couldn't lead her along such a tenuous, psychic journey.

Or could he?

What was it she had kept repeating that horrible night? He remembered. *Can't you see what I have become?* John stopped meandering through the sand. It suddenly occurred to him that maybe he *could* see what she had become. He grinned. Of course, that was the answer! If the compulsion came over her again, he would be there with his sketch pad, his colored pencils, and a tape recorder.

So armed, he would reproduce the ugliness that was inside her mind.

*   *   *

When Melanie got home, she was surprised that John wasn't there. He had left her a note, reminding her to pick up the kids from nursery school if he weren't back in time. For a moment, she was sad. She had wanted to share her fears and frustrations with John and to find him gone, well. . . . Then she decided she had been expecting far too much of him. He was always home; he spent more time with the boys than she did; except for a cleaning lady twice a month, he did most of the housework; he even cooked sometimes. She took too much for granted and had no right to ask anything of him, especially now. She blushed, then shuddered.

Suddenly, she felt faint and realized that she hadn't eaten all day. Grateful for the diversion, she went into the kitchen and made herself a cheese sandwich with plenty of lettuce and mayonnaise. As she munched on it, she wandered out onto the verandah, started to sit down, but saw the mailman by the front gate. With a casual wave, he drove away. She walked out to the mailbox, gathered what was inside, and started back for the verandah, finally feeling relaxed. There's something about picking up the mail that makes you feel more at home—like you really belong. She finished her sandwich, then flipped through the usual collection of bills and advertisements. No bills, nothing interesting, not even—her heart stopped.

She held a postcard. On it was a representation of the Vladimir castle in Transylvania. With a trembling hand, she turned it over and read.

Dear Melanié—
    I was up here the other day because I had been away too long and I thought of you. I hope you are well. Say hello to America for me.

                                        Yours,
                                        M.

And just when she thought she had put him out of her mind forever. Her face burning with shame, she ran inside the house. Glancing at the postcard once more, she ripped it up and dropped it into the trash. Troubled now, she swept her hair back and went upstairs to the den in search of refuge. She lay down on the sofa, gathering her body close in a tight ball and stared out the patio doors at the soft skies beyond, angry with herself. *I didn't need that. I didn't need to be reminded of the vile things I did with another man halfway around the world. Mihail*

Popescu and Melanie Ross. She felt sick. *And I don't even have the courage to tell John and take the consequences. I don't deserve him. I don't deserve any of my good fortune.*

Minutes later, an idea occurred to her. Still gazing out the patio doors, she abruptly sat up. *Could that be it? Was my affair the reason I went temporarily insane?* She doubted that guilt could explain a smashed mirror; the scratches on her body; driving around naked. *Although*—she wasn't certain.

She thought harder. Sure, adultery was a powerful emotional medicine, but could it make people go berserk or change to alien personalities? She frowned and shook her head. None of the women she knew had ever suffered from committing the sin. If anything, they would always come off like *Vogue* reprints, telling how the experience had improved their marriage. Yes, adultery could create jealous rages and violent crimes, but she hadn't been a party to any of that. (At least she didn't think so.)

No, she concluded, *my affair didn't bring on the horror of four nights ago. Something else did. Something deeper.* She sighed heavily. *Great. I'm right back where I started. My mind is turning in upon itself, full of confusion.*

Exhausted, she closed her eyes, leaned back on the sofa, and was about to drift off when a lurid image of Mihail flashed through her mind. She bolted up and scowled. Cursing, she went downstairs looking for busy work—anything to keep her mind off the guilt and despair.

"John," she whispered to herself. "Please come home."

*   *   *

Late that afternoon, John drove up to the house, his hair wind-blown, his skin covered with a fine layer of salt spray. He went inside quietly through the back way and saw that Melanie had dinner started. A salad reposed on the kitchen island, and the smell of a roasting chicken wafted out of the oven. He was about to call out when he heard laughter coming from the game room. He crept to the door and peeked inside. She and the boys were playing a form of kick ball they'd obviously just invented. The room was in shambles, but it didn't matter—there was joy on their faces. John grinned with relief and his knees went weak. Just like old times. Maybe the trouble has passed.

After dinner, he watched while she cleaned up, then read the boys a story and put them to bed. He was amazed—it was as if she had never stopped being a mother. The three were completely natural together. He was convinced that something instinctual, something good was afoot. With a chuckle, he went out onto the verandah, appreciative that no one needed him. Right now.

Tiberon was there on a redwood chair, his aloof body curled up in the last patch of sunlight coming through the trees. John sat down next to the cat and stroked him, expecting him to yowl indignantly, jump down and saunter away, tail switching. Instead, he purred and lifted his head, asking to be scratched. John wasn't surprised—the only consistent thing about Tiberon was his unpredictable nature. Then Melanie came out with two cups of coffee, and the cat ran off.

She looked at him askance. "Sorry for living, Tiberon." She turned to John. "What'd he do? Change sides?"

John shrugged. "Beats me, sweetheart. You know him better than I do."

"I'm not so sure any more."

He laughed and couldn't resist. "I've always told you that he was an arrogant son of a bitch."

Laughing too, she handed him his coffee, then sat on the same chair with him. She held her cup with both hands and blew into the steam.

"Thanks," he said.

"Don't mention it."

"You seem better." He paused. "Less preoccupied."

"I'm keeping busy, if that's what you mean."

"I hope it's because of the psychiatrist."

She made a face, then smiled ironically. "It's a way to forget what transpired."

"What do you mean?"

"We paid him a hundred dollars to tell me that I had a vivid imagination and realistic nightmares."

"Oh, no," he said quietly and shook his head.

"At first I was angry, then—" She set her coffee down and put her head on his shoulder. Her voice became soft and vulnerable. "John, what am I going to do?"

He caressed her arm. "Hey, take it easy. After all, you had a good day and that means there's hope."

"What if something happens, though?"

"Nothing's going to happen. And if it does, we'll deal with it."

"But what if I?—"

He waited for her to finish. When she didn't, he glanced at her, then asked gently. "What, sweetheart?"

She shook her head. "Nothing." Then she moved away from him, folded her arms across her chest and stared vacantly at the mountains. In the deepening twilight, they were black silhouettes against the sky with a splash of pink soon gone.

John sipped his coffee reflectively and listened to the choruses of crickets grow louder. Somewhere nearby a mockingbird shrieked. Rather than push her to talk about something painful, he remained silent and made himself content with the way things were. She was beside him and the evening was tranquil. A warm wind whistled through the pines, making his skin tingle pleasantly. As he watched the sky darken, he felt optimistic. It had been a good day. Sure, there would be future anxieties and problems, but right now there wasn't too much wrong with anything.

"Melanie," he said and reached out to touch her.

She wasn't there.

Surprised, he sat up straight and turned. When he saw her, he gasped. She was on her hands and knees beside the chair, silently retching.

"My God, Melanie!"

She looked up at him. Her eyes were anguished; sweat streamed down her face, causing her hair to stick to her skin. As her body convulsed, she forced herself to speak, the words coming out in a hoarse whisper. "Do something, for Christ's sake! It's happening! I can't . . . it's happening. . . . I can't—"

*   *   *

Riding the hard edge of the nausea, she stood tall on the verandah, her face lifted to the moon, which had just risen above the trees. Shuddering she caressed herself and was glad to be a creature of the night again. Then she hunched over and paced the verandah, assuming her form to be hideous, slimy, and crablike.

Suddenly, lights went on. A man came out of the house, carrying things—a man who seemed familiar. She gnashed her teeth and growled at him, but he was not startled by her presence. Instead, he studied her and occasionally sketched on a pad. She scowled and took several menacing steps toward him. He remained motionless—almost impassive. Surprised, she backed away, wondering why this man was not frightened by her. *Does he have something magical he thinks will protect him? Is that why he isn't groveling like the one the other night? Bah! Nothing can resist my strength.* She growled again, but he didn't retreat. *Must I prove how loathsome I am? Must I demonstrate my power?* She clacked her tongue pensively. *Do I have to kill him?*

"Melanie?"

"How do you know my name?"

"I'm your husband, John."

"What do you want?"

"I want to know how you feel inside."

She laughed, her lips flaring so her teeth showed. *He wants to know what? He wants me to reveal my hatred? What shall I tell him? How contemptible the human race is? How all people wear cloaks of righteousness and deserve to die? Including him? All right, I'll play his game for a while.* Then she shoved her face close to his and glared at him. He did not flinch.

Rather, he produced a hand mirror and asked her to describe herself. Shocked by his boldness, she rocked back on her heels and did not immediately comprehend. Then she stared foolishly into the mirror, contemplating her twisted, piebald face. "You blind or something?" she said sarcastically.

"Yes," he answered quickly.

She regarded him quizzically. *Maybe that's why he doesn't run while he has a chance.* In a sing-song parody of a church litany, she described her features, embellishing those parts she found unusually disgusting. After she finished, she closed her eyes and imagined her face melting away. She told him that, too, then threw the mirror away and waited impatiently for a response.

Instead, he continued drawing on the pad, his own face glistening, belabored, and intense.

"Well?"

"Wait a minute," he whispered, his eyes wide.

She stepped back. *He's not blind! He lied to me!* She moved away, growing more and more angry. *Why would anyone want to deceive me? Am I not wretched and grotesque? What could he possibly hope to gain?* Snarling, she looked back at John from the comfort of the shadows; her pent-up rage needed release. As she squinted at him her breath quickened, and she wondered how it would feel to claw his face. Slash his throat.

Grunting, she scuttled out of the darkness toward him. He seemed not to notice; he was staring at the large pad, his face a mask of horror. She paused by the chairs, gathering her strength for the final charge, then leapt forward, hands clawing at him.

At the last moment, he whirled around brandishing the pad like it was a crucifix. She stopped and looked at it, befuddled. He had drawn an accurate representation of what she had seen in the mirror. Yes, it was her likeness.

"Is this what's inside you?" he asked, his voice trembling. "Is this what you truly think of yourself?"

She didn't know what he was insinuating, so she just nodded.

"Then remember that you have become a creature, a monster, an abomination. And may God help you." He lowered the pad and stared into her eyes feverishly.

Then he began crying, and she was amazed, for she had never seen a man weep before. Whether it was the drawing or the tears, she didn't know, but she no longer wanted to kill this man. He already seemed destroyed. She sprung off the verandah and ran aimlessly toward the trees, her feet rustling the dry grass. Suddenly, there was noise in the bushes to her left. She stopped, turned and crouched. A silence. She grinned and stalked forward, her feet gliding now, making no sound.

*   *   *

St. Jude's of the Cross was a Spanish-style Catholic church secluded in one of the small valleys between the Pacific Ocean and the Santa Monica Mountains. Basically, it served the religious needs of the Malibu community, which in a lighter time Melanie had said was a contradiction in terms. She had been to St. Jude's twice—both times attending the Christmas midnight mass, more for the candlelight show than anything else. She did not know the resident priest, so she was very grateful when he had agreed to see her without a referral. She had no place else to turn.

As she parked in the lot underneath a row of giant eucalyptus trees, the night before came back to her in vivid detail and she slumped over the steering wheel, trembling. How could she tell anyone, let alone a priest?

At first light, she had come to her senses wandering in the mountains, her clothes ruined, her body scratched and bruised from crashing through heavy underbrush, she guessed. The most frightening thing was that she was covered with dried blood. At first, she thought she had attacked the boys—or even John, himself. When she finally found her way home, though, she was extremely relieved to learn that no harm had come to them. Still, the blood wasn't hers.

Somewhere in the area there was a victim.

After she cleaned up and dressed, John questioned her, but like before she had no answers. Then he told her how she had threatened him and showed her the drawing he had made. She locked herself in the bedroom, unable to deal with the horror of it. She thought about committing herself to an institution, but knew instinctively it wouldn't help. Then there was only one thing left to do. She got a bottle of Valium and a razor blade out of the bathroom.

When John had finally broken the lock and rushed in, he had found her sitting on the bed, studying the pills and the blade, trying to decide which to try first. Suicide? he'd said. No, that was unacceptable, and reluctantly, she had agreed. An hour later, she decided to call St. Jude's because she was too afraid to phone the police and ask them if any murders had been reported last night.

Determined, she got out of her car, crossed the empty parking lot, and climbed the steps to the parish house. A breeze from the ocean gusted, and she had to hold onto the large hat she'd worn to hide her face. She pulled it tight over her eyes, then went inside, looked around and saw no one. Grateful to be alone, she seated herself in the reception area and leafed through a *Catholic Digest*.

Eventually, the priest came, stood in the mouth of the hallway and studied her. He was tall and thin and wore a brown sackcloth monastery robe and sandals, instead of the more traditional cassock. Clutching the talisman of a crucifix, he leaned forward slightly like a bent nail. With haunted eyes, he could have been the reincarnation of a medieval priest except he was a black man.

He glanced behind him as if a large, invisible hand had just settled on his shoulder, then shook off the apprehension and spoke in gentle, moody tones. "Melanie Ross?"

She rose, nodded, and removed her hat.

"I'm Father Beckett. Father Earl Beckett." He motioned with his head. "This way, please." He turned and walked silently down the corridor, hunched into himself.

She followed, puzzled by his expectant nature. She had told him nothing on the telephone, yet he seemed preoccupied—pursued, even—by an impending sense of doom. Was he always that way or did he know something about her?

Father Beckett had a spacious, modern office in the rear of the parish house, made comfortable by hundreds of books that lined the walls. Scowling, he switched on the fluorescents, apologized for them and the lack of windows, then gestured for Melanie to sit on the couch across from his desk. He began by asking general questions about her life and whether or not she was religious. She answered honestly.

She replied truthfully about her troubles, too, which it seemed fair to say had started in Romania.

"Was there anything unusual about your trip to Eastern Europe?"

"I had an affair."

He nodded and half-smiled. "Mrs. Ross, many people have affairs and are extremely remorseful about the experience."

"I was a happily-married woman and I want to remain so, Father."

"I'm sure you will," he said softly, "as long as the basic foundation of love and mutual respect is solid."

"It is."

"Then you have more than most, believe me."

"Father, if John hadn't broken into the bedroom this morning, I would have killed myself."

A silence. He studied her for a moment, drumming his fingers on the desk. Then he sighed and reached for a leather-bound address book. "I can refer you to a competent psychiatrist."

"I've tried."

"Perhaps you should try again."

"It won't help."

"Nothing is absolute."

She shrugged and looked away. "I didn't come here to argue about psychiatry."

"Very well. As long as you are aware that contemplating suicide indicates a serious emotional disorder, which is more in the province of a doctor than a theologian."

"I'm aware."

He leaned forward, his eyes glittering. "You should also understand that traditionally people always blame adultery as the source of their troubles."

"And?"

"Properly it should be viewed as a symptom." He paused. "It is an effect rather than a cause."

"Meaning?"

"Something else is at the heart of it."

"All I know is that before I left everything was fine!" she exclaimed.

"I'm sure it was," he agreed. "And I certainly would not rule out the possibility that something, which you do not recall, happened to you when you were in Romania."

"But how do I find out?"

"The Lord works in strange ways, but always with a purpose. Have faith."

Frustrated, she clenched her fists. *How can I have faith when I am not even sure who I am? When I don't know what I do? He thinks I'm just another guilt-ridden Catholic housewife.* Tears welled up in her eyes. "Don't you understand?" she whispered. "There is a demon inside me that takes over sometimes!"

He smiled. "There is one in all of us."

"I'm serious!"

"So am I."

"You—you don't believe me, do you?"

"On the contrary, I believe in all things."

"Father!" she cried. "What am I going to do?"

"Pray," he said softly. "Prayer always helps."

"But I can't!"

"And why not?"

"It wouldn't be right. I feel—" Tears rolled down her cheeks. "I am dead in spirit."

"What did you say?"

"I am dead in spirit!"

Father Beckett recoiled as if in the presence of an enemy. "Are you quite certain, Melanie Ross?"

"Yes!" she hissed.

He crossed himself and then his eyes went dull and hard. "You must find your soul, your true self."

"How?"

"You must make a spiritual quest. A pilgrimage," he replied somberly. "In my opinion, if you fail, you are doomed."

"Doomed?" Her face turned ashen.

"Perhaps for an eternity."

*   *   *

John sat in his studio and stared at the illustration

he had made of Melanie, sadly wondering where he went wrong. When he had shown it to her, he had expected her to see something in the likeness that would give her a profound insight, hence a cure. Instead, she had almost attempted suicide.

So much for the theories of Carl Jung.

Fortunately, he had stopped her, then urged her to see a priest because he could think of nothing else. After she had left, he called the police and asked about disturbances in the area; none had been reported, which was a relief. Yet, the mystery remained. What had Melanie done last night?

He took a beer out of the small refrigerator in the corner, opened it and sipped. Should he call the Woodview-Calabasas psychiatric hospital and ask them if Melanie should be taken there? He scowled and shook his head, hating even the thought of the idea. He drained his beer and got another one. But what if she'd already killed someone?

Finally, he sprawled in a lounge chair and just stared at the sketch. With morbid fascination, he scrutinized his technique, realizing ironically that it was the best work he'd done in years. Perhaps ever. He knew right then that he would paint the drawing on a large canvas and that very possibly it could be a breakthrough for his career.

"Jesus Christ," he muttered and closed his eyes.

He heard her drive up and for once was grateful to leave his studio. It was a flight from sanctuary. He went through the house and met her outside by the driveway. "How'd it go?"

"It went fine," she replied.

But he could see that she was frightened and pale. He touched her arm. "Mel—"

"Where are the boys?"

"They went next door," he said, gesturing at the

neighbor's house, a half-mile away through stands of pine and oak.

They went to the verandah, rather than the den, both knowing that the den was reserved for good times and pleasant conversation. They sat opposite each other in the redwood chairs, and she took his hand in hers.

"I'm going back to Romania."

"No."

"Yes."

He scowled, glanced down, and shook his head vehemently. "You're not well. You shouldn't go anywhere."

"John, I have to. You know I have to. It shouldn't be something that needs explanation."

Looking away, he considered what she was saying and decided he wouldn't try to stop her. She had to slay the proverbial dragon, he supposed, and she wasn't going to find the monster here in the Santa Monica Mountains. He nodded quickly and gulped. "I don't want you to go, but if you think it's for the best. . . ."

She smiled with relief. "It's not forever, John."

"Yeah. I know," he said, but his mind was filled with doubt and worry. What if she didn't return? What the hell would he do then? He didn't want to live without her. All he wanted was for her to be the way she used to be.

Suddenly, he realized that by allowing her to go to Romania, he was taking the easy way out. There would be no dilemma; he wouldn't have to deal with it. Actually, he was surprised that a decision of such importance had been made so quickly. He wanted to go back and argue with her except it was already too late. He had said yes. Still, he offered a quiet protest. "I don't think it's a good idea, though."

"I don't think I have a choice," she whispered.

"What do you mean?" he asked, startled.

"I'm afraid for you and the boys as much as I am for myself."

Before he could respond, he heard Mark and Todd coming across the field and turned to look. Mark's face was white with fear, and he carried what appeared to be the body of a dead rabbit. Todd stumbled along behind, sobbing, eyes downcast, waving haplessly at the droning flies accompanying them.

"Mommy, Daddy, look!" said Mark. He stopped at the stairs to the verandah, carefully laid the body on the ground, then started crying. "It's Tiberon."

John felt the nausea build in his stomach. The cat's unseeing eyes were open and his mouth was frozen in a shriek of agony.

Four

The Pan-Am jumbo jet made a sweeping turn over the Black Sea and began its final approach to Bucharest's Otopeni International Airport. Reluctantly, Melanie turned away from the window, fastened her seat belt, then put on dark glasses so no one could see that she had been crying. She sighed and shut her eyes, but the attempt to relax was in vain; everytime she closed them, she saw the drawing that John had made and then the mangled body of Tiberon. Her tears started anew. How could she have murdered Tiberon? She loved that animal more than she did herself! She had saved him from so many bad ends; she had cared for him when he was sick; she had pampered him.

Of course John had been quick and glib with the excuses. "Don't even think that you could have possibly done that, Melanie. It was the coyotes. Or the owls. Wild dogs. A mountain lion, perhaps. They're still around, you realize." Only she knew. John knew, too, even if he wouldn't admit it.

Somewhere inside her unconscious mind a demon lurked. And somehow—at its own whim or fancy— that creature could make Melanie forget who she was and allow her to do unspeakable acts. She shivered. She was a prisoner of herself; she was ruled by darkness. And she must find out why lest the somber prediction of Father Beckett come true.

Doomed for eternity.

The jet touched down on the runway with two slight jerks of the wheels. Melanie lifted her head and nodded. Once again, she was in Romania, the land of her ancestors. *If nothing else,* she thought, *it's a beginning.*

After passing through customs and leaving the terminal, she took a tram for the other side of the airport. Loudspeakers on the cars blared an association football game from Bucharest's 23 August stadium, the announcer's voice rising and falling with the flow of the play. Occasionally, passengers applauded with enthusiasm, while others whistled to show their displeasure. Melanie recognized the reactions. In many ways life was a symphony regardless of where you were. People always listened or played no matter how familiar the melody, for the outcome was never certain. Hope—or the lack of it—was common to all men. Wasn't that why she had returned to this land, the wellspring of mystery?

Since she had a four-hour wait at the Tarom terminal before her flight to Brasov departed, she went into a gift shop, browsed and found a tourist guidebook in English with simple phrases in Romanian spelled phonetically. So armed, she decided to contact Mihail Popescu, the logical first step in her search for answers. She went to a telephone booth and dialed the National Studios of Cinematography in Bucharest, glad that all of Romania's film industry was confined to one huge facility and she wouldn't have to make dozens of phone calls. After twelve rings someone finally answered, and she asked for Mihail Popescu.

"*Stai nitel.*" The phone clattered down, and she could hear the person on the other end of the line, impatiently leafing through a directory. Finally, he came back on the phone. "*Ce departament?*"

"Camera," Melanie replied without thinking.

"*Camera?*" the person said, astonished.

Panicked, Melanie scanned her guide book and discovered that "*camera*" was the Romanian word for "room." She looked up the proper term, then said, "*Cinematografie,*" while blushing crimson.

"*Stai nitel.*"

She heard sharp static as he plugged the line into an extension. The phone started ringing again. This time she sat through twenty-five rings, before realizing that it was Sunday in Romania and no one would be working. Frustrated, she hung up, then dialed information and asked for Mihail's home telephone number. Since the operator understood a smattering of English, Melanie had no trouble making herself clear and for once didn't mind the interminable wait. Except the operator came back on the line full of apologies—there were seventeen Mihail Popescus in the city of Bucharest.

"*Aneti un adresa de strada?*"

"*Nu inteleg,*" Melanie said haltingly.

"*Aneti un . . .* street address?"

Melanie shook her head, embarrassed. "No, I'm sorry."

"*Scuzati,*" the operator replied and the line went dead.

Cursing, Melanie slammed down the phone, left the booth and strode across the wide terminal. As she opened her purse and dropped the guide book inside, she saw that her hands were shaking badly. *Am I that angry or just desperate?* It made no difference. She stopped and surveyed the terminal.

The signs were incomprehensible, and she couldn't understand the announcements coming from the speaker system, either. A helpless feeling settled over her; she was alone; she might as well be lost. Before when she was here, the production company had insulated her and made her lavishly comfortable. Now she was left to her own resources in a strange land. She had an urge to run back to the Pan-Am terminal and jump on the first plane home. Only that wasn't possible. She could not return. Not now. Maybe never.

Suddenly, she laughed. The absurdity of it! None of this was possible! Here she was halfway around the world, surrounded by unfamiliarity, supposedly searching for her soul? And a cure for a schizoid mutation that possessed her without rhyme or reason? *My God*, she thought. *And I don't even have the vaguest idea of what to do next!*

Her laughter attracted the attention of a uniformed security guard who questioned her. She handed him her passport and plane ticket, then smiled, shrugged and shook her head as he repeated his questions. Finally, he shrugged back at her, then led her to the gate for the flight to Brasov and wished her bon voyage. She was embarrassed by her outburst in a public place until she realized that if she hadn't laughed, more than likely she would have gone to the wrong gate and missed her plane.

The speakers droned again, only now everyone around her was standing and heading for the doors leading to the aircraft. Melanie got in line, assuming that the flight to Brasov was about to leave. When the Tarom agent gave her a boarding pass in exchange for her ticket, she knew she'd guessed right and felt good.

The flight was short and uneventful. The small,

twin-engine jet circled above the city, then banked in front of Mount Timpa, now a dark purple in the sunset haze. Melanie looked down and saw the profusion of whitewashed buildings and red-tiled roofs. She felt a surge of recognition and relaxed. Brasov. Romania's second city. The gateway to Transylvania. A jewel at the foot of the Carpathians. Then she glanced up and saw the black silhouettes of the Fagaras Mountains to the south. Against a pink sky, they seemed mysterious and forbidding. She looked away.

After the plane was down and Melanie had collected her baggage, she rented a car, feeling confident enough to navigate the narrow streets of Brasov on her own. Without mishap, she drove the Dacia 1200 sedan to the Carpati Hotel, parked, went inside and requested a room. The hotel clerk remembered her, became animated, and reached for the telephone with a flourish. When she asked him what he was doing, he replied that he was phoning the manager to tell him that the renowned film star had returned. Shaking her head, she stopped him, then whispered urgently that she needed to stay incognito. Discreet.

"*La locul lui?*" he said, slipping back into Romanian.

She nodded. "*Da. Poftiti.*"

He agreed and so she registered, this time taking the cheapest the Carpati offered—a room on the third floor with a view of the boulevard at fifty dollars a day. She was grateful and did not notice that behind his respectful air, the clerk was very curious—perhaps troubled that she would show up unannounced, hiding behind dark glasses.

Once unpacked, Melanie showered, dressed in fresh clothing, then poured herself a glass of the

Carpati's complimentary white wine. She opened the draperies, sat down, sipped her wine, and stared out at the city. The expanse of the boulevard and the dark shapes of the buildings seemed much more real from the third floor as opposed to a suite ten stories up. *Intimate?* she wondered. No, that was the wrong word. She did feel closer to everything, but not warm or amicable. Rather, cold and vulnerable. In that sense, right now Brasov seemed—*menacing*.

Abruptly, she got up, closed the draperies, then turned, switched on a lamp and noticed the telephone by the bed. It reminded her of the frustrating experience at the Otopeni International Airport that afternoon. Just getting around in this land was going to be difficult. But to search for something both spiritual and baffling, while not speaking the language—that was impossible! She resisted a wave of panic, closed her eyes and thought logically. She did have the phone number of the studios in Bucharest; she'd just have to wait until tomorrow when people went back to work and call then. If she had any problems, she'd just ask for someone who spoke English. In the meantime, she should telephone John and tell him that she had arrived safely. Suddenly, images of Tiberon filled her mind. Ugly, powerful hands reached for him. *Hers.* He yowled with fear, but could not move. Then she had him and was bending him like a tree branch.

Melanie stifled a cry and hurried to the telephone as if that instrument were her last connection with sanity. As she reached for it, a surge of nausea forced her to drop to her knees. She retched.

Over and over.

Then she was on the crest of it, the transformation happening quicker than before. She rose to a crouch, went to the window and glared out, imagining that her eyes were dissecting the ancient city. Someone was out there who deserved her lethal claws and teeth, someone who maybe even wanted to die. She must find that person and stalk him. Now.

Before she left the room, she looked into the bathroom mirror to make sure that she appeared as hideous as she felt. Yes, there was the gnarled nose, the fur, the growths, the jagged rows of saw teeth. Satisfied, she went out the door, slammed it behind her, and hurried down the long corridor to the elevators.

After leaving the hotel, she drove sedately through the streets of Brasov, humming an eerie, discordant tune. She had no idea where she was going, yet an instinctive force told her what direction to take. She might as well have driven the route everyday, so familiar did it seem.

At the end of *Bulevardul V.I. Lenin*, she turned into a quiet neighborhood, then made a left onto *Cala 16 Februarie*, a twisting lane of cobblestones with an occasional pot hole. She parked next to a high wall, got out of the car and was accosted by a dog who barked and snapped at her. Scowling, she feinted at the cur, and he turned tail and ran away whimpering. She grinned, then quickly looked around to see if anyone had noticed. No lights went on suddenly. Except for the soft patter of a television somewhere, the neighborhood remained quiet. Peaceful, even. *But not for long*, she mused.

Something made her glance up at a second story balcony across the street. Had the shutters behind the French doors moved ever so slightly? She frowned and stared at them for a long time, but could detect nothing. It must have been her imagination. She shrugged. What did it matter? No one could stop her, anyway. Her hideous presence was invincible. Inevitable.

Get on with it, she thought. *Do not keep them waiting. It had been much too long already.*

And then she was trotting down the lane at a quick but comfortable pace. Around a bend was a cul-de-sac and behind a wall was a modest house. It seemed to be the right place. She tried the gate, but it was locked so she scaled the wall and dropped to the ground on the other side. She paused briefly to get her bearings. In front of her was a small, yet bountiful vegetable garden. With a snarl, she uprooted all of the ripening corn; whoever lived here wouldn't be needing food any more. Then she bounded over to an acacia tree and from that vantage point studied the house. No lights were on. One window was open, presumably for fresh air. *And a personficiation of the grim reaper*, she added, crossing to the window, hoisting herself up, and slipping inside the house.

She found herself in a sitting room. In the traditional fashion of peasant lodging, padded benches lined all four walls. Woven tapestries of abstract design hung above the benches, and near the ceiling a shelf held a plate collection. Should she break one deliberately, causing her victim to become worried? Or should she surprise him? An interesting choice. One that deserved a moment's reflection.

She sniffed the air. The house smelled musty and the slight odor of canned peas wafted from the kitchen. She turned and looked at a cabinet in the corner. On it were photographs. Family portraits. A quick perusal told her that she would be dealing with *two* people tonight. An elderly couple certain to be in bed right now, asleep. She grinned. No, she would not break a plate first, striking terror into their hearts. The shock might kill them, and if they died before she got to them, she would be disappointed. *Quit dallying. Now is the time.*

She padded lightly down the hallway. At the bedroom door, she stopped and decided to kill the wife first because women aged better than men, and the old lady would be the strongest. After nodding to herself, she burst into the room and turned on the light. Snarling, she lunged forward, lips curled back and teeth glistening.

*   *   *

Paralyzed, Melanie stood in the bedroom, staring at the rumpled bed covered with blood. The wife, a bulbous woman, lay there dead, pain and surprise etched on her face. Her husband, a shriveled relic, had tried to get away but had been caught by the window. He was crumpled beneath the organdy curtains dancing in the breeze, his throat and belly slashed.

Moaning with horror, Melanie averted her eyes, then had to look back at the murdered couple, desperately scanning the scene for something recognizable—a tangible sign—*anything* making sense! But her mind was fogged and she could not remember how she had ended up in this strange bedroom with two dead bodies.

Had she killed these people?

Hysterical, she staggered back against the wall, mumbling to herself. Trembling. This was no joke, no nightmare, no hallucination. She closed her eyes and forced herself to think clearly. She remembered the hotel. She was drinking a glass of wine. She was going to telephone John to tell him that she had arrived safely. She reached for the phone and . . .

And found herself *here*? She moaned again. The

conclusion seemed inescapable. She had committed two grisly murders. With what, though? She slowly looked down at her hands, opening them as if they were windows of comprehension. They were clean and told her nothing. There wasn't any blood on the rest of her, either, except for her feet and she could have walked in it when she came into the room. How could she murder anyone if she had no weapon and wasn't covered with blood? *Technicalities. If I were the police, I would arrest myself for murder and question myself and find out exactly what happened. The police have ways.*

Only she didn't know if she had done it! She didn't believe herself capable! Only who knew what happened after the retching started and she changed?

A noise.

She whirled around, whimpering, terrified that someone would find her here. Guilty. She held her breath and listened.

Another noise.

Panicked, she bolted to the window, grateful that it was open. She swung through it, fell to the ground and rolled, then scrambled up and looked around. There were fruit trees, a chicken coop, and no moon. *Thank God, the night is black.* Afraid, she ran around the side of the house to the gate in front. She hesitated there, realizing that if she went outside, she risked being caught. She had no choice. No time. She had to get out of there and pray that her car was nearby. With trembling hands, she lifted the bolt and opened the gate.

It creaked.

Heart pounding, she went through it in a crouch, eyes wide and frightened. The lights went on in the house next door. Melanie gasped, then sprinted down the lane, repressing the urge to scream.

*   *   *

Lieutenant Constantin Goga had been enjoying a breakfast of boiled eggs, sausages, and rolls when he got the telephone call from the police station. Although the news of a double murder did not please him, he was used to such unsettling phone calls and finished eating. He pushed his plate away, drained his coffee, went into the kitchen and took a fresh supply of hand-rolled Humberto Upmann cigars out of the refrigerator. These he put into his Naugahyde briefcase, which was as slim as he was portly. At the front door, he kissed his wife tenderly, said good-bye pleasantly, then left the house and drove to the location of the murders instead of his office. All things considered, he was in a decent mood.

Well aware of his importance, he parked in the middle of the street, blocking access. He got out and strolled toward the house on the cul-de-sac, chewing on a cigar. A cream-colored Fiat rested alongside the curb, the engine still groaning. Goga shook his head and smiled contemptuously. The car belonged to his thorough, but apolitical assistant, Sergeant Ionescu. Goga had told him many times that the Fiat was an inferior Western product, yet he still drove it. In his opinion, Italian automobiles had shorter lives than occupants of the Vatican.

A uniformed officer by the gate snapped to attention as Goga approached. "*Buna dimineata, Locotenent,*" he whispered.

Goga scowled and did not reply. His decent mood vanished. When the *ofiter de politie* at the gate showed the proper respect, it was usually a bad sign. This meant his homicide team, which he assumed had arrived an hour before, had encountered an unusually nasty situation.

Inside the gate, Goga studied the vegetable garden and the ruined corn. His grayish-black eyes narrowed and he felt an uncharacteristic anger building in his ample belly. During his long, distinguished career as a policeman, the last seven years as head of Brasov's homicide division, he had always managed to remain detached from his investigations. Already he knew he would become involved in this one and he hadn't even seen the victims yet. He salvaged an ear of corn, stroking it sympathetically before pocketing it. He had grown up poor on a small farm in Wallachia, and it distressed him to see deliberate waste. Murder was one thing, perchance justifiable at times, but vandalizing food? Never!

Full of sarcasm, he asked the officer at the gate why he hadn't found a bag and picked up the corn. Surprised, the policeman shrugged, a gesture Goga hated because it implied sloth. He suggested that if the policeman waited too much longer, he'd also be watching his severance pay rot on the ground.

The lieutenant turned on his heel, crossed the yard, went up the steps and rolled into the house. He had a feeling he wouldn't get any lunch today. The corn was a sign. Only it wasn't just vegetables he'd miss. He'd be passing up his usual tin of black caviar, too.

Sergeant Ionescu met him at the door, his eyes wide. "Where have you been, *Locotenent*?"

"Bodies keep, don't they?"

"But one of their children is coming!"

"Children!" Goga hissed, turning red. "*Mei doamne!* Have you lost your mind?"

"He is the *Viciu-Primar*," Ionescu explained. "The *Capitan* felt an obligation."

Goga just stood there, clenching and unclenching his fists. Cold sweat ran down his flanks; his thick neck muscles jumped and twitched, too. All right, so the *Viciu-Primar* was coming. He, Constantin Goga, still had an investigation to conduct; he still had to find out what was going on. Finally, he nodded coldly at Ionescu, meaning for the man to bring him up to date. Ionescu gulped and obliged, although there wasn't much to say. The elderly couple were retired members of the Brasov people's council, an organization Goga had always held in utmost esteem. He, himself, was a delegate of the National Party Congress, and he took his socialism as seriously as he did his job, which was rare. In his opinion, good communists were hard to find these days. But Ionescu was still talking. So far, according to the sergeant, the homicide team had found no clues. The crime seemed senseless. When Goga had heard enough, he moved his bulk forward.

Ionescu cautioned him, whispering, "It is evil. Pure evil!"

"Nonsense, Ionescu! I don't want to hear any of your speculative pig manure about the supernatural!"

With that, Goga pushed past his assistant, thinking, a murder was a murder, simply that. While some might be more vile or bizarre than others, all such crimes had motives and could be traced to some defect in the brain, not a deficiency in spirit, as Ionescu would suggest!

But when he saw the bodies, he wondered about his convictions and was forced to turn away and gag, his handkerchief held to his broad face. Stomach churning, he looked again and nodded mechanically. This one, he must admit, went beyond a defective brain and perhaps even a deficiency in spirit, too. If there were any logic or motive here, it escaped him.

The horror, the brutality! His men, usually quick

and impersonal, could not move. As one, they waited helplessly, looking to him, their faces white and sick, their eyes hollow.

"Bag them," he said flatly.

The team responded sluggishly, and he emitted a long sigh, then pulled out a small notepad and methodically began describing the scene in his own words. It wasn't that he didn't trust his photographer; rather, he always liked to compare his own utilitarian view to reality farther down the line when people had trouble recalling details. He heard his men cursing softly and glanced up. Three of them struggled to get the old lady into a bag. Suddenly, his knees went weak. The corpse reminded him of his mother who still lived on the farm, did her chores, and pulled a cart to market everyday. No doubt, this woman had worked just as hard. She had not deserved to suffer such a horrible death. Goga's anger returned; his jaws tightened and his impassive face resembled a brick, both in color and texture. He had to leave the room.

Shaken, he stood in the front room, staring at the tapestries so painstakingly woven years ago— probably before the old lady's hands had been crippled by arthritis. Who would want to kill such venerable, noble members of the Romanian working class? He shook his head, convinced his men would find no motive. There were no signs of robbery or even a dispute. Just pure savagery. Had Western decadence finally come to Brasov? Eyes downcast, Goga began pacing. The brutal murder of the peasant in the village outside Risnov just a month ago— there had been no motive, suspect, or evidence in that crime, either. Just vandalism and violence. He pursed his lips and shook his head sadly. A psychopathic killer was loose in Brasov. He couldn't ignore that fact any longer. No diligent, hard-working communist could possibly have committed such a heinous crime. Goga relit his cigar and puffed on it doggedly, while thinking of a plan of action. He heard voices and frowned.

Sergeant Ionescu led a thin, well-tailored man into the room, and Goga knew immediately that it was the Viciu-Primar. Without speaking, he formally embraced the man, then extricated himself and said, "Imi cer extrem scuze."

"Do you have any idea who could have done such a thing, Lieutenant Goga?" The man asked, his voice anguished and choked.

"No."

"What about the *lumpen proletariat*? Their members have been increasing lately."

"No." Goga scowled at the floor.

"A Gypsy, then? They have been causing trouble for centuries!"

"No."

"Don't tell me a *Szekler* was involved! My parents made no secret of their *Vlahi* ancestry!"

Goga looked up at the man, his eyes cool, but sympathetic. "A stranger is responsible for this crime, *Dommule Viciu-Primar*."

"What?" said Sergeant Ionescu, astonished that his superior would make such a bald assumption.

"An alien." Goga turned to the sergeant for confirmation. "*Dreptate*, Ionescu?"

"As you wish, sir."

Goga turned on his heel and left, then walked around the outside of the house, looking for a clue. As he neared the bedroom window, he became more meticulous, expecting to find a footprint. Instead, he discovered something else and scowled.

A crude, baroque figure had been scratched into

the windowsill. It was the same grotesque etching Goga had seen on the gate of the peasant house outside Risnov.

*   *   *

Melanie awoke with a start, sat up in bed and glanced around, eyes blinking. The beige walls with their modern art reprints, the vanity made of real maple, the desk, the—the telephone, and next to it sat the wine bottle now empty because she'd had to drink all of it in order to sleep. With a groan, she fell back onto the pillow, stared at the ceiling, and remembered. She had raced down *Calea 16 Februarie* so blind and frightened she almost went right past her car. Something made her stop and climb inside just before lights were turned on in the house across the street and the curious peered into the lane. She huddled on the floor until the shutters were closed and the lights were off. Then she drove out of the neighborhood, but soon was hopelessly lost. Since nothing was open, she stayed in her car until morning and then asked a sleepy-eyed petrol station attendant for directions to the Carpati Hotel. Once there and locked in her room, she started shaking badly, seized with the terror of not knowing what she had done. For lack of something stronger, she drank the wine. With it came mild relief and then— thank God—sleep.

She sat up again, pushed her hair out of her face and reached for the telephone. *No more. I am not going through this any more. I will not succumb. I will fight and win. Or die.* She placed a call to the National Studios in Bucharest and, after struggling past the usual language barriers, finally got through to Mihail Popescu.

"Hello, Mihail? This is Melanie Ross."

There was a long silence.

"Can you hear me?"

"Yes, of course!" he replied in a voice full of surprise and confusion. "Where are you?"

"I'm in Brasov and I have to see you."

"Why, that is . . . that is wonderful! Except I am working and I don't know what to do." He sounded uncertain. "Tomorrow, perhaps?"

"It can't wait for tomorrow."

"Very well. I'll think of something. Give me several hours to drive up there."

They agreed to meet for a late lunch at the Cerbul Carpatin, a famous restaurant, which had been a gathering place for the city's merchants 450 years ago. At the appropriate time, Melanie took a taxi into old Brasov because she didn't want to risk getting lost. The Cerbul Carpatin was in a medieval cellar near the Black Church. The interior of the restaurant was a slice of ancient Transylvania, including a Gypsy band playing folk music, and Melanie temporarily forgot her problems, enchanted by the atmosphere. Alas, when she looked up at the barrel-vaulted ceiling and saw the centuries-old carving of a dragon on a wooden stave, reality returned. Somehow the surreal representation reminded her of the drawing John had made just a few days ago, halfway around the world. Shivering, she instinctively turned to leave, but was greeted by the maître d' who graciously ushered her into the bowels of the place.

Mihail was already waiting at a table in an antechamber where the stone was moist and cool. He had ordered wine. When he saw Melanie approaching, he rose, exclaiming how delighted he was to see her again. Then he kissed her hand, waved the maître d' off, seated her and poured her a glass of the chilled Moldavian white. He was acting as if they were old friends meeting harmlessly to share a pleasant moment out of the day, only his performance was forced. He ran his hands through his blond hair once too often to be relaxed. Occasionally, his blue eyes darted off to see if they were being observed. She grew annoyed. *He's nervous that someone will think we're lovers. How ironic. I want nothing more to do with him. I should tell him that and get to the point.* Except she couldn't think of how to say it, and they were silent.

He ate garnished veal with fried potatoes, while she had roasted chicken—more for the sake of appearances than anything else since she wasn't hungry.

"You should eat," he said low, pouring them more wine. "You look gaunt."

"Oh, really. And why do you suppose I look gaunt?" She studied him, waiting for his reaction.

"A lack of food and love," he said quietly, and she burned under his adoring gaze.

"Stop it," she whispered.

"Stop what?" He set his fork down, spread his hands and smiled. "I am very flattered that you have returned to Romania. Forgive me for being presumptuous, but don't you—like me—want to share a blissful moment from our recent past?"

She shook her head firmly, but couldn't look him in the eye. "No."

He leaned back, puzzled and unsure. "No? But why—"

"I want to know what you've done to me," she pressed.

"You want—"

"Mihail!" she exclaimed in a hiss and glared at him. "I want to know how you've cursed me and why!"

*   *   *

Mei Doamne! Mihail thought, staring at her, his jaw slack. What did she mean? How treacherous could a woman become? She had come to him and he had unlocked the passion hiding inside her, and now, there she sat, impaling him with her eyes and saying he had *cursed* her? He had *loved* her! He remembered what had transpired since he had last seen Melanie Ross. With visions of the west dancing in his head, he had gone to the American embassy for a visa only to be informed coldly that he needed a sponsor. Certain of Melanie, he had returned to Brasov only to find that she had gone and left no message, no explanation, nothing. His heart was broken; his dreams, shattered. Morose, he went home again, and his wife, Ioana, accused him of infidelity (even though she had no proof), then threatened him with a divorce, a move that could create a scandal. Ever since, his life had been taut, grim, automatic. Often he had nightmares of walking through a maze of electronic eyes that revealed his soul. He felt Melanie Ross had deserted him. She didn't even appreciate the risks he was taking right now! He made a nervous shrug, wishing he hadn't begged off work, telling the producer that an emergency had come up at home and he had to leave work immediately. This woman didn't realize what would happen to him if people learned of his affair with an American actress. His superiors (no doubt envious) would condemn him as untrustworthy. He might as well forget about a promotion to director of photography. Also, he would be a prime candidate for political re-education. And she was saying he had cursed *her*? Confused, Mihail shook his head and stared off, trying to order his thoughts, but one question kept recurring in his mind: What had she come back for?

Obviously, another affair, no matter what she had said moments ago. He closed his eyes and recalled their times in bed together. Such beauty. Such passion. Such satisfaction. Nothing in his life compared, and he yearned to taste Melanie Ross once more. Still, should he be so willing to tempt fate again? Frowning intently, he took stock of things and told himself he had to face it. Since she had left, his life had resumed its boring, predictable pace. His marriage was a mutual silence as usual. His children were whining again as usual. His sex life was banal as usual. His work on a film about tractors was ordinary as usual. Bah! If he ever did get promoted, he'd end up lighting and photographing steel mills instead of actors! So if this woman had come back to Romania for him, why should he be afraid? Why should he hang onto mediocrity? His life hadn't changed without her! Perhaps it would change with her! (Could he trust her?) Yes. (Was he wrong?) No, he decided.

He sighed and relaxed a little. As the notion blossomed in his mind, he felt warm, then excited by the prospects. He would court her. He would treat her like a princess in bed and out. True, for the present he must remain discreet, but once she agreed to sponsor his emigration to America, then it wouldn't matter. He could see her when and where he pleased. He shuddered with pleasure. And once in the States he could become a director of photography, with the mystique of the Eastern European *artiste*. Except he would take it seriously. He would make a significant, magical contribution to the cinema of the future.

He looked at her as he would a prospective bride, then raised his glass in silent tribute. No, he had not cursed her; rather, he was coming into her life again.

"Well?" she asked, rather puzzled by his silence.

Eyes soft and innocent, he smiled and replied, "If love is a curse, then I suppose I'm guilty."

"*Love?*" she responded, aghast. "How can you talk about love?"

He leaned toward her, intimately so. "I thought that was the subject of this conversation."

"In that case, there is nothing more to say."

"Speak for yourself, Melanie Ross. If you dare."

She sighed with exasperation. "Will you please forget this . . . this nonsense? I don't want anything to do with you!"

He straightened up, hurt and bewildered. "But why? What about the beautiful moments we shared?"

She half-stood and leaned over the table, an intense, desperate frown on her face. "I'm not interested in repeating past mistakes, Mihail, so *forget it! Please?*"

A silence. If there had been anyone else within shouting distance, Mihail was sure that they would have heard. His ears burned. She sat down again and drained her wine glass. He could see her hand shaking so he poured her more. She did not refuse it. "Then what do you want?" he asked.

"You don't understand, do you?"

He grinned sheepishly and shrugged. "I have done my best, but I must confess that I do not."

"Ever since we met and I . . . and I—"

"Slept with me?"

She nodded quickly. "Something has happened to me."

His heart surged with joy, yet he was still confused. If she was trying to tell him that she was in love with him, she certainly was choosing a strange method. *Mei Doamne*, these American women, he truly did not understand them!

"I am filled with self-loathing. I am—" She touched her forehead, closed her eyes and once again recalled the drawing that John had made. Then she looked at Mihail, her face impassive, almost placid. "I am a monster."

He wanted to laugh and say, "And you blame these feelings on my love for you?" Instead, he listened respectfully. When she explained that she could arbitrarily change into a hideous, evil creature, though, he could not hold back his astonishment. She was completely serious! His intentions were momentarily forgotten. They dissolved with the enormity of what she was saying, and he began to think on her behalf instead of his own.

Had she taken a drug? He scrutinized her actions, but she appeared normal. Then he figured she was making up her story, except . . . why would she tell him something that was so obviously phantasmagoric? To repel and disgust him? Perhaps.

He smiled slowly and felt his mind being pulled into something he did not understand, yet was pleasant nonetheless. He realized her strange tale was absorbing and involving him. He *wanted* it to be true! Yes, how perfectly marvelous that his lover should be a marionette of the supernatural! It seemed fitting for an affair that had started in Transylvania, the very cradle of the occult. And so he gazed into her eyes and took her hand in both of his, nodding all the while.

"Have you thought about seeing Doctor Schadt?"

*   *   *

My God! she thought, *I don't believe it! He actually understands! I don't know whether to laugh or cry!* She frowned abruptly. *Hasn't this man—in some way—already cursed me before? Why am I so willing to trust him?* She read his face and discerned genuine innocence. Then she remembered his total amazement just a few seconds ago when she had told him that she was a monster. There was no way he could have faked either reaction. She was an actress, she knew. Was she wrong, then? She nodded inwardly. The conclusion was inescapable. He was *not* responsible; he had not cast a spell over her or cursed her. *Except with his love?* She blushed crimson and did not know what to say. That same bittersweet melody played in her mind—that same song of inevitable sorrow.

When she realized he was still holding her hand, she was embarrassed further, then shook off the feeling. It was all right; he felt sorry for her; he seemed willing to help; he had recommended someone. She slowly pulled back her hand, in the process, allowing her fingertips to graze his palm, although she was not conscious of what she had done until it was too late. His eyes lit up, but she glossed over his response by taking pen and pad out of her uncluttered purse with a breezy flourish.

"Who is this Doctor Schadt?"

"He is a Dutchman who moved his practice to Timisoara many years ago. Romania has always been a haven for medical and pharmaceutical revolutionaries, and Dr. Schadt specialized in mysterious, heretofore incurable diseases. Until recently, I suppose, his reputation was obscure."

"How did you find out about him?"

"He was mentioned in an article my wife saw in a Western magazine." Mihail paused, suddenly looked pained. "Shall we go? I would love some fresh air."

"All right," she said cautiously.

"A drive in the country?"

She nodded.

They took the highway to Poiana Brasov, and he

continued speaking of Dr. Schadt, although she noticed that his voice was slightly strained and his words forced. *He is uneasy,* she thought. *I wonder why.*

Mihail explained that for the last five years, he had been plagued with insomnia and migraine headaches, conditions looked upon with suspicion by the bureaucrats. More recently, he had been having nightmares, which only aggravated the insomnia, so when he learned of Dr. Schadt, he was quick to make an appointment. At first, he was appalled because the good doctor charged a thousand *lei* per treatment for patients not referred through official channels. In retrospect, the cost had been worth it, however; better to spend hard-earned savings than to have illnesses of a psychological nature on one's state medical records, no?

"Surely the authorities don't hold emotional problems against citizens, do they?"

"Why take the chance?"

"So did Doctor Schadt cure you?"

"Yes!" he exclaimed enthusiastically, then paused to negotiate a steep exit off the highway.

They drove along a narrow, but recently-paved road that meandered through a mountain valley lush with the green of early summer. Mihail explained that after six extended psychotherapy sessions, he was better, except for an occasional blackout.

"Why do you get those?" she asked, absorbed. "Did you have them to start with?"

"No. They are a side-effect of the drug he gave me." He grinned self-consciously. "Sometimes I forget to take the pills. Then the headaches come back and I know I've been remiss."

"But what do you have, anyway?"

"He diagnosed my condition as a rare dysfunction called *schizincroniza.*"

"What's that?"

"There is no English translation." He laughed strangely. "I don't even know what it means in Romanian."

Melanie fell silent and stared out the window at a small farm with horses and cows grazing nearby. Behind the pastures, forests of beech, oak, and fir covered the mountainside. *If you let it happen, the beauty here could overwhelm you,* she thought idly.

At the western end of the valley, Mihail turned up a long driveway that led to a chalet and cabins, now almost deserted because of the off-season. He parked in the lot near the main entrance.

"Why are we stopping here?"

Leaning against the steering wheel, he turned toward her and smiled. "You said you didn't want to repeat mistakes of the past," he stated solemnly, while caressing her hair, "but we never talked about what delightful moments the future might hold for us."

Before she could respond, he pulled her to him and kissed her. She placed her hands against his chest and tried to push away, but her strength failed. Then her resolve crumbled, too, and she felt her thighs go weak, then hot and moist. Head swimming, she returned the kiss, only without energy; she had none. Her last thought of any clarity was that the moment was an exaltation of sorrow.

He left the car to rent a cabin. She just sat there waiting, her jaw slack, her vision fogged from tears that came easily. *What am I doing, anyway? Why am I allowing this to happen? I hated myself for this before; I despised him, too. And yet the ultimate truth is: right now, it doesn't matter. There is something about him. Something I want.*

He came back, helped her out of the car, then

took her hand and led her across a freshly-cut expanse of grass toward a cabin. Insects jumped and buzzed and flew in the late afternoon sun. She followed numbly, waving her free hand in front of her, trying to dispel an aura of haze. *Was it the wine I drank or am I sleepwalking?*

"By the way, before I forget, there's one thing you should understand," he said.

"What?" she replied, vaguely aware that he was only making conversation to get them over the awkward space that lay between where they were now and the bed inside the cabin.

"One of Doctor Schadt's preoccupations is demonic possession."

"What?"

"It is a little known fact, but according to his research assistant, he is the only doctor in the world who treats it as a disease."

Five

At precisely six o'clock A.M. at 23½ *Grivita Rosie* in the quiet city of Timisoara, a large white cat with slate eyes leaped onto the chest of the sleeping Dr. Fritz G. Schadt and yowled in his face. On cue, eleven other cats, of all sizes and colors who lived in the flat, began meowing and trotting into the kitchen for their breakfast.

Mumbling, Schadt rolled out of bed gracefully, his feet hitting the cold floor the same time his eyes blinked open. He slipped into a heavy wool robe that he had inherited from his father, a missionary in South Africa who had been murdered by colonialists. Then he padded to the bay window, raised the shade and squinted out at his flower beds in back. He beamed, his freckles crinkling generously. The black rose bush had finally blossomed. With a sigh of pleasure, he turned and moved his short, but lithe frame into the bathroom, nimbly avoiding cats zigzagging beneath his feet. For privacy's sake, he shut them out and took his constitutional. When finished, he shaved, washed his face, brushed his teeth and combed his blond hair, which did not yet have a trace of gray, even though he was fifty-seven. Next, he opened the medicine cabinet and took out a bottle of Gerovital H-e, a Romanian wonder drug that he was convinced kept him looking fifteen years younger. More important, he thought while swallowing three, the pills made him *feel* fifteen years younger. Although he hadn't analyzed or tested the drug personally, sometimes he speculated that it would triple his productive years.

He left the bathroom, hopped over a persistent calico, then dressed in his usual light-brown tweeds. As a final touch, he donned a powder-blue bow tie, selecting that particular color because his buxom research assistant, Tanya, said it matched his eyes. Flexing his hands, he walked through his cavernous study made smaller by comfortable chairs and a good library. He went into the tiled kitchen, which—when he needed to entertain someone—seemed stocked with nothing but exotic herb teas and cases of cat food.

Greeted by choruses of meows, he went to the sink and began the precarious ritual of opening six cans while surrounded by felines, some swatting at others so they could get close to the horrendous odor of cooked fish parts. He thanked God for American ingenuity everytime he pressed down on the electric can opener.

Later, Schadt strolled down the gentle curve of his neighborhood street on his way to work, enjoying the bright sunlight and the singing birds. He passed one of the old city's many parks and admired the sculptured gardens. An elderly gardener saw him and they exchanged nods before Schadt continued on. After crossing *Bulevardul Politechnii*, he entered the center of Timisoara, which was every bit as quaint and well kept as the residential neighborhoods. It was, truly, the city of gardens, and that was one reason Schadt had come here fifteen years ago. For him, life in Timisoara was a rebirth; he had seen too much of death in his time. He shuddered, then frowned and did not understand why the memories were coming back now on a typical Tuesday morning walk to work.

Fifteen years. He couldn't help but smile. Fifteen years of peace. Before, existence had been a constant struggle. He had been a student at the Sorbonne during World War II. Then came medical school in Amsterdam when it seemed all of Europe would sell its soul for a chocolate bar and a carton of American cigarettes. Next was a residency in the moralistic, opulent midwestern United States, plus a disastrous first marriage to a cheerleader with a degree in psychology. And finally, the years with Father on the dark continent and the battles with the Afrikaaners to establish health care programs for the blacks. As a result, he had become political, and they began speaking out. His father was assassinated and he was banished.

When he tried to go home, the Netherlands refused to let him into the country on the grounds that he was an international anarchist and troublemaker. While floating helplessly at sea, he applied to countries like a prep-schooler in search of a good college. Months later, he was accepted by Romania, a nation he had long admired for the risks they took in medical science. After a brief residency in Bucharest, he finally made his way to Timisoara, a center for some of the most advanced research in pharmaceutics in the world. He found it fitting that Timisoara was a city of flora and fauna, too. In his opinion, gardens and drugs should complement each other.

He had always known that he would end up in Timisoara, hadn't he? Even though he had been born in the Netherlands and grown up Dutch, he had never felt as though he belonged anywhere until he had come here. He was comfortable. He had found his soul in Timisoara. After so many, many years. If he weren't so old, he would consider raising a family here. A sudden thought made him pause, then chuckle with delight. Given the ongoing experimentation with geriatrics in Timisoara, that was a distinct possibility, anyway. Perhaps when this current business was over, he would make an undignified pass at the voluptuous and (he hoped) innocent Tanya. He sucked in a lungful of air heavy with the perfume of rose and jasmine blossoms. Yes, soon he would indulge in the pleasures of youth that he had never taken much time for when he was young.

After passing another park, he turned down *Bulevardul Michelangelo*, a short, tree-lined street just off the main plaza. He loved the name, which was why he'd leased offices here. Also, he was close to all the big laboratories, yet no one really took notice of him and that was how he wanted it. Except now he had to be careful or else he'd be forced to move to protect his anonymity. A frequent lunch and backgammon partner was the physician, Vasile Boici, famous for discovering space-age pain killers and mood enhancers. Six months ago, Boici had introduced him to a *Psychology Today* contributor. The result had been a favorable article mentioning his work with pharmaceutics applied to moral and spiritual disorders. A rash of correspondence and phone calls followed, which Tanya handled with aplomb, but the experience left Schadt wary. His findings were too volatile and revolutionary to share with the world right now. There were too many proverbial toes to step on: the church, the state, the orthodox medical profession, the communist party, the university paranormal investigators. If any of them deemed him dangerous, he would be crushed instantly. And he wasn't finished yet; his mission wasn't complete. Too much was at stake right now. Better to indulge pleasant thoughts of his cats, his flowers, and Tanya than to do any more babbling about his research.

As he approached the two-story, baroque building, he swelled with pride. Once it had been a townhouse for the Hungarian royal family. During the war, it had been headquarters for the German General Staff and then the Russians. Now it was his. Tasteful wrought-iron letters above the entranceway read: *Institut de Medical si Farmaceutic a Dr. F. G. Schadt.*

He went up the steps, through the door and into the spacious foyer, where he was greeted by his receptionist, Peter, who always insisted upon taking his coat and hat. He put up with the show of deference, rather than protest and risk offending the young man. Then he trudged up the spiral staircase and hurried down a long hallway. His personal office was at the end in a circular room with windows offering a view of an intimate courtyard below. Beyond the wall was a park of gentle slopes and flowering trees and then whitewashed buildings with slate roofs sparkling in the sun. He closed the door behind him and immediately went to the windows, avoiding the stacks of paperwork on his huge desk. Hands behind his back, he absorbed the beauty and longed to be outside. He glanced down. Tanya was in the courtyard, taking her morning tea. Schadt gazed at her, wishing that he had the talent of, say, a Rembrandt so he could paint her. He shook his head sadly. No such luck. He had been cursed with the abilities of the scientist. All his life those skills had haunted him, forcing him to sacrifice for their benefit. Sometimes he enjoyed it, but not when the external world—the land of sight—was so appealing. He bit his lip, turned away and faced his desk. With a sigh, he marched behind it and sat down, consoled by one thought. Soon, his work would be over, and he could spend the rest of his days leisurely documenting his findings in an autobiography. He would call it *The Memories and Discoveries of a Displaced Dutchman*. Weather permitting, he would write the tome outside, eschewing laboratories of all kinds. He would, of course, continue to help out the local veterinarian who saw his twelve cats. Some chores made his heart sing.

He picked up a pencil to rework some formulae, which he thought might be the pharmaceutic equivalent of the golden rule, then frowned abruptly and stared off. Vasile Boici had often remarked fondly that the reason they were such godawful backgammon players was they both had become slaves to medical research. "Bah!" Schadt snorted. What Boici didn't know was that he was a slave to the past. He had *always* been driven by medical research.

Suddenly, he straightened up, closed his eyes, and automatically touched the bridge of his nose, a sign that something remarkable was about to happen. Yes, a premonition was coming to him. He wondered if it were connected to the memories he'd had so unexpectedly while walking to work. Probably, he mused. Destiny had a way of making the events in one's life like stars blinking randomly on a celestial spiderweb.

Someone knocked softly on his door.

"Come in," he said wearily.

Tanya stepped inside and smiled demurely, her

intelligence belied by a round face, brown eyes, long red hair, and curves that made her blush frequently. "Buna dimineata, Dr. Schadt."

"Buna dimineata, Tanya." He gazed at her body, admiringly.

She looked down and her cheeks reddened. "You have a telephone call, sir."

"Already?" He dropped his pencil and spread his hands. "But I haven't done any work yet! Who is it?"

"A lady calling long distance from Brasov. Someone named Melanie Ross."

*   *   *

Heart pounding, Melanie hung on the line and waited. She hated phoning blind, but under the circumstances she had no choice. She could only hope that Dr. Schadt would not turn her away. Eyes downcast, she watched a muscle in her hand twitch spasmodically. It was a renewal of guilt. Ever since she'd come back to the hotel late last night after her episode with Mihail, she had been compulsively restless. Once again she had to drink herself to sleep. Now she was bleary-eyed and groggy, yet remained on edge. The mere act of waiting for someone to come back on the line was torture in itself. She had no patience left.

An inner voice told her to hang up and forget about Dr. Schadt. *He can't help you. No one can. Used and dirty, you are beyond redemption.* Bitter tears welled up in her eyes, and she deliberated with herself. The longer she sat there, ear nervously glued to the receiver, the more insignificant and depressed she felt. *He doesn't want to talk to me.* She moved to hang up the phone, then suddenly stopped. *Dammit, I need help! I must talk to him! I'll wait forever if I have to!* Finally, she heard a click and held her breath expectantly.

"*Alo?*"

She was surprised, for she had expected him to sound somber, erudite, or condescending. Instead, his voice was pleasant, musical, and droll, and she thought that he sounded more like a philosopher than a doctor.

"*Alo?*" he repeated.

"Hello, Doctor Schadt?"

"*Si aceasta e Dr. Schadt a vorbi. Cu a servitati?*"

There was a long pause while she flipped through her guide book to the telephone section.

"*Cu a servitati?*" he repeated patiently.

"*Nu inteleg,*" she said haltingly, feeling like an illiterate schoolgirl. "Uh . . . *scuzati. Va rog repetati. Nu vorbesc Romaneste prea bine.*"

(Was that a chuckle she heard?)

"That is quite all right, Miss Ross. I speak English fluently, although I suppose my diction and syntax can be faulted by someone who uses the language everyday, no?"

"Oh," she replied, surprised, embarrassed, and then very relieved. "Oh, thank God."

"Now, how can I help you?"

"I'd like to make an appointment to see you at your earliest convenience," she said in a rush.

"Regarding what?"

"Well, I don't really know how to say it. Something's wrong with me, only I can't remember what it is or exactly what happens to me!"

"Perhaps you are experiencing a temporary emotional upset?"

"That, too."

"I'm sorry to say, but you don't need me for such a common condition." He sounded suspicious all of a sudden.

"Please," she asked desperately. "I mean, I know

I'm not saying it right, but you must understand that it's difficult for me to talk on the telephone to someone I don't know."

"You are not alone."

"Then can I please make an appointment?"

"Miss Ross, I'm sorry, but I have too many patients as it is, so if you must have an interview with me, the least you can do is give me an idea what is wrong with you, no?"

"I have become a *monster!*" she cried. "Don't you understand?"

A sudden hush.

"How did you find out about me?" he asked quietly.

"Someone gave me your name."

"Ah, a referral. Why didn't you say so in the first place? May I ask who?"

"Mihail Popescu."

*   *   *

The telephone still to his ear, Schadt stared at the windows, mouth agape. His mind raced, trying to make a connection between the memories he'd had on his way to work, the sudden premonition just before Tanya came in, this woman, Melanie Ross, whom he did not know, and now, Mihail Popescu.

He failed.

The events, the people remained random. Isolated. He needed more information. Still, he sensed that something significant was happening that he had not anticipated. He frowned. Destiny was muddying up what had seemed a clear trail to the horizon. Cynically he considered: Since when has the path to righteousness ever been smooth?

"Doctor Schadt, are you there?" she asked in a tiny, fearful voice.

He opened his calendar and began crossing out

appointments scheduled for the afternoon. "Can you see me at five o'clock?"

"Yes. Oh, yes," she said gratefully.

He gave her the address, wished her a pleasant trip, then hung up. Cursing softly, he closed his eyes and put his head down on the desk. Why was this woman *really* coming to see him? And how did she know Mihail Popescu? Maybe Popescu had become dissatisfied with his treatment and had talked to the medical review authorities. Schadt's innards tightened and cold sweat beaded up on his forehead. And maybe, if that were the case, he was being set up by a sweet-sounding young lady who was posing as a foreigner. He would know soon enough, he supposed.

He paused for thought and shook off his paranoia; his instincts told him that Melanie Ross was genuine. She represented an unexpected, unknown complication he must deal with. Nothing more. So Popescu had referred her? So what? People did it all the time. Even he was guilty of referrals, having urged the widow Bantas to take her precious Siamese to his veterinarian because the man had an uncanny ability to put cats at ease.

He scowled, muttering under his breath, "Don't deceive yourself, Schadt! This is no ordinary referral!" She had said something about becoming a monster and not remembering what had happened. Her dark experience could be the first hard evidence that he, Fritz G. Schadt, had actually tapped into the supernatural. But how could he have affected her? He had never met the woman. There was no way she could have had access to his writings or experimental pharmaceutics, either. Everything he did was kept under lock and key. (Much to his chagrin, he had even been known to lock up grocery lists on occasion.) He shrugged. Right now he had no answers. All he could do was wait and try not to fear the worse.

He heard knocking and turned, grateful for the interruption. "Come in, please."

Tanya entered with his morning edition of *Romania libera*, a pot of tea, and a stack of computer read-outs. She was her normal buoyant and cheerful self until she saw his face. Instantly sympathetic, she took a chair across from him and asked if there were anything she could do.

"Cancel my afternoon appointments. A woman will be coming at five."

She nodded soberly. "I will stay past seven if you want me to."

"It isn't necessary, Tanya," he said with forced joviality. "As a matter of fact, why don't you take the day off? Have a good time while you still can."

"Whatever you wish, sir," she replied wistfully.

"Come, come now! Where's your enthusiasm?" He gestured at the windows. "Look outside! The weather is perfect!"

"You are still working, sir."

"There is much to do," he replied vaguely.

"Then I will stay."

"No. I insist that you indulge yourself! You are young and frisky, no?"

She rose and half-smiled. "Very well. I will go home, write poetry, and pray that someday you will enjoy inner solitude." She blushed. "Forgive me for being so bold, sir, but youth is nothing without wisdom."

*   *   *

When she found out it was a six-hour drive to Timisoara, Melanie knew she would never make

her appointment, so she went to the airport only to
discover that there were no flights to Timisoara that
day. Not to be dissuaded, she bought a ticket to
Arad, a city just north of her destination, then decided to have lunch since she had a two-hour wait.
In the cafeteria, she wondered why Dr. Schadt hadn't
told her that she wouldn't have time to make the
trip by car. Perhaps it had been an oversight. Maybe
not. She was thoughtful. As far as she could tell, Dr.
Schadt's reaction to Mihail's name had been one of
shock. But why? Had Mihail already told the doctor
of their intimate conversation at the Cerbul Carpatin?
She scowled. Something mysterious was going on,
only she didn't have a clue. She felt like a pawn on
an iridescent board that changed realities if tilted
slightly.

The flight to Arad was quick and pleasant. They
served beer and *tuica*, so when Melanie landed, she
was more relaxed and confident. Even though no
one in the local ACR office spoke English, she rented
a car anyway by using sign language and pointing to
lines in her guide book. Triumphantly, she drove
out of the agency and headed south on a two-lane
highway that took her through the rolling hills and
farmlands of the Banat.

She made it to Timisoara by 4:30, fully expecting
to encounter rush-hour traffic, but there was none.
Except for a light stream of bicycles and small cars,
she might as well have driven in during the dead of
night. She found a parking space with no problem,
got out of her car, and was astonished by the beauty
of the inner city. Long shadows gave the trees and
buildings a magical quality. Pedestrians moved lan-
guidly through hazy sunlight, and the air was ripe
with pollen. Melanie longed for the tranquility of

Timisoara to touch her life and thus went up the steps of Schadt's institute encouraged.

The receptionist greeted her indifferently, then led her into a waiting room on the ground floor, which had once been a formal library. She hoped that her conservative dress, dark glasses, and floppy hat didn't make the man think that she was a desperate woman in search of an illegal prescription, although wasn't that exactly why she was here? She blushed, sat down and waited, admiring the original paintings and antiques in the room, thinking the decor was more in keeping with an estate in France than the waiting room of an enigmatic doctor in Eastern Europe.

A grandfather clock with a gold pendulum struck five, and the muted chimes did not echo. Melanie heard children laughing, so she stood, gazed out the window and saw three boys bouncing a soccer ball back and forth with their heads. Charmed, she smiled, became lost in the moment, and forgot her troubles. Silently, she urged them on, wishing that the ball would stay in the air for an eternity. Then she felt a presence, turned quickly and was startled. A small man with blue eyes and a freckled, cherubic face stood there scrutinizing her and chuckling.

"Doctor Schadt?"

He gestured at the window. "You watch them and I watch you and we both hope their delight is infectious, no?"

She nodded hesitantly.

"Yes, I am Doctor Schadt." He bowed slightly and indicated a door in the far corner. "This way, please."

She followed him into a room of quite a different character. There were no windows. Light emanated from frosted panels in the low ceiling. Plush leather furniture abounded and a long table was against one wall. They were in a conference room. Schadt indicated that she should take a chair, then sat across from her and pulled out a small notepad. She gulped, leaned forward and held onto her knees so he wouldn't see that her hands were shaking. When she looked up at him, she could not see his eyes.

"You are an American, no?"

"Yes."

He made a note.

"And you?" she asked timidly.

"A displaced Dutchman," he said lightly, then waved his hand as if to dispel any curiosity she might have about him. "What brings you to Romania, Miss Ross?"

"I am not well. I am—" She exhaled in a rush, considered lying, then decided to withhold nothing. Too much was at stake. "I am in search of my soul, for I am dead in spirit."

Taken aback, he paused and stared off. "Those are not your words."

"No. I spoke with a priest. In Southern California. When I was home last. You wouldn't know him."

"His name?"

"Father Earl Beckett."

He wrote it down, then spoke without looking up. "And how do you know Mihail Popescu?"

"I worked on a film with him, I—" She blushed. "I was his lover."

"*Was?*" he asked, not conscious of his emphasis.

"I suppose I still am," she said sadly.

He glanced at her wedding band. "You're married."

"It wouldn't matter whether I was or I wasn't! Mihail Popescu touches something inside me I don't understand! He is—" She paused and then the word just came out. "Irresistible."

"Why is he so irresistible?" Schadt asked, leaning forward.

She remembered following Mihail trancelike across the grass to the cabin, then being pulled inside. He had locked the door, kissed her tenderly and started undressing her. She had found him impossible to fight because he touched her with love and consideration like an angel. Soon, she was on the bed, overcome by sadness, confused that she didn't feel ugly or dirty. When he had stepped away to take his clothes off, she had begun crying and begged him to leave her alone. Concerned, he had held her close until the emotions passed. While caressing her hair, he had whispered that he would respect her wishes, then had gotten off the bed and turned his back until she was dressed. He had told her that he wanted to see her again, but he would have to work things out. She had nodded dumbly. Embracing her, he had said that sex wasn't that important to him— his feelings for her went beyond anything physical. Bewildered, she had nodded again and touched his lips. At the door, he had kissed her one last time, and she had felt herself melt into him willingly. If he hadn't taken her back to the car, she knew what she would have done. She hated the memory because she had lost control.

Only more so: *I understand none of it.*

She frowned at Schadt. "Why are you asking me about him?"

"He referred you."

"Are you a psychiatrist?" she said indignantly.

He smiled. "Of course not."

"Well, then, just what is your specialty?"

He touched the bridge of his nose. "Let me think."

He has to think about it?

"In English, I suppose the medical profession would label me a psychopharmaceuticologist." He smiled. "Although you must understand that I don't make insignificant moral judgments."

"Oh." *What the hell is he talking about?*

"Personally, I'd rather be called a *philopharma-ceuticologist*. It has a nicer ring, don't you think?"

"Doctor, please," she whispered.

He frowned. "Rest assured, Mrs. Ross, that my cases are kept in the strictest confidence. Nothing you tell me goes beyond the sanctity of my files. So if I choose to ask you about something potentially scandalous, you must cooperate regardless, or I cannot help you. Is that clear?"

She gulped and nodded.

"So if you don't like Mihail Popescu, then why on earth are you involved with him?"

"I don't know." She paused and thought. "I do like him, I guess. No, that's not it. I think—" She sighed, then tried again. "I feel compelled to—I am compelled to—to run amok?"

"Why are you asking me?" he said, fascinated.

"Because I can't remember what happens to me!"

"With Mihail?"

"No," she said impatiently, not seeing the glint in his eyes. And then she explained about the compulsions that had smitten her at home and finally in Brasov. Schadt became more and more interested, frequently stopping her and asking her to repeat things so he could make note of them. He paid particular attention to her description of the drawing John had made, although it seemed to confound him. For a long time after she finished, he just stared off, preoccupied, his eyes half-closed. Was he meditating? Or in search of something buried in the subconscious? Finally, he sighed with frustration, then began lecturing quietly about delusions and hallucinations not induced by synthetic drugs.

"Are you telling me that my experiences are not real?" she asked, astounded.

"It is quite possible," he replied. "You see, the human body produces some of the most powerful organic substances we know of. It is, if you will, the original pharmacy, and if the subconscious mind wants a certain chemical to create a particular situation, more than likely, it happens. I suppose you could call a dream or a nightmare an organic hallucination. And more often than not such experiences are beyond the capacity of our reasoning powers. Sometimes, I think the entire universe can be found inside our minds, yet we understand little of it. Ironic, no?"

"Dr. Schadt," she said in anguish, "I hardly think that the mangled body of my favorite cat is a hallucination!"

He stiffened.

She began crying. "And I hardly think that finding myself with a murdered elderly couple is a hallucination! Especially when the hotel desk clerk tells me about the crime the next day and says the Brasov police are investigating!"

Distressed, he got up and began pacing. "You're sure that you were there?"

"Yes!"

"Did you kill those two people?"

"I don't *know* what I did!" She began sobbing.

Schadt sat on the arm of her chair and patted her shoulder. Had she looked into his eyes, she would have seen that he was calming himself, too. "You must not think it true," he said softly.

"But what if I did it?" she whispered hoarsely.

"Reality is of no consequence right now," he soothed. "And if you think you are a murderer and dwell on it, your condition will worsen. That I can guarantee."

She gazed up at him, her eyes red and swollen, her face, tear-stained. "Do you know what's wrong with me, then?"

"Not yet." He stroked her hair, clinically so. "But I will find out."

"Oh—thank you." She took his hand and pressed it to her face. "There's hope, then?"

"Humanity will always have an eternity of second chances," he pontificated. "And then one day it will end and we will not know why."

She hadn't heard him, which was just as well. "You'll give me something to stop the—the compulsions?"

"I wish I could. Right now I don't know enough. I'll have to start with Mihail Popescu and go from there."

She straightened up and frowned. "Why him?"

"Because he is symptomatic of the disorder. He is the tip of the psychological iceberg, so to speak."

"I've already seen a psychiatrist," she said defiantly.

He smiled. "Conventional psychiatry will do you no good, Melanie." He got up, crossed the room and sat on the table, facing her. "Your Father Beckett, the priest, was right. I must cable him my professional congratulations. The key to your therapy is rekindling your spirit."

"How do I do that?"

"By searching for your roots and identifying your past."

Puzzled, she looked at her hands. Had she glanced at Schadt, she would have seen that he was nervous. "But what good can come of?—"

"Don't argue with me, Melanie Ross!" He slammed

his fist down on the table. "Don't you *ever* question a diagnosis of mine, even if it is only partially complete! or, for that matter, what I might prescribe for you!"

"I'm sorry."

"Why do you think you were drawn to Romania and the hometown of your ancestors?"

"I never thought of that."

"Did you think your disease was a human virus? Did you think that I would be listening to you if an ordinary doctor could cure your illness? Bah!" He threw up his hands, paused, then softened the tone of his voice. "Somehow, my dear lady, you have gotten tangled up with the supernatural, and somehow we must unravel the mystery."

"But why me?" she cried.

"Why anyone?" He resumed pacing. "You may ring me day or night. Your condition could worsen suddenly." He glanced at his watch. "Christ! Where does the time go?"

"I didn't mean to make you late for another appointment."

"It doesn't matter. I'm late for everything. It comes from knowing in your heart that time is relative."

He left the conference room. She followed, surprised that he walked so quickly. While crossing the elegant waiting room, she glanced out the window and saw that the street was gray and cold in a misty twilight. She shuddered and hurried to catch Schadt. When she came into the foyer, he was halfway up the stairs.

"Excuse me, Doctor."

"Yes?"

"If you don't mind me asking, what is your fee?"

"For you? Nothing."

Stunned, she stood at the foot of the staircase

and stared up at him, her jaw slack. "Nothing?"

He grimaced, then bowed slightly. *"Nu te lega la cap cind nu te doara."*

She shook her head helplessly, not understanding. "But isn't there something I can do?"

He thought and shrugged. "You might pray that destiny is on our side." He smiled pleasantly in spite of himself. "And stay away from Mihail Popescu."

*   *   *

Muttering, Schadt walked down the corridor to his office, turning on the lights as he went. When he was locked inside, he let himself in a sideroom, which, when in a grandiose mood, he referred to as the "medical records division of the Schadt institute." He switched on one of the computers, keyed in, then asked the machine to find Melanie Ross. The response was a compilation of news items from the Hollywood trade papers. Aside from a birth date and place, there was nothing about her personal life or history. Disgusted, he asked for a read-out anyway, then posed the same questions regarding Mihail Popescu. This time the information was much more extensive, only Schadt knew it already, since most of the data came from his own files. For convenience sake, he got a second read-out then retired to his desk, grumbling about being overworked.

After reviewing his notes, he recalled Melanie saying that she'd come to him because he treated demonic possession as a disease. Bah! That rumor came from Mihail Popescu, no doubt. If only her case were so simple. Demons were easy. He had the molecular structure and chemical essence of many on file. All he had to do to rid people of them was use a time-release synthetic, which was poison to the demon in question. In those cases, the problem was the victims. Since they were possessed, one could hardly get them to submit to an examination, let alone stand still for treatment. No, Melanie Ross's problem was of a different sort. He did have a notion what was wrong with her, but didn't want to proceed until he knew more. If he treated her for the wrong thing, the results could be disastrous. Just as his was no ordinary medicine, neither was just her life at stake. The ramifications were such that if the proverbial stone were tossed into the wrong pond, the ripples would be tidal waves when they reached eternity.

So he must play medical detective, which was one reason he had insisted that she search for her roots. She might discover something that would ring a bell in her personal psychic totality. And that would save him time and agonizing effort.

Schadt leaned back and rubbed his tired eyes. At this point, there was little he could do. Unless, of course, he had overlooked something.

Cursing, he went to his bookshelves, removed a stack of volumes and carried them back to his desk. He sat down again, opened the first one, perused a few pages, wondering if this was really necessary. He lifted his head, sighed and muttered to himself, "Yes, you old fool! You must find out if she is, in fact, infected with this horrible creature she describes. You must find out who she is. You must—you must protect yourself. You must find out whose side she is on."

*   *   *

After consulting her guide book, Melanie drove to the Continental Hotel in Timisoara, since she had to wait until the next day for a flight back to Brasov. It was one of the few modern buildings in the city, and she didn't care for the look of stacked concrete *au soviete*, but the place was convenient, and the management spoke English. She took a room for the night and spent a long time by the window, gazing out at the muted lights of the city. Despite Dr. Schadt's ominous warning, she felt mildly elated. For once she was not so horribly alone; for once she had talked to someone who could find out what was wrong with her; for once hope soothed her weary mind. She nodded slowly. She fully intended to follow his instructions religiously, no matter how frustrating it might become. So what if the language was foreign, the archives restricted, and the bureaucrats officious? She would find a way. She grinned devilishly. Hadn't the crusades come through here once before?

She remembered that she hadn't eaten anything all day except for a plate of *mititei* and a *baclava* at the Brasov airport, so she called room service and ordered dinner. While waiting, she lay back on her bed, feeling warm and relaxed. She thought it would be nice if she could share her good mood with John; there had been so few. With a burst of energy, she sat up, dialed the international operator and gave him her home phone number. The wait was interminable, but eventually John came on the line.

He sounded lost and flat.

She frowned darkly and then tried to reassure herself. Of course she knew that the electronics of long distance could strip a voice of its resonance and emotion; of course she knew that it was ten o'clock in the morning there, and she was into the night. Still, why hadn't she heard a spark of enthusiasm over the static when he'd said hello?

"John! she cried. "It's me!"

"Melanie?"

"Yes! How are you?"

"I'm just fine. The kids are all right too. Are you coming home soon or should I ask?"

She shut her eyes tightly and conjured up his image. *Please don't forget me; please be there; please keep a special place for me in your heart, John. I'll make it up to you.*

"Are you?" he repeated.

"I hope so. God, I hope so."

"Well," he said slowly, "everything's the same here."

She scowled. *Why does he feel it necessary to say that? Something's going on there I know nothing about. He's being too casual and distant. Cagey. Except I have no right to question him.* She shook off the paranoia. "John, I've found a doctor."

"Great."

"I think he understands what's wrong with me."

"Can he do anything?"

"He's going to try."

"Then God bless him."

"Yes." She nodded.

"You know, Melanie?"

"What?"

"I don't know."

"What?" She was suddenly fearful again.

"I could still come over there, you know? I could come over there and be by your side. I could help you, Melanie. If you'll just say the word, I'll be on the next plane."

She could not respond.

"What is it?" he asked cautiously. "Has it . . . happened again?"

She nodded, then whispered. "Yes."

"Are you in trouble?"

"No."

A long pause.

"Mark and Todd miss you very much, but I could try to get someone to look after them."

"John—"

"You don't want me to come, do you?"

"No."

"You're probably right. I guess all I'd do is get in the way. Forget it."

She clutched her head with her free hand. All she could think about was Mihail Popescu! Guilt surged through her.

"It's just empty around here," he said. "I suppose it's my fault, but—hell, it's just empty."

"I miss you, John." Jaws clenched, she resisted the tormenting images of her lover. The tension made her want to scream, *John, if you have any sense, you'll take the boys and walk away! I am a hypocrite! I am unworthy of you! Only—only if you go I'll have nothing left.* "I really do."

"I miss you, too, Melanie. Just let me know what's going on, will you?"

"Yeah."

"Honey," she whispered. "I love you."

*　　*　　*

"I love you, too."

Only the connection was broken before he could finish speaking. He swore and slammed down the phone, but missed. The receiver smacked onto the hardwood floor in the den and rocked, its buzz matching the drone of a plane overhead in the cloudless blue sky.

"Fuck it," he said softly, then took a long pull off a bottle of beer—the fourth one he'd had since dropping Mark and Todd off at summer camp an hour before. He rolled his head on the couch, gazed out the patio door past the deck and laughed hollowly. At lease he didn't have to worry about picking up the kids. The lady from across the way, Margaret, would bring them home, drop them off out front and all he'd have to do was wave to her. He didn't have to drive anywhere, either, which meant that today he could drink comfortably with no nagging responsibilities.

He rose unsteadily, left the den, and headed downstairs, intent on getting another beer. He grinned facetiously. Melanie had called. So this time, in honor of her desire to speak with him, he would set up a shooter or two of tequila. He shook his head and laughed again, this time sadly, knowing that Melanie didn't want him over there, that she was probably worried that she'd go crazy again and try to hurt him—either that or she didn't want him to see her so debilitated. He drained his beer, got another one out of the refrigerator and opened it mumbling to himself, "Well, John, old man, if it's any consolation, you should be thankful she said no because in your shape you couldn't make it to L.A. let alone Romania." He got out the tequila, poured a shot, set it on the kitchen island next to the beer and studied it philosophically. Booze. The only other time he'd ever lost control and wallowed in it was when he'd finally made it out of Vietnam to Hawaii. He'd stayed drunk for two weeks, and they'd had to scrape him off the rocks after he'd sneaked into the International surfing championships and taken a twenty-foot wave that crashed instead of rolled.

How long would it last this time? There was no way of telling. His life seemed to be coming apart faster than he could get from one day to the next. And he hadn't even made a conscious decision to let himself unravel. Like all moments of importance, it just fucking happens. He'd spent years gathering strength and building defenses—character, as they call it—and now he felt he could lose it all overnight. He wondered if great men reacted the same way? Great artists? He laughed. Hell, no. They were the most vulnerable of all. They were the true poets, for they used bad habits to hide from themselves, and their terrors. He tossed down the tequila, chased it with beer and shuddered. The jolt straightened him up a little and his vision cleared. He scowled and wondered if his thoughts were making sense. Then he nodded fiercely. Of course they were.

Tiberon. A chill went through him and he poured another shot. The cat was an omen. He had been one of the most resilient animals John had ever known. Now he was dead. God help us all, what was next? If Melanie didn't come home soon, if she didn't find a cure—well, who knows? Despite the love he felt, was it time to move on down the road? Even if she did come back her old self, would their life together ever be as good as it was? There is a time for every season. He frowned.

"Poor Tiberon. . . . Shit!"

He drank the second shot and chased it with beer, too. Only this time his eyes didn't exactly open. He felt himself sinking, and he knew if he didn't find a chair soon, he was going to fall down. He went into the living room and dropped onto the sofa. The draperies were pulled, making the room dark and depressing, which fit his mood. Outside, everything was so damned beautiful it was painful. The oaks, the pines, the mountains, the houses from afar, the road, even. Even beauty could not interest him; it struck no responsive chords inside him. Not any longer. Not since that fateful night when he had made the sketch of the beast Melanie said was her. He could safely say that it had driven him to drink.

There. The colors in his mind stopped swirling and out of the blackness that creature materialized, familiar now. She had been his constant companion; now she was waiting for him to define her and reveal her mystery. Suddenly, he opened his eyes and groaned. What if all this blew over and Melanie came home and everything was fine again, but every time he would look at her he'd see that grotesque monster?

"Then you damned well better get it out of your system, John Ross," he said out loud.

He lurched to his feet, went into the kitchen for a six-pack of beer, then strode purposely out to his studio. He took the six by eight canvas he'd stretched the first day Melanie was gone and placed it on his large easel. After focusing his opaque projector on it, he got the sketch out of a portfolio and put it onto the projector. He looked up and gasped. Even though he'd seen it on paper and in his mind a hundred times, the image was still startling. First, it grabbed his attention then hinted at a horror so unspeakable that it filled him with despair and empathy for anyone who had ever endured pain. John nodded slowly. There it was. His work. The bold outlines of a masterpiece. He gazed at the image and calculated how he would proceed. He must keep the aura of mystery so an audience would sense the unknown and be partially lost. Yet, for the work to have meaning, he must unlock the terror and ugliness there. He must describe, he must paint the unspeakable.

Still squinting at the canvas, he opened another beer, drank, then grinned broadly. It suddenly occurred to him that if he succeeded with this work, then he would understand what had happened to Melanie; he would know what she could not remember. And by so doing, he would come to know himself. He shuddered. There was no higher goal than an artist could set.

He went over to the workbench and organized his brushes and trowels, spurning his air compressor and air brushes because he wanted every stroke of this one to be by hand. Next, he began mixing paints, then turned to eye the canvas again. So this was it, was it? John Ross was to show the world the horror that lurked inside one beautiful woman.

And perhaps all of mankind.

Six

Melanie left the Brasov city hall at noon. For three hours she had been shunted from office to office and had been subjected to a whole host of bureaucrats (of all shapes, sexes, and sizes, who did in fact have faces) spouting streams of Romanian. Usually, they ended their remarks with a timeworn shrug and a smile. She responded in kind, not having understood one word, and would get elaborate, pantomimed directions to another office. Eventually, she ended up waiting for an audience with Octavian Bogdanovici, a senior official who was chief liaison to the local People's Council. She got to see him simply because she refused to go away and come back later as his secretary suggested.

Bogdanovici was a small, bald man with an imposing black moustache who frowned a lot. He listened impatiently as Melanie explained in pidgin English and broken Romanian that she had come to his country to make out her family tree, and she wanted permission to see the city's records. Bogdanovici told her she didn't need permission, then took a phone call, assuming that she would leave. She didn't. Exasperated, he mumbled apologies into the phone, hung up, spun around, threw up his hands and asked what she wanted. A letter of permission, she replied, indicating with her moving fingers that he should type it up right now. Which he did.

Flushed with triumph, she returned to the hotel, deciding to freshen up before a quick lunch and then an afternoon at the hall of records. Once in her room, she gazed at the letter bearing the official seal of the city of Brasov. She understood nothing except her name, but the document was her first major accomplishment, and she was proud.

Someone knocked softly on the door.

Startled, she turned, waited until the knocking was repeated, then slowly went to the door. "Who is it?"

"A wise man from the east bearing gifts," came the muffled, but musical reply.

Frowning, she opened the door. There stood Mihail Popescu grinning foolishly, holding up a bottle of champagne and flowers. He handed them to her. *"Pour vous."*

"Thank you, but you shouldn't have." Blushing, she took the gifts and backed into the room. "What are you doing here?"

He followed her inside and closed the door behind him. "I had an unusually bad case of loneliness yesterday. Everytime I looked through the lens I saw your face. Since then, I have been unable to stop thinking of you." He shrugged. "That is why I am here."

She ignored the personal side of his comment and asked, "Aren't you supposed to be working?"

"I took a sick leave."

"Oh." She was embarrassed. "You should have called first."

"If I had telephoned, you would have said don't come." He started to open the champagne.

"Don't."

"No?" he asked with surprise.

"I'm on my way to the hall of records."

He raised his eyebrows, but did not question her. Meanwhile, she went into the bathroom, got a glass of water and put the flowers in it.

"Good wine always keeps," he said, setting the champagne on the table. "Besides, it is a perfect day for the hall of records. May I go with you?"

"Mihail, please," she said softly, "you're not making this any easier."

"They don't speak English at the hall of records."

She almost said yes, then hesitated, remembering Dr. Schadt's final warning, which she didn't understand. Mihail Popescu was charming; he respected her; he offered companionship in the face of a tedious ordeal. Maybe they could become friends. Besides, a translator would make her afternoon much easier. Just this once. *I don't have to let him touch me.* "All right."

Beaming, he ushered her out of the room, took her arm, and led her down the hall to the elevators. She was conscious of his warmth and felt like she was walking a high wire. *Nothing has been said, though, and something has to be said!*

At the car, he opened the door for her, but she stopped him, placing her hand lightly on his arm and looking into his eyes. "Mihail, you must understand that I can't be your lover any more."

"Whatever you wish." He bowed slightly and smiled, but the gesture was forced. There was a hint of coldness in his voice. "May I ask why?"

"It is too painful."

"I would agree. That is how I felt this morning

when I was in Bucharest and I knew you were back from Timisoara. Then again, all things must pass. Even pain."

They got into the car, and in the close quarters, Melanie caught whiffs of his scent. Her palms were moist and she got that weak feeling in her belly again. She closed her eyes and let her head fall back on the seat. *Please, God, give me the strength to resist.*

"So how did it go with Schadt, anyway?"

"It went fine."

"Do you think he will be helpful?"

"Yes. Very."

"Did he tell you that you have been imagining things?"

"No. He listened very intently. He made no conclusions."

"So what are you supposed to do?"

"Go to the hall of records and search for my roots."

"*That* is why!" He laughed uproariously. "I suspected as much! Schadt is a genius! He can make people do anything!"

"But you believe in him, don't you?"

He nodded. "Yes. I was only laughing with admiration."

They drove along in silence for a while and when unnoticed, Melanie studied Mihail and catalogued his small, automatic expressions: the quick frown, the flash of a smile, a lifting eyebrow, jumping neck muscles, wrinkled forehead, hand flexing on the steering wheel. *He is more nervous than he lets on. Less jovial. Perhaps sad. He is a man in search of—of an explosion that will propel him in a different direction. A decent man who met me when it was too late for both of us.* She sighed. *If nothing else, I hope I'm not getting him into any trouble.*

Suddenly, she straightened up and turned toward him. "Mihail, where did you tell your wife you were going?"

"She thinks I'm on location again."

"What if someone sees us together?"

"I don't care."

"Well, I don't want to accidentally mess up your life."

"There is not much to mess up."

"You have your career."

He chuckled bitterly. "Yes, but I am not fully appreciated."

"You could always go elsewhere."

"It is not easy to establish oneself somewhere else without credits and references."

"True."

He turned toward her, his face shadowed by a monolith, making it dark. She could not see the blue in his eyes. "Don't forget that one advantage I have over most is that I am fluent in several languages."

"Yes."

At the hall of records, they were greeted by a stout, myopic young woman who was clearly offended by Melanie's grace and beauty, but could not ignore a letter from Octavian Bogdanovici or her dedication to the Romanian civil service. She reacted zealously to Melanie's request, and Mihail had to slow her down so he could translate and Melanie could respond. Armed with the names of Melanie's grandparents, Anton and Maria Magda, the woman pulled the microfilmed archives for the village of Vladimir, like they were bad teeth. Into the viewer they went and on came the light. Focusing, the woman asked a question.

Mihail translated. "When was your grandfather born?"

"I don't know exactly," Melanie replied, embarrassed.

"Was it before nineteen-seventeen?"

Melanie calculated quickly. Her father was born in 1928, so, yes, it must have been. "Definitely."

There was a brief, hushed conversation between Mihail and the bureaucrat. Then he shrugged at Melanie and explained, "She cannot help us. When the Germans occupied Brasov during World War One, they destroyed records. She only has vital statistics dating from nineteen-seventeen."

"What am I going to do?" Melanie asked, crestfallen.

"She suggests we try the Brasov museum of history."

*   *   *

Mihail drove her to the museum. By the time they arrived, it had closed for the day. Melanie was upset, but there was nothing anyone could do. Mihail pledged that he would bring her back in the morning, and, reluctantly, she agreed to leave.

"Besides," he said as they drove away, "there is a perfectly marvelous bottle of champagne waiting for us at the hotel."

She shook her head. "I really shouldn't, Mihail. You know it's not right."

"I don't understand. What is wrong with two friends sharing good wine and conversation?"

"Nothing, I suppose."

"Well, then?"

"But I feel like I'm taking advantage of you!"

"Why don't you let me worry about that?"

They made the rest of the crosstown trip in silence. He escorted her from the car and into the hotel, his hand pressed lightly against the small of her back. They went up the elevator, then down the hall toward her room. He realized she would still insist that they mustn't be lovers again, and knew that her husband must have quite a hold on her. That was good. He had to be prepared for such challenges if he was to be worthy of a new life, a new stature. And never would he forgive himself if he acquiesced now. There was too much at stake. Oh, it might take time to win her heart, but then, nothing good ever came easily.

Once in her room, he opened the champagne, poured them both glasses, then pulled the draperies back so they would have a view of the sunset. He sat down at the table and took out a pack of cigarettes. "Do you mind if I smoke?"

"No." She drained her glass, refilled it, went to the window and gazed out.

He wondered if she was trying to see beyond the moment—beyond reality? He studied her exotic profile lit by the orange haze of late afternoon and once again dreamed of photographing her, only this time he was in Hollywood surrounded by the lavish excesses of a big budget feature film. Smiling, he waved his cigarette back and forth so the smoke would diffuse and soften her image. If all he had to do for the rest of his life was paint her with light, he would have been gloriously happy. Life could be so simple and beautiful. He chuckled inwardly. Beautiful, if properly lit.

Then he realized he needed an opening gambit. Something to put her at ease. Something close to her yet removed from them. Something safe. He leaned forward—open and sincere—started to speak, but noticed she was refilling her glass. He relaxed.

It was perfect. She was nervous, therefore ripe for nostalgia. He knew exactly what to say. "Melanie?"

"Yes?"

"Tell me about your children."

She stepped back, quickly turning away to hide her surprise. There was a long silence, where any movement seemed languid and took on exaggerated importance. He snubbed out his cigarette and waited. Inside his head he heard a drone occasionally punctuated by flat squawks. She swept her hair back and faced him, her eyes downcast.

"I—I can't talk about them. They are not part of this."

He grimaced and drank. So much for opening gambits.

"Would you care to tell me about yours?" She was at the window again, gazing out, slightly swaying.

"I have a boy and a girl, eleven and nine." He paused. "The boy is the best football player in his class, and the girl is being groomed for the science academy. If one of them were a gymnast, we would be advertised as the all-American family of the new Romania."

She laughed with delight, and he realized that she was tipsy. Now, he was sure the time was right, the moment magical. He slipped out of his chair, crossed to the window, stood behind her, but did not touch her. "And I would give it all up in a second to be with you."

"Mihail." She turned to him and brushed against him, her eyes glazed and dreamy. "Dear, sweet Mihail." She lifted her face, parted her lips and touched his cheek with her fingertips.

He started to reach for her.

A sudden pain stabbed into his trapezius muscles, ran up his neck, and exploded in the back of his head. He closed his eyes and gritted his teeth. Gathering momentum, the pain enveloped his skull and throbbed just behind his eyes. He staggered back, groaning, remembering he hadn't taken his pills for several days. In fact, he had been remiss ever since that day he and Melanie had lunch at the Cerbul Carpatin.

"What's wrong?" she cried.

Waving her off, he hurried to the table, grabbed his glass, drained it, then frantically rubbed his temples. Why, he wondered, did he keep forgetting the blasted medication? Was it the blackouts? Everytime he took a pill, he subjected himself to a blackout! That must be why. Well, something was wrong. He had to get back to see Schadt and get another drug that had no side effects. The pain did not subside. It came on in ferocious waves that left him weak and sick. For one agonized moment, he imagined his head was an accordion between the hands of a vindictive four-year-old.

"Please tell me what's wrong!"

"My head! It's killing me!"

And then he ran from her room, angry that he had ruined a romantic moment, a chance with her, but not caring because the only thing that mattered was his head bursting with pain. He fled the hotel, intending to get his pills out of his suitcase in the borrowed car.

The headache went away just as swiftly as it had come, leaving him surprised and grateful. Sighing with relief, he slumped down on a bench and waited for his strength to return. Now he didn't need the pill and its concomitant blackout. Perhaps that was a good sign.

Then he slowly went back into the hotel and took

a room for the night. Key in hand, he headed for the bar, hoping that in the morning he would have the courage to face Melanie Ross and try again.

*   *   *

The next morning, Melanie was surprised when Mihail met her in the lobby as she was leaving for the museum of history. Concerned, she asked if he were all right. He said he was feeling fine and was ready for the day. The headache had been a temporary discomfiture but now was of no consequence.

"Shall we go, Mrs. Ross?" he said with a bemused smile, offering his arm.

She took it and they left. Traffic was light, so they made it to the museum by nine o'clock.

Eventually, they were steered to an assistant curator named Peter Drajan. He was a gentle, middle-aged man who wore his spectacles as loosely as he did his dark suit. While Melanie explained her mission and Mihail translated, Drajan listened, nodding and touching his fingers together.

"Romania has a contiguous history of two thousand and fifty years," he said in English. "Much of it is thoroughly documented and readily accessible. I cannot make any promises, but I will be glad to help you."

She was delighted. When she turned to look at Mihail, though, she saw hostility in his eyes. It suddenly occurred to her that he was jealous. She almost laughed, only she didn't want to be cruel. She patted his arm and smiled at him reassuringly. "Mihail—"

"So the man speaks English. It is not necessary for you to comment."

"If there's something you'd rather do—"

"No, no, please! Three heads are better than two, am I correct?"

"If you will come with me," said Drajan.

"Don't you need this?" She handed him her letter of permission.

He read it quickly, looked up and smiled. "Congratulations. You are official."

He led them up to the second floor, where they entered a large room with reading tables lit by fluorescents. His desk was in the front and several collections of Mark Twain were on it. He pushed them to one side, saying, "I am making a study of the world's great humorists." His eyes twinkled. "Isn't it amazing that none of them are Russian?"

They all laughed nervously. Drajan looked around to make sure they had disturbed no one, then indicated that Melanie and Mihail should sit down, which they did. He sat behind his desk and took out a clean legal-sized notepad.

"It is true that the Germans bombed most of Brasov's records during the first war," he whispered sadly. "In many ways they are as bad as the Hungarians." He raised his eyebrows and frowned. "You must understand, however, that Romanians are obsessed with their history." He looked to Mihail for confirmation.

"Most definitely," agreed Popescu. "It is our mandate."

"And through the efforts of the government and various museum staffs, we have managed to restore most of the records circumstantially."

"Good," said Melanie, nodding.

"We've always had the *letopisete*, of course."

"*Letopisete*?" she asked.

"Manuscripts," translated Mihail.

"Chronicles," stated Drajan, correcting him, then

was quick to add, "but we have manuscripts also." He leaned forward and turned to Melanie. "Now, if you'll just give me the names of your grandparents, we'll get started."

She did, and he wrote them down, then stood. "This shouldn't take long."

They went into a small, windowless room across the hall that was filled with ponderous computer equipment of soviet manufacture.

"They keep promising us new machines from your IBM corporation," Drajan said apologetically. "But no one can afford them any more. Not even Americans, no?"

He sat down at a keyboard console, turned it on, typed in the names of Melanie's grandparents, then pressed a button. After a brief hum and click, the screen lit up, and Drajan beamed as if he'd discovered an old friend.

"What?" Melanie whispered, trembling with excitement.

"Your grandfather, Anton Magda Jr., was born in Vladimir in September of 1900. The exact date is not given because the information comes from a cousin in Oradea who wasn't sure."

"That's all right!" she cried.

"Now," he said with relish, "let us see how far back we can ascertain the genealogy." He typed in questions, then hit the button again. While the screen flashed, he looked up and smiled, his forehead shiny with perspiration. "I have also asked for a readout." He pointed across the room. "It will materialize over there."

Almost immediately, the machine began spewing paper, but Drajan kept his eyes glued to the screen. When the computer stopped, he frowned and mumbled with surprise. "No, that is not possible."

"What's not possible?"

Instead of responding, he reformulated his questions, typed them on the keyboard, then leaned forward and peered at the screen anxiously. His glasses slipped down his nose and a lock of hair hung in front of his eyes. He pushed both back into place, took a deep breath and hit the button.

This time when the machine stopped, he stared at it for several minutes, then finally shook his head. "Remarkable."

"What's remarkable?"

He looked at her with genuine admiration. "Congratulations again, Miss Ross. You are a descendant of Nicholae Razdy."

"Who is Nicholae Razdy?"

He chuckled. "A medieval man worth reading about. Come. You will have the pleasure of examining some fifteenth-century *letopisete*."

*   *   *

Nicholae Razdy scooped up one last mound of freshly-cut hay with his pitchfork and tossed it into the sun-bleached wagon. With a satisfied grunt, he leaned his large frame against the side, causing it to creak, and rubbed the dust and pollen off his face with the sleeve of his loose blouse. He watched his smaller (and slimmer) son working nearby and grinned with pride. All four of his children were good and selfless. While the eldest labored here in the fields with him, the others were inside his comfortable farmhouse, helping their mother.

Pushing his straw hat back on his head, Nicholae stared off across the valley at the mountains. The late afternoon haze made them seem distant and unreal. Unattainable, perhaps? There he went again, harboring philosophical notions, a weakness developed when he had gone to the church college in Brasov as a young man. He had enjoyed those days and he supposed if he'd stayed with it he could have become a priest, but his parents did not have enough money to buy him an office. Besides, then he had owed allegiance to the old count (long since dead) who had chosen him for an education because he had displayed wit and promise as a child. Unconsciously, Nicholae felt the signet ring on his left hand; the band had a black stone set in silver, upon which was carved the Vladimir seal. The old count had given him the ring when he successfully finished school and offered him a chance to become a lieutenant of the castle guard. He had respectfully declined and pursued his affinity to grow things and revel in majestic thoughts.

In retrospect, he figured his life hadn't been so terrible. He had prospered as a *taran*, where most failed. God had been good to him, providing him with a loyal wife, children, and the desire to help others. At forty-one, he was realistic enough to understand that he didn't have many years left, but if they were as peaceful as life had been so far, that would be enough. If only.

He frowned and kicked at the ground, his contentment shattered by a premonition that trouble lay ahead. His current lord, the young Count Vladimir II, was becoming overly zealous in his attempts to please the Hungarian devils who had occupied the lands and exploited the Vlahi for generations. (By Hungarians, Nicholae meant specifically the fierce nomadic Magyars and Szeklers used to "guard the frontiers," which meant intermittent reigns of terror against the local peoples.) As a result, Nicholae and his fellow commoners (the *taranime*) were expected to work harder and to pay more rent so the count could send more tribute to the indolent monarch, Sigismund, in Buda. There was talk that soon they would be forced to work five days a week in their lord's fields instead of the traditional four.

Nicholae squinted at his fields. It was all he could do to farm his own with three days a week, let alone two! There were also rumors that the count was going to hire a troop of the hated Szeklers to augment his employ of knights and infantry. Nicholae shook his head sadly. The thought of those pigs in the Vladimir castle, drinking wine he had produced, eating food he had grown, consorting with women he had defended. . . . It made his blood boil, and he was a gentle soul. His friends would not stand for it; that he knew.

His son had finished pitching his row and waited patiently behind him. He apologized for daydreaming, and the two led the mare and the wagon piled high with hay toward the barn. Nicholae took a deep breath of the heavy, sweet air and felt intoxicated. He savored the moment and hoped that he was wrong about the brewing unrest.

A week later when he was preparing to harvest his grapes, a neighbor's boy ran up the path to Nicholae's house screaming for help. Nicholae could not get the child to speak coherently, but went with him, regardless. In the neighbor's yard, he saw four horses and frowned with concern. The *taranime* didn't own such fine horses. What was going on? A closer examination told him that one of the horses was the personal mount of the count's bailiff. The other three wore Szekler accoutrements. Nicholae gasped. So the rumors were true! The Szeklers had been hired as deputies! He crept to the door of the house, peered inside and was horrified. One Szekler had a sword at the neighbor's throat, while two others held his wife.

The bailiff was raping her, his fat body jiggling with each thrust.

Indignant, Nicholae strode into the house and demanded an explanation. Annoyed, the bailiff pushed the violated woman aside, pulled up his breeches, then told Nicholae that if he didn't leave, the same fate would befall him and his wife. Nicholae turned to the neighbor who reported hollowly that the bailiff wanted more rent. Since he couldn't pay, they had taken his wife. A Szekler swaggered up to Nicholae, called him a miscreant, and roughly pushed him back through the doorway. He fell off the steps and sprawled in the yard, and the Szekler laughed.

Which was the wrong thing to do.

Enraged, Nicholae scrambled to his feet, jerked a

rung out of the balustrade and attacked the Szekler, using the wood as a club. Much to Nicholae's astonishment—for he was not a fighter—the man fell, knocked unconscious. The other Szeklers came for him and he knew they intended to kill him, so he picked up the fallen man's lance and ran through the Szekler who rushed him first. The other was not so foolhardy, and he and Nicholae circled like dogs, feinting at each other. Meanwhile, the liberated neighbor grabbed a dropped sword and hacked the bailiff to pieces, then swung at the Szekler from behind. Distracted, the man wheeled, which was a fatal error. Nicholae impaled him, too.

Having regained consciousness, the first Szekler saw what had happened to his comrades, scurried out of the house and escaped. Although the neighbor was grateful and jubilant, Nicholae knew that what they had done was irrevocable. Soon, the count would hear the news and would dispatch a posse of knights wearing light armor. Most probably, more Szeklers. They would burn his fields and home and rape his wife and daughters, then murder him and his sons. The pastoral life that he had carved out of the bountiful hills was finished. Moreover, he only had a few hours to save himself and his loved ones and to salvage his possessions.

Apparently, the neighbor had also realized what was going to happen for he was holding his wife, and both were crying. Then he broke free, grabbed a bag and began stuffing it with a few meager belongings, preparing to flee. Nicholae asked him if he could outrun horses. The hopelessness of the situation dawned on him and he stopped. Instead of waxing hysterical, he looked at Nicholae and with much dignity asked him what they should do.

"Resist," Nicholae replied, remembering that as a young man he had seen armies march past to fight the infidel Turks in the land of Bulgaria. Well, he figured, if men could fight and die for the cross, they could also do battle for themselves.

"Resist?" asked the neighbor, incredulous.

"We don't have much time," said Nicholae, his thick face impassive, but his eyes glowing with resolve.

And so they sent out their family members to spread the word among the *taranime*. That evening just after Vespers, about 600 men gathered in a clearing on the edge of the forest by the river. As they exchanged greetings, Nicholae stood alone on a hillock, gazing across the valley. He could see smoke billowing in the distance, and tears rolled down his face, for he knew that they had put the torch to his house and barn and fields. All his life he had taken pleasure in the fruits of his own hard work, not just for himself, but for others, too. To see it destroyed so quickly made him heartbroken and angry. They might as well have burned his patience along with his worldly possessions.

He called for the men to assemble, and after they quieted down he began speaking. He told them of the incident with the bailiff and the Szeklers who now wore the Vladimir crest on their tunics. His voice passionate, he reminded them that their fathers had defended themselves against the Szeklers, more often than not dying while the outlaws plundered their farms and ravaged their womenfolk in the name of the King of Hungary! And now they were supposed to work *five* days a week and pay more rent to provide for those very same Szeklers? Had the count lost his mind? Why hadn't he asked them, the *teranime*? (Because he treated them like slaves and never asked them anything!) Wasn't Vlahi blood good enough for the count any more? Why did he pander to the Hungarian devils? Was he trying to become one of them?

The men roared their approval. Never had they heard such eloquence spoken by one of them. After years of hardship and misery, they were finally listening to someone who made sense to them! Why should they put up with a greedy noble who had hired their enemies to police his territory? Why not just legalize rape and robbery?

"It is time for a new leader!" proclaimed Nicholae Razdy. "It is time to drive the Szeklers and *all* the Magyar pigs back to where they came from! It is time for justice, my friends! We are on the threshold of a new century! Let us make it a golden age for the *taranime!*"

Again the men roared approval, their voices rolling across the meadows, like wind through the grass. Then Nicholae asked for silence, had them kneel and told them to pray for guidance and God's will. Finally, he told them to go home, say good-bye to their families and prepare for war. At first light they would march against the Vladimir castle.

The men dispersed, and a lone bat flew out of a giant oak, heading south. Disturbed, cuckoo birds in the same tree woke up and cried.

Nicholae dared not go near the settlements in the valley or the town of Vladimir, fearing the Szekler patrols would recognize and arrest him. So he spent the night in the forest by a low fire, planning the next day's action with a handful of friends who now were "trusted lieutenants." Toward midnight, he was finally reunited with his family and thanked the Lord they were all right. After urging the children to sleep, he went off with his wife and stayed with her for the rest of the night. Wide-eyed and frightened, she did not fully understand what her man had done. She begged him to be his usual wise and prudent self. As befitting a man of destiny, he told her that unusual circumstances begat unusual men. He was committed and there was no turning back. Because she loved him, she accepted his decision without question.

At dawn, the *taranime* gathered in a grove of oaks on the plain below the castle, but above the town. The men were armed with pitchforks, scythes, and even barrel staves. Nicholae viewed his "army" with trepidation. Out of the 600 he had spoken to the evening before, only half had shown up. He had his first misgivings then, but decided to march anyway rather than totally lose momentum. If they did not, the Szeklers would hunt them down and slaughter them one-by-one. And so he divided the men into three companies, each led by former soldiers who had fought for the Count at Nicopolis against the Turks. The ragged but determined assemblage started for the castle, keeping to the gulleys and trees in

order to maintain surprise. Also they were blessed
by a light mist that concealed and muffled their
approach. And then they were scrambling up the
mountainsides and through the forest, their confidence growing, the closer they came.

Nicholae halted them just behind the ridgeline a
half-mile above the castle ramparts and reconnoi-
tered. The forest would cover them to within 500
yards of the gate. Then they had to cross an open
plain to get inside, but he wasn't worried. Down
there the mist was heavier, blanketing the ground.
And no sentries patrolled the castle walls. Filled
with optimism, Nicholae dreamed of usurping the
count, without taking one casualty. He ordered his
men forward.

At the edge of the plain, they paused once more,
while Nicholae and his lieutenants conferred. They
decided to maneuver on line and without reserve
since they were only 300. Nicholae was well aware
that their initial show of force would do more to
panic the count and his mercenaries than anything
else. Once again, he signalled the *taranime* forward,
blessing one and all in this, their final assault.

The rough-hewn peasants went across the plain,
crouched like hunters, but continually whispering
to each other, making sure that they were on line
since it was difficult to see. Their breeches were
wet from the dew of the knee-high grass, and some
shivered from anticipation, while others sweated
with fear. Now they were 400 yards away ... 350
... 300 ... 250. Half the plain was behind them
and victory was just ahead, the bold ones asserted.
They could smell the stale odor of venison roasted
the night before, and many grumbled quietly—they
only got meat twice a month.

Suddenly, there was a whoosh. Then another and
another and another. The *taranime* stopped advanc-
ing, confused. One hundred yards in front of the
castle, pyres had been lit. Nicholae was befuddled,
too, and briefly wondered what the count was doing.
Then he gasped with horror. The heat from the
flames caused the mist to lift.

The *taranime* was caught bunched in the open.

Nicholae ran along the ranks, screaming at them to charge the castle. Most of them obeyed, raising their voices in a thin, exalted wail that seemed to come from the earth itself. Closer, closer they came. Just as most of them sensed victory and forgot their private fears, a company of archers leaned over the wall and unleashed volley after volley of arrows. Half of the peasants fell dead or mortally wounded. The others turned and ran despite the rallying cries of Nicholae and his lieutenants. Suddenly, two mounted troops of Szeklers materialized to the rear of the panicked men. Swords and lances glinting in the early morning light, they galloped forward and butchered the remnants of the *taranime*. Nicholae stood his ground, an arrow in his shoulder and another through his side. When the Szeklers closed on him, he killed the first three with mighty swings of his great scythe. And the next and the next. He fought furiously and defiantly, realizing that since all was lost he had nothing more to lose. And in those final moments, the carnage all around him, he discovered that he had the instincts of a born warrior and a supreme one at that. He swelled with pride and began singing the lullabye of the cuckoo he had learned as a child. Elated, he killed five more Szeklers before a dozen lances found their mark and he toppled to the ground. *Moarte.*

The Szeklers were so impressed with the performance of the fierce peasant, Nicholae Razdy, that they severed his head and placed it atop the guidon, which carried the colors of Count Vladimir II.

*   *   *

Count Vladimir II betrayed his own people, Melanie thought as she left the museum, exhausted and dazed.

Mihail helped her into the car and then they eased into traffic and headed toward the hotel. She stared out the window, awestruck by what she had learned, thanks to the painstaking, line-by-line translation of Peter Drajan. He had called Nicholae Razdy the first true Romanian hero, a man who sacrificed his comfort, his privileges (implicit in the *Letopisete*) and finally his life for the common man. He said that she should be proud, and, indeed, she was. Only how could her genealogy mysteriously end with Nicholae Razdy, a forty-one-year-old educated peasant leader, an enigma in itself? She must go back and search farther; she must learn the antecedents of that remarkable man, because they were hers too. Drajan had said that further investigation might be frustrating, since Nicholae Razdy had been adopted as an infant by a modest couple; his real parents were unknown. Still, the assistant curator had been willing to keep searching tomorrow, and that gave Melanie heart.

"Well," said Mihail, "you have quite an ancestry."

"Yes, but I can't believe the injustice, the treachery."

"I don't follow you."

"Count Vladimir II was a *Vlahi*, a Romanian, and yet he courted the favors of the Hungarians and held his own people in contempt! Why, he even hired the enemy of his mercenaries!"

"True, but all history has two sides. Look at it from his viewpoint. If he had not given the Szeklers employment, wouldn't they have overrun his territory anyway? Of if not them, then the Turks? Perhaps all he was doing was keeping the peace."

"I don't see it that way," she replied coolly.

"You don't understand Romanian practicality. It is a common trait bred by centuries of coping with foreign domination."

"Wouldn't duplicity be a better term?"

"Ah, Americans!" He laughed and threw up his hands. "You are so intense!"

"Let's just forget it, okay?" She stared out the

window again, but her mind was too tired to have coherent thoughts. Then her anger subsided and she turned back to Mihail. "I'm sorry."

"Your apology is humbly accepted."

"Look, I'm not making this very easy, but it's hard for me. Still, I want you to understand that I appreciate your help."

"I understand completely," he said, then suddenly gasped and gritted his teeth. His vision blurred into a red haze.

* * *

The pain was overwhelming. *Mei Doamne!* He couldn't understand what was happening to him. It had never been that bad before. He lost control of the car and narrowly missed colliding with an oncoming bus. Melanie screamed, and he pulled over and stopped. Groaning, he scrambled out of the car and walked in circles, massaging his temples. The pain subsided to a dull ache, and he could see clearly again.

"Are you all right?" Melanie asked, beside him now.

"Yes, yes," he said impatiently, his face etched with despair.

"I'll drive the rest of the way."

He nodded, got into the car and slumped in the passenger seat, unable to talk or even think.

The first thing he did when he got back to the hotel was go to his room and take a pill. Magically, the pain disappeared completely, and he sighed with relief. Still, Melanie insisted that he come to her room for a rest. He hated people to see him in a weakened condition, but in this case he agreed—he did not want to be by himself. He followed her to her room, worried, eyes downcast. He couldn't live with these attacks any more; he didn't want his life governed by medication, either. Especially, when he was supposed to be already cured. He must make an appointment with Schadt. He needed answers. He could not stand any more pain. It was enough to—

They were in her room, and Melanie was pushing him down on the bed and taking off his shoes. The thick comforter felt good and cool against his skin.

"You are so kind," he whispered, studying her face, now half in shadow. For a moment (he wished it were timeless) she gazed down at him, softened, and lost her composure, so he reached up for her, while saying, "and beautiful."

"Mihail!" She stepped back. "You need rest."

"And you, Melanie," he said quietly. "Don't you have feelings?"

"Yes," she said lightly. "And right now my body is telling me to take a shower because I smell like old paper."

He forced a laugh, knowing he'd lost again, except this time it was annoying. She hadn't rejected him because of her husband. Rather, she was distracted—entranced—by tracing her roots back to a medieval peasant revolutionary. He watched her go into the bathroom, thinking how ironic it was. She had gotten five centuries of names, dates, and and places, and she still wanted more. A genealogic madness, that's what it was—and how quickly that sickness grew. It was like the compulsion to gamble, only in this case the fever was cloaked in self-righteousness. And all because of that ubiquitous Dutchman, Doctor Schadt. When he had talked to him, the Dutchman had asked him if he'd ever been to Africa since he'd seemed familiar to the doctor. What nonsense! To send people into the stale dust of history in the name of medical science. He wondered if he should have recommended someone else to Melanie, but he had no idea who. Despite Schadt's eccentricities, Mihail still believed in him. Nevertheless, he wondered if the doctor knew what he was doing.

Mihail gingerly touched his head where the pain had been. The skin was tender and tight, like a balloon on the edge of elasticity. He shuddered. Carefully, he got off the bed, went to the table by the window and poured himself a glass of wine. He looked out at the lengthening shadows of the city, reflected, and frowned. He hadn't talked to his wife since leaving home two days ago. He should ring her up. Just then he heard the water go on in the bathroom, grinned, and went to the telephone. Now was the perfect time.

"*Bucuresti 14.31.74, poftiti.*" He waited, humming a nameless tune.

"*Alo?*"

"Ioana, my dear, it's me. How are you? And the children?"

"Oh. Hello." Her voice went flat and alien.

He gulped and felt uncomfortable. "What is the matter?"

A long pause.

"How was work today?" she asked.

"Oh, fine," he replied, fighting panic. From her tone he knew there was something she wasn't telling him. What did she know? "Just fine," he insisted. "You know how it goes. The usual boring stuff."

"Where are you anyway?"

"I told you yesterday! We are in the Turda Gorges."

"And they don't have telephones where you are staying," she stated sarcastically.

"We keep moving around!"

"You're not camping out, are you?"

"Of course not!"

"Who are you working with, darling?"

"You know! The usual crew." Cold sweat ran down his sides. "Why so many questions?"

"And Martin Tetranovich—is he directing?"

"Don't I always work with him?"

"Of course you do, darling, except I believe Martin Tetranovich is in *Bucuresti* this very moment."

"What do you mean?" he snapped defensively.

"He called today and asked if you were feeling any better."

Caught. Mihail closed his eyes and almost dropped the receiver. His heart sank. He was at a complete loss for words.

"You might have told me that you were supposed to be sick so that I could have said the right thing."

"What did you tell him!" he demanded, his voice hoarse and strained.

"Does it matter?"

"It matters!"

"Why did you lie to me, Mihail?"

"I—"

"What are you hiding? Another woman?"

"No! How could you possibly think that? Ioana, please, you must believe me! I—I just wanted to get away for a while! I didn't think you'd understand so I didn't tell you, that's all! There's nothing wrong with taking a little vacation, is there?"

She laughed. "Mihail, don't be absurd! What do you take me for, an utter fool?"

"I'm not lying!" he said hotly.

"It is of no consequence, but if you care about your future, I suggest that you be back to work by tomorrow morning."

"I have an entire week of sick leave," he replied stupidly.

"Well, then, perhaps you'd better discover a miraculous cure because Martin Tetranovich is starting preproduction on another film and he wants you to be the director of photography."

Mihail gasped. His mouth fell open and he stared off, eyes blinking. By the time he could think of something to say, Ioana had hung up on him, and he found himself listening to nothingness. He slowly hung up the phone, then rose and paced the room, confused. His emotions were a jumbled mess of terror and euphoria. One the one hand, Ioana knew there was another woman; on the other, he had finally received his promotion. His mind whirled. He could see himself locked out of his apartment, a disgrace to his neighborhood, just as he could envision himself becoming the premiere cinematographer in all of Eastern Europe. He groaned. What a terrible dilemma!

He sat down at the table and composed himself. Although it would take some time, he was certain that he could patch things up with his wife. He was also sure that if he didn't show up at the studio in the morning, he would never get another chance to become a director of photography. His choices, then, seemed rather clear. Except for one thing.

Melanie Ross.

He loved her madly. And he wanted the life she represented. America had become a dream for him, an obsession. It was a land of riches, possessions, sophistication, excitement, and travel. A land of color. The cultural center of the universe. And he knew he was an artist.

He shook his head. The news from Ioana could not have come at a worse time. Melanie Ross was not yet his, and he had to make a decision. His hand was forced. He had to make his choice—so what was it to be? The millstone of Ioana *et al*, or the good life in the West with a goddess at his side. He assured himself he deserved the latter. It was in his blood, and he couldn't deny it. He sighed and lit a cigarette, leaned forward and placed his elbows on the table. She turned off the water; he could hear her stepping out of the shower stall and drying. His heart began pounding. This was his last chance.

She came out of the bathroom fully dressed in a loosely-fitting pastel-print blouse and jeans, but with a towel wrapped turban style around her wet hair. "You must be feeling better."

"Yes, I am." He snubbed out his cigarette. "Thank you."

She gestured at her head. "Sorry for the image, but I had to wash my hair."

He rose, smiled and bowed. "Don't apologize. For a moment, I could not believe my eyes. I thought you were Princess Nefertiti."

"How sweet of you."

"Would you like some wine?"

"I'd love some wine." She sat down at the table.

He poured a glass and handed it to her, then went to the wall by the television, where there was a built-in radio. He tuned in music, and the room was filled with the romantic harmonies of Franz Liszt's *Les Preludes.*

Melanie was delighted. "I didn't even know it was there!"

He laughed and winked. "That is because music is invisible."

"How clever of you."

He waved his hand back and forth. "Music and

feelings. Yet we always think of beauty in terms of a visual image. Like yourself."

She laughed, blushed, then set her glass down, folded her hands and looked away.

"If you would like, why don't we have dinner tonight at the Cerbul Carpatin?"

She glanced at him curiously. "What's the occasion?"

"Who needs an occasion?" He shrugged. "But since you've mentioned it, why don't we celebrate your discovery of Nicholae Razdy?"

She smiled at him and touched his hand. "Why are you so nice to me?"

"Because I love you," he whispered, choked with emotion.

"No, don't." She shook her head. "I don't want you to love me!"

His face twisted; tears ran down his cheeks, hot against his cold skin. He knew that he had lost control and perhaps ruined everything, but it felt good to cry. So good. There was something peaceful and strong at the heart of it. "You cannot ask me to stop loving you. It is unfair. It is not natural. It is unfeeling."

"Mihail, please!"

He put his face in his hands and wept. She came up behind him, and he felt her hands on his shoulders, then around his chest as she embraced him. Soon, she was crying, too, her face pressed against his. He turned and, quite abruptly, they kissed, lips slipping clumsily upon lips until they got it right. He could taste her tears and then smell them. He was reminded of a dark country road after a light rainstorm. His tears became joyful.

Still kissing, they rose as one, stumbled to the bed and fell onto it. He caressed her body, unbuttoned her blouse, slid down, kissed her belly and then her breasts. Moaning softly, she was trying to push him away except every time he obliged, she pulled him back. Never, he imagined, had uncertainty been so painful. But he was a patient man and a considerate lover. He would let her find her own way to him.

Once more, he kissed her on the mouth, and she flattened against him. Intent on arousing her even more, he unsnapped her jeans and started to slip his hand inside. Then he stopped and was astonished with himself. He suddenly knew how he would play it. When she took his hand and placed it on her belly, he knew she had given him a clear sign to proceed, which was what he was waiting for.

But he did not move his hand.

She pulled back and looked at him, her eyes wide and black, her chest heaving. "It's all right," she whispered. "Go ahead. I can't fight it any more."

"No." He rolled up and sat on the bed, his back to her. "It's not right."

"What do you mean, it's not right?" She frowned and sat up, still breathing heavily.

"I have feelings, too."

"I don't understand," she said, bewildered.

"I love you."

"Then why did you stop?"

"Because I want more than just a good time in bed with you," he replied glibly, even though he knew if she got any closer, his courage was going to crumble. Yet he was afraid if he made love to her, she would no longer need him. He got up and walked to the window, straightening his clothes. "I love you and I want you to love me."

A long, heavy silence.

"In a way, I suppose I do," she said in a tiny voice.

His heart surged, but he did not turn to her. It was too soon—he was not quite there. "Then we can be together?"

"Right now, yes."

"For how long?"

"As long as I'm here."

"And then?"

"I don't know."

It was maddening! If only he had more time! In a week, he was sure she would be his.

"Mihail, do we have to talk about this now?" She came up behind him and put her arms around him.

"What about your husband?"

She sighed. "He isn't here."

"What about him?"

"Are you trying to humiliate me?"

"No. I'm trying to make you follow your heart."

She went back to the bed and sat down, her hands in fists, her face tense with frustration.

Suddenly, he turned in a beseeching manner. "Darling, I want to go to America with you. I want to share your life, don't you see?" He went to her, held her face in his hands, kissed her until she responded, then stopped. "I will give up everything I have for you!"

Passionate, confused, she shook her head. "Well, I—I can't make that choice yet."

"Melanie." He kissed her again, this time running his hands over her breasts.

She pushed away and started crying again while buttoning her blouse. "Really, I can't!"

"Bah!" He turned away, disgusted and embarrassed. Even though he had made her desperate to make love, he couldn't break her. For a moment he felt he should hate her. He shrugged away the thought.

"Mihail, please, let's not quarrel. All I need is a little time."

He spun around. "Well, I don't have any more time!"

"Dammit! I can't make a commitment yet! I'm too confused!"

He pointed at her, waving his finger. "No one keeps Mihail Popescu dangling like a paper doll! Not even you, Melanie Ross!" He started for the door.

She got there first and blocked his path. "Please don't leave this way."

"I will ask you one more time. Are you going to take me to America with you?" He waited, angry he was in this position. He felt desperate. Cornered.

She hesitated, then shook her head. "No."

"Then it's good-bye." Furious, he pushed her aside, started to leave, then turned and ripped open her blouse.

He spit on her breasts.

*   *   *

Melanie saw him go quickly out the door. It swung shut and she was alone.

She dropped her hands to her sides. Her breasts receded, and she watched the spittle run from then down across her belly, cold on her skin. Curiously calm, she wiped it off, then went and sat on the bed and considered her humiliation. She supposed it was her honesty—more with herself than with him. Yes, she had wanted him to make love to her, even though he had manipulated her and defiled her. He could have beaten her and she still would have found him irresistible.

Why?

She supposed that one part of her loved John and

the children, whereas another desired Mihail. It really wasn't a question of love or hate, though. He was her compulsion. She had found him charming (until just a few moments ago), but she did not like him; she did not hate him; she did not love him. She wanted him. She needed him to soothe some dark corner of her soul.

And she hadn't a clue.

Now things were complicated. Mihail had wanted a commitment, which was only natural if he loved her. And John wanted to be with her, which was only natural because they were committed to each other. She had rejected both of them. Would she end up alone? . . . Because of a frustrating quest into her past? How much more could she lose? She shivered. The most important question was, she guessed, how much longer could she remain anonymous? The third part of her, she meant. The one that lurked inside, occasionally raising its ugly head and driving her to—unspeakable acts.

She went to the table, sat down and opened her notepad, intending to record what she knew of her ancestor, Nicholae Razdy. As soon as she wrote his name, the nausea seized her stomach, and she was forced to lurch upright, knocking over the table. Groaning and retching, she dropped to her hands and knees, hunched, then rolled on the carpet. It was awful.

I am dying.

When the sensation blossomed into strength, Melanie grinned and scrambled to her feet. She went into the bathroom and squinted into the mirror just to make certain—her grotesque image stared back at her.

Like before, she left the hotel sedately, got into her car and drove off, then followed her impulses.

This time they led her to a secluded neighborhood in the hills just below Mount Timpa. She parked her car under a huge oak tree by a bridge that spanned a creek, got out and smelled the dank odor of moss. Curious, she peered over the bridge and saw a stagnant pond beside the creek. Frogs croaked and crickets chorused there.

She ran across the bridge and went down the twenty-foot embankment in nimble jumps. As she neared the pond, she heard a car approaching. She whirled and crouched, but the car rattled across the bridge and continued on. She had not been seen. Grunting with pleasure, she deftly removed her clothes and lowered herself into the black water, enjoying the moss lifting between her toes and the slime brushing softly against her skin. She rolled in the pond, then took great handfuls of mud and smeared her body with it. Satisfied, she got out of the water, dressed, climbed up the bank, then trotted into a residential glen, keeping to the trees and ignoring an occasional barking dog.

Soon, she came to an estate separated from the rest of the neighborhood by a high wall and a spiked iron gate. Lights blazed from the three-story house, and the gabled, slate roof cut a jagged silhouette against the moonlit sky. She studied the scene and clacked her tongue. *Someone prosperous is master of this household. Someone comfortable. Dignified and famous, perhaps. I will fill his last conscious moments with horror, and he will die, wallowing in his own filth.* Snarling, she scaled the gate, vaulted over, and dropped to the ground, landing lightly in a half-crouch. Then she ran across an acre of lawns that sloped up to the house.

She was drawn to a room with windows on three sides, and one glance told her it was a library. She peered intently into the room, her face so close to the window that her breath fogged the glass pane and she had to wipe it clear. Floor-to-ceiling bookcases lined the walls, and most of the volumes were leather-bound. In the far corner, by a fireplace, a man sat in an overstuffed chair, reading and occasionally sipping port from a crystal glass. He was white-haired, distinguished, and wore a tie and shirt, the sleeves rolled up. She grinned, confident that his flesh would cut like soft butter.

A branch broke and twigs snapped.

She spun around and squinted into the darkness, growling defensively. The noise had come from a thicket, which meant that something menacing lurked in the bushes. She decided to investigate, stepped forward, then felt a presence and turned around.

The white-haired gentleman was at the window, staring at her.

Startled, she forgot the noise in the thicket and instinctively crouched. Instead of threatening her, the gentleman was speaking to her gently, asking her if she needed assistance. She scowled. Rather than a grotesque creature, he undoubtedly saw her as a pretty young woman who had gotten wet and filthy in some way. Well, she would show him! She stepped back and coiled for her charge. Only at that moment he turned and called out. A door opened into the library and a butler entered. The gentleman said something to the butler, and she knew that he would want to find her and offer help. Disgusted, she shrank into the darkness, ran for a grove of trees and hid there. After a moment, the butler came outside with a flashlight, its beam sweeping slowly across the grass. Calling softly, he began a dutiful search of the grounds. Melanie worked her way behind him so she wouldn't be caught by the light.

All she had to do was bide her time and wait for the butler to reach the far side of the property. Then she would slip into the house and kill the white-haired gentleman. Shivering with anticipation, she almost laughed. *Perhaps they will think the butler did it.*

*   *   *

A cold wind sighed through the brittle foliage stinging Melanie's flesh—scratched from crawling through a thicket. She looked around quickly and discovered that she was surrounded by thorn bushes. Her arms and legs were bloody and she smelled so bad she gagged. How had she gotten so filthy? Dried slime covered her skin, her—face! She moaned. It had happened again. *At least there aren't any corpses at my feet. Thank God. At least—*

"Ce cineva acolo?"

She flattened to the ground and froze. Someone was waving a flashlight around! The beam passed inches over her head, came back again and hesitated. She held her breath.

"Domnisoara? Esti la aparat?"

She felt bugs crawling on her, but dared not move. She itched. She stung. Her skin crawled. She began twitching spasmodically. Finally, the light was switched off, and she heard the man's footsteps receding across the grass. Relieved, she waited until he had gone around the house, then stood and carefully sidled through the bushes, gingerly pushing them apart. She slipped and a branch snapped back, its thorns raking her neck and face. She hissed and resisted the urge to cry out.

Once free of the thicket, she ran toward the front gate. Her angle took her past the library windows, and she was compelled to look inside. She gasped.

"No! Oh, God, no!"

A white-haired gentleman was sprawled on the floor in a pool of blood. He rose slowly, then flopped back with a groan of assignation. A faint aura hovering above him turned black and dissolved.

Melanie lurched away and sprinted to the gate, sobbing hysterically. Somehow, she climbed over it, then ran down a street canopied with trees. In the distance she could hear the shouts of someone discovering the body. Her lungs hurt; her legs felt dead; her throat was dry; she became dizzy. Yet she ran on and on.

Finally, she saw her car by a small bridge. She jumped inside, slammed the door and started it. Jerking the wheel, she spun around in a tight U-turn and accelerated up the road, not bothering to turn on her lights or check her rearview mirror.

Had she looked behind her, she might have seen a man walking his dog, now staring after her, amazed by what he had seen.

Seven

Dr. Fritz G. Schadt pushed himself away from the mountains of books and papers on his desk, rubbed his unshaven face, yawned, then got up and poured himself tea he'd made hours ago. Sipping the luke-warm liquid, he padded to the windows so he could watch the sun rise. He enjoyed the solitude, although he wasn't thrilled about spending two days and nights in his office. One lost touch with reality. Frowning, he remembered to ring Mrs. Banta at a more respectable hour and ask her to feed his cats again. It was a chore he loved doing himself, but right now there wasn't time.

Thanks to Melanie Ross.

He paced in front of the windows, wondering if he would ever discover the key to the mystery. Why was the truth so damned elusive? She hadn't phoned either, which was not a good sign. He supposed he should telephone her soon. She could be in danger. She could be—

Scowling, he reviewed his theory. Melanie Ross said she had been at the scene of a brutal crime, yet she did not remember how she had arrived there. Her experience, thus, could have been a hallucina-tion, even though the murder actually occurred.

People did get visions of events happening else-where—in the past, present, or future—due to their collective unconscious. The complication was she also said she felt herself changing into a hideous creature *capable* of murder. Some sort of transfer-ence was going on from the supernatural to the human that he didn't understand yet, despite re-reading all the important literature on the subject. Back to basics, then, and, thank God, for the notions of that great man, Dr. Carl Gustav Jung.

Melanie Ross's unconscious mind had two dimen-sions: repressed personal events and—in common with everyone—archetypes of the collective uncon-scious. Somehow, the interaction between these two spheres was creating a psychological monster. That was the key. That was one reason he had asked her to look into her past. He wanted her to uncover events that would unlock that critical third dimen-sion of the human mind, the *personal* collective unconscious. Schadt sighed, drank his tea and smacked his lips. Armed with that information, not only would he cure Melanie Ross, but he would have a clear path from the human into the super-natural. If she—if *they*—could just get over that barrier.

He stood motionless at the window and watched the sun slip behind a massive black cumulus. He was pleased that soon a summer rain would wash Timisoara. Perhaps he could persuade Tanya to go walking with him. He loved the rain—always had, for it meant that life would go on. A summer rain . . . Tanya. They would go through the park on the way to his flat. Once inside, she would be thrilled with the cats and would play with them. While waiting for the tea to brew, he would pluck her one black rose. She would sit in the window holding it

while he—a sudden thought ruined the image, and
he scowled.

Mihail Popescu.

Somehow the specter of that man was flitting
around behind this entire affair. Like a weevil, he
had bored inside Melanie Ross's otherwise healthy
brain and his presence there was causing the wrong
pharmaceutics to combine. Was that it? Was the key
to her disease that simple?

Schadt returned to his desk, jerked open a draw-
er, turned on a small cassette recorder and heard a
transcript of his interview with Melanie Ross for the
fifth time. Sitting down, he picked up his pen, ready
to write down something crucial he had overlooked.
He nodded impatiently as he listened.

Why was she having an affair with Mihail Popescu
if she were happily married? She found him irresistible. Why was she the man's lover if she didn't
particularly like him? She didn't know. Schadt
frowned and massaged the bridge of his nose. As
before, there was no clue, not even a telltale inflec-
tion. He would have thought that Popescu had brainwashed her, except he didn't think the man that
resourceful. He blushed, realizing that he was supposed to remain objective about patients, and, tech-
nically, Popescu was a patient. Still, on a purely
intuitive basis, he didn't really like him very much
and when this was over, he hoped he would have
good reason for feeling that way.

The telephone rang. Since he was alone in the
building, he answered automatically. "*Alo?*"

"Doctor Schadt!" cried Melanie Ross. "Oh, thank
God, you're there!"

Despite her desperate tone, he allowed himself to
comment drily. "Normally, I'm sleeping at such an
ungodly hour. I hope you have a plausible excuse?"

"It *happened!*" she shrieked. "It happened *again!*"

He stiffened.

"You've got to do something! Please! I can't go on!"

"Melanie!" he shouted into the receiver. "Compose yourself! Now!"

A long silence.

"I'm sorry."

"Tell me about it."

In a rush, she recounted another tale of horror, and Schadt found himself drawing on his legal pad.

"And you did not recall driving to this, ah, estate in the foothills?"

"Not at all."

"And you say you don't remember being in the library with the white-haired gentleman?"

"No!"

"Then perhaps you weren't," he suggested without conviction.

"Don't tell me I had another hallucination! I've got scratches from thorn bushes to prove I was there!"

Schadt exhaled slowly, closed his eyes and held his head. He could feel the helplessness, the panic growing inside him. In all good conscience, he could not tell this poor, distraught woman that she was innocent of murder because now he believed she was guilty. If she couldn't recall the act, her brain was simply erasing it from her consciousness to protect her sanity. Somehow, Melanie Ross had become a killer. Except there were no motives and the victims had obviously been selected ones! She hadn't gone on a rampage! He shuddered. There was much he didn't understand—far too much. He threw up his hands.

"Well?" she asked angrily.

"Well, what?"

"Isn't there something you can do?"

"Melanie, you must stay calm," he said hollowly. "I'm doing all I can!"

"Isn't there some drug I can take?"

"There are innumerable drugs you can take, my dear, but none of them will do you—or me—any good."

"Doctor Schadt, I am a murderer!"

"Not without cause," he said blindly, his voice quavering.

"What do you mean?"

"You chose those particular people. The violence was not mindless."

"Why them?"

"Ask yourself. There is a reason for everything."

"Oh, great. I really needed to hear that."

"You must—you must look into your past."

"I am!"

"Then you must *continue* to do so!" he shouted.

She began weeping. "What if it happens again before I'm finished? What if . . . I get *caught*?"

He froze. By all means, what if she did get caught? What would happen to Schadt's messianic vision then? What about Melanie Ross? Could he use her affliction in his own search into the supernatural and just ignore her humanity? Aside from its chemical equivalent, what *about* the golden rule? He frowned and vacillated. Since he hadn't fully discovered its pharmaceutics yet, perhaps it didn't apply in this case. Besides, no question about it, she was a murderer and that was justification enough. The thought made his ears burn. Bah! That kind of thinking made him unworthy of the loftiness of his medical inquiries.

"If you are caught, Melanie Ross, I will use every conceivable means at my disposal to set you free."

"Aren't you forgetting that I'm guilty?"

"You are not guilty, my dear, you are but a pawn in a game that has been going on for a long time." He assured her, hoping he was right.

"I am not a chess piece, Doctor Schadt, I am a human being!"

"Remain calm."

"I *can't!*"

"Calm yourself," he persisted, gazing out the window. "Think of the ocean."

"What do you mean, the—"

"Waves. An eternity of waves. Sculpting, molding the beach. Think of each grain of sand as a world of calm. There are billions of them. Billions and billions of calm. C-a-l-m. Spell it, my dear."

She did so.

"Now think it." He sighed. "Breathe it." He sighed again. "Be it."

After a long silence, he said good-bye and hung up. Then he leaped up, yelling with frustration, and swept all the books and papers off his desk. He raged around his office, occasionally charging and kicking a book toward the door as if to score a goal. He missed.

Something horrible had happened to the woman! Something he couldn't control or even understand! In spite of all his papers, all these books! He booted another one. They meant nothing if he couldn't grasp a bizarre circumstance and even explain it to himself! Lord God, he wondered, was he that inferior?

Eventually, he was back at the window again, befuddled, his mind riddled by half-convictions. If his patient was a murderer and he didn't telephone the Brasov police, then he was an accomplice. He laughed bitterly. Still, in the final analysis, who was to say? He couldn't quite believe it yet, and he didn't think she had accepted it, either. So, if he called the police now, they would never know.

He picked up his books and papers, annoyed with himself for being susceptible to tantrums. Suddenly, he saw what he had drawn on his notepad. It was a caricature of a cheshire cat with the tail shaped in a question mark. He studied it, admired it, then pinned it to the wall between his Romanian medical license and his degree from the Sorbonne.

Tanya entered the room with fresh tea and the newspaper. When she saw the mess, she stopped short and gasped.

"Tanya, *buna dimineata!* How lovely you look this morning!" He gestured at the sketch of the cat and beamed. "Come here, my dear, and look at my latest discovery!"

*   *   *

At her lowest ebb, Melanie sat on the bed, her face in her hands and confronted reality alone. Remaining calm did not help.

She was a schizoid killer.

Dead in spirit, cursed—whatever—she could not escape that fact. Why, then, didn't she go to the police and turn herself in? Somehow she must find the strength; she must be punished for her crimes. Could she stand being locked up and tried, though? *No. I'll go mad. The beast inside me will take over completely. They'll have to drug me and I'd almost rather be a monster than a vegetable.* Were there no answers? She had already called Dr. Schadt. *What a great help he was! The man is only good for gibberish about "an eternity of waves." He says I'm tangled up with the supernatural. A lot of good that does me.* Except she knew he was right.

Only that did not lift the pain, the despair, the

hopelessness. She went into the bathroom, rummaged through her toilet articles and found a cartridge of razor blades. Nodding, she decided for a second time that suicide was a quick way to solve her problems, but as she was taking a blade out, she remembered her promise to John, then the words of the priest. *In my opinion, you shall be doomed for an eternity.* She looked into the mirror, studied her filthy, haggard face and thought, *Do you want to die in that condition, Melanie Ross? Or do you want to finish what you came back to Romania for?* She dropped the razor blade into the wastebasket. *I will accept retribution when I discover why I am what I am.*

She shuffled to her bed and sat down again, dizzy with fatigue, but determined to see herself through this ordeal. She had to put last night's scene out of her mind so she could go back to the museum and dig farther into her past. As weird as it seemed, that was her therapy, and she would pursue it doggedly. And then?

Retribution or—redemption?

She stared off. It suddenly occurred to her that if she wanted deliverance, then she better prepare the way, which meant taking responsibility for herself. True, she wasn't ready to go to the police, but she was finished with deceiving John. Even though she had not ended it, her affair, her infatuation, was over. She needed to confess and accept the consequences. She grabbed the phone, dialed the international operator and gave him the phone number. She waited, rehearsing her words. Her hands were shaking badly.

A busy signal.

Frustrated, she slammed down the receiver. And five minutes later when she tried again, the lines of the transatlantic cable were tied up. Muttering, she paced the room. *How ironic. I finally decide to do something, which will irrevocably change my life and I can't get through.* She smiled sardonically. *If Dr. Schadt were privy to this, he'd say I'd been placed on hold by destiny.*

* * *

When Constantin Goga burst through the double doors into the squad room of the homicide division, the *ofiter de serviciu* leaped to his feet and saluted. "*Buna ziua, Locotenent Goga!*"

Goga did not acknowledge the man. Scowling, he hurried across the room, removed his trenchcoat, and hung it up in mid-stride. Just before going into his office, he took off his straight-brimmed Panama hat and flipped it back at the coat rack, without looking. As always, it ringed a hook and spun there. He kicked his door shut, and the glass rattled. Jaws working, he rolled behind his desk, took a fresh cigar out of his briefcase, cut and lit it, but did not sit down. He was too nervous and angry. The alien killer had struck again, and this time the victim had been a Supreme Court Justice. The pressure to find a suspect didn't bother him. Rather, it was the crime itself. Gritting his teeth, he put his hand to his head and pictured the scene once more.

The Justice had been found on the floor, books all around him, the decanter of port smashed, and the light overturned. There had been a brief struggle but it was all for naught. The Justice's throat and belly were slashed. Goga seethed inside. Once again, there had been vandalism too. Original oils on the wall were cut and broken. And once again, no motive was evident other than the murder for the sake of murder and destruction for the sake of destruction—

both capitalist aberrations, which did not belong in the new Romania. He picked up the latest edition of *The Spark* and flipped through it, but only saw words. His mind was on capturing this alien killer. This animal that had no place in his society. He would make an example of him, *asculta de mine!*

Someone was knocking softly on his door.

He turned. "*Cu ce va pot servi?*"

Sergeant Ionescu stuck his head in the door and half-whispered, "The *Viciu-Primar* is on the phone, sir. Line three."

"You answer, Ionescu."

"He wants to know if we have made any progress. What do I tell him?"

Goga planted his feet and threw back his shoulders, an ironic twinkle in his black eyes. "Yes, we have made progress. Tell him we have a lead."

"We do, sir?" Ionescu was astonished.

"Of course. There has been another murder, hasn't there?"

"That's a lead?"

Goga nodded soberly. "It means that the killer will strike again, Ionescu."

"Yes, sir."

The lieutenant glanced at his watch. "I want the division assembled in the *garnizoana* in five minutes."

"Yes, sir." Ionescu closed the door.

Then Goga sat down and collected his thoughts. So far, the *modus operandi* of the crimes was identical. Even the victims were similar in that all three had served the state. Therefore, the murderer was conforming to a grand design not yet apparent. But that wasn't what bothered the lieutenant; he was confident that he would catch the killer, sooner or later. In the interim, he was worried about the effects the crimes would have on his beloved city.

With that thought in mind, he left his office and strode into the briefing room. He sat on the table in front, causing it to creak. Ionescu closed the door and called the roll. Meanwhile, Goga made eye contact with each of his men, affording them silent but respectful acknowledgment. He might be the boss, but they were the team, and without them, he was nothing, and he knew it.

When Ionescu finished, the indomitable Goga began. Quietly, but forcefully, he told them that as of right now the homicide division was a crisis situation. Until the alien killer was apprehended, all detectives would be on duty twenty-four hours a day and could take their shifts from the *sectie de politie*.

There were no groans of dissent—only respectful silence. Every man in the room knew that Constantin Goga was not to be fooled with, especially when he was angry.

Then the lieutenant explained his radical decision. They weren't just dealing with a bizarre multiple murder case involving the personal life of the *Viciu-Primar*. Rather, they were dealing with a crime that could profoundly affect the local citizenry. Fortunately, there had been no official news stories due to the political importance of the victims. Nevertheless, the lieutenant continued, rumors had circulated. He punctuated the air with his cigar. "Rumors, gentlemen, which have originated in the homicide division!"

Some shifted uneasily in their seats. Others coughed nervously. Ionescu looked at the floor, expressing a collective guilt, since he was usually the lieutenant's most accessible target.

"And do you know what is happening, comrades?

The populace is reviving the old superstitions! The folk tales and legends that used to frighten us all when we were children!" He could not resist sarcasm, even though he was deadly serious. "Ghosts, gentlemen! The citizens are murmuring about ghosts! Not only ghosts, but ghouls and werewolves and druids and satyrs!" He got up and paced. "Vampires, gentlemen! Yes, vampires, too. Aren't they part and parcel with Transylvanian sovereignty?"

The men were smiling sheepishly now.

"The next thing we know, you, yourselves, will be exchanging tales of Count Dracula, instead of working for the benefit of modern Romania!"

The room exploded with nervous laughter.

"*Ei dracia draculiu, Gura!*" Goga shouted.

Silence.

He relit his cigar, then issued a stream of orders. "Between the hours of eighteen-hundred and oh-eight hundred, foot and motorized patrols will be tripled. All public figures will have a personal guard. All suspicious people will be apprehended and interrogated. And finally, gentlemen, there will be absolutely no mention of these murders to anyone! If this story gets out, it will be picked up by the Western press, and they will have a field day, talking about ancient demons terrorizing a progressive socialist republic!" He started for the door, then turned for one final remark. "And that will not happen, will it?"

They all murmured assent; they were with him.

He smiled briefly. "The comrade who brings me the alien killer automatically gets his stripes. *La revedere*, gentlemen."

He left the room and headed toward his office. Ionescu followed, pad and pencil poised, ready for the flood of particulars that Goga would dump on him. Neither got that far. An interrogator approached them with professional indifference, although his eyes were downcast and he could not hide an embarrassed smile.

"Lieutenant Goga?"

"Yes?"

"I have a citizen in my office, who was walking his dog in the vicinity of the murder last night."

"So?"

"He keeps jabbering about a beautiful woman covered with slime, leaping into a brown Dacia sedan. Perhaps he has seen an apparition?"

Goga looked at the man coolly and raised his eyebrows, yet contained his growing interest. "Bring this citizen to my office. Immediately."

*   *   *

For lack of something to do, John Ross watched the late news on TV. As he did so often lately, he considered calling Melanie. It was 9:30 in the morning there; he'd probably catch her. He reached for the phone, then abruptly stopped himself, shaking his head. He couldn't bring himself to make the call. Certainly, he wanted to know how she was, but his real reason was to ask her about the demon that lurked inside her. He had that goddamned painting out there in his studio and couldn't finish it. Something was missing, and Melanie had the key, except how could he even think of questioning her when she was fighting for her life and sanity? He felt guilty and cheap. Still, he was obsessed with the painting. He knew that it was by far the best work he'd ever done. He couldn't let it go, yet he knew he was exploiting her ordeal for his own benefit. How fucking ironic that her personal horror could produce greatness.

Muttering, he clicked off the TV, checked to make sure the kids were sleeping soundly, then took a six-pack of beer from the refrigerator and went out to his studio. He sat down on a stool, stared at the magnificent painting, and drank. Although the grotesque was evident, if one looked at it long enough from a particular angle, one could see the impression of an exotic, beautiful woman, which was the effect he wanted. One should be repelled, then compelled, then entranced. He sighed.

The eyes were hollows of white canvas. So was the mouth. And they would remain that way until he could finish the work. Which meant talking to Melanie. Which he refused to do.

He drained his beer and with a cry of frustration threw the empty bottle. It smashed against the wall. Instead of releasing tension, the gesture galvanized him. He leaped up, ran to the workbench, found a matte knife, then faced the painting, breathing hard. Tears welled up in his eyes. The hell with his career! He loved her too much to finish this—this goddamned masterpiece! He stepped forward and raised the knife, intent on cutting the painting to shreds.

The telephone rang.

He slumped and stared at the knife. The phone rang five more times. Finally, he dropped the knife and answered, wondering who the hell was calling him at midnight.

"Yeah?"

"John, it's me."

"Melanie!" He closed his eyes and was flooded with warmth.

"Did I get you up?"

"Hell, no, you know me! How you doing anyway?"

A pause. Then, "Not well."

"Jesus. What does the doctor say?"

"John, I . . ."

"What?"

"I've had an affair."

At first, he laughed. "Come on, don't jive me! Is that your 'hysterical' way of saying you're coming home?" He waited. "Melanie?"

Another pause.

"You're not kidding, are you?"

"No."

His knees gave way, and he sank into the old leather chair beneath the phone on the wall, not knowing how to respond. He closed his eyes and just listened, growing sick inside.

She was speaking rapidly now—between bursts of sobs—telling him that she didn't feel worthy of his love any more and that she would understand totally if he didn't want to have anything more to do with her.

He nodded cynically at all her obligatory statements. The fact was, it had happened; and, in itself, such an event was not unusual, he figured. After all, most people succumb to the wanderlust of their flesh. So she'd had an affair. Really, only one question remained.

"Do you love him, Melanie?"

"No."

"Do you love me?"

"Yes."

"Then we'll survive. Somehow. Some way."

"John—" Her voice was tiny and fearful again. "There's something else."

Another pause.

"I'm here," he said quietly, his heart pounding, his throat suddenly dry.

"I've killed people."

He bolted upright, his eyes wide. "Are you sure?"

"There doesn't seem to be any alternative."

"Are you sure, Goddamnit?"

"No."

"You're not in jail, are you?"

"No."

"Thank God for that."

"John," she sobbed, "what am I going to do?"

"I'll be on the first plane to Romania I can find."

After he hung up, he opened another beer and drank long and deep. So Melanie had slept with someone else. So his wife was a killer. He supposed it mattered, yet he was still on her side. His instincts were to do all he could to make sure she remained free. What did that say about him?

He left his studio and went back into the house to pack. In the morning, he would arrange to take the boys to his parents. As he organized his things, he wondered why he was so detached from her admissions. Why wasn't he jealous that another man had been with her? Why wasn't he shocked that she might have committed murder? He knew the answer—it was because she wasn't herself right now.

Had she become the painting?

He had a vague notion that whatever happened in Romania would enable him to finish his masterpiece. Melanie's confessions, then, were premonitions. Besides, how could he judge her—how could anyone—when she was caught up in something no one understood?

*   *   *

Melanie showered and dressed, then did what she could with cosmetics to disguise the horror that had etched her face. She discovered some gray hairs—she had aged considerably since coming back to Romania. Her dark glasses and large, floppy hat were a definite comfort.

Talking to John had been good, for it renewed her faith in herself. If nothing else, she was still capable of honesty. No more lies, no more deceit. Sullied for so long, the love she had for John engulfed her, making her shiver with pleasure. Smiling, she left her room, went down the elevator and started across the lobby, a spring to her step that hadn't been there recently. She was going to the Brasov museum of history—hopefully for the last time.

* * *

The Hotel Carpati restaurant on the mezzanine offered a splendid view of the lobby below. Constantin Goga sat at a table there, eating black caviar on wedges of rye bread soaked in butter. Occasionally, he turned to Sergeant Ionescu and the citizen he had interviewed earlier and told them how remarkably good the food was; they should eat their *sarmale* and not just play with it. The citizen took an unenthusiastic bite and chewed slowly. Goga smiled and understood. He had made the man nervous because he had questioned him brutally and thoroughly, yet it had been a fruitful session. After checking with O.N.T. and customs, he found out that the only foreigner in Brasov, who came close to the citizen's description, was a Mrs. Melanie Ross. And now they were here, waiting, the first positive move Goga had been able to make since the murders began.

The hotel desk clerk looked up at the lieutenant and nodded furtively. Goga nudged the citizen who craned over the table and studied the lobby below.

"Yes," he whispered, pointing at Melanie as she

headed toward the double doors and the *bulevardul,*
"that's her."

"Are you quite certain?"

The man hesitated. "With the hat and the glasses,
I cannot be sure, but I think that I am."

The lieutenant snorted with disgust, dabbed at
his mouth with a napkin, then pushed Ionescu impatiently. "What are you waiting for? *Era iadul pe
pamint?* Follow her!"

"I don't understand why we cannot arrest her
now," he protested, getting up nonetheless.

"Because she is an American film star, you idiot!
And Constantin Goga is not going to provoke an international incident unless he is certain that she is the
guilty one!"

"Sir, why would the Americans object? They don't
like criminals any more than we do. If a Romanian
citizen were arrested for murder in the United States,
it would not bother me."

"You never did understand politics, Sergeant
Ionescu."

"What do politics have to do with it?"

"They make criminals into heroes and vice versa.
Now shut up and get going! If you lose her, you'll
be in real trouble!"

"Yes, sir." Frowning, the sergeant hurried for the
stairs.

Goga pulled Ionescu's unfinished plate of *sarmale*
over to him, stabbed a forkful and grinned at the
citizen who was now thoroughly intimidated. "My
mother has spent half her life, keeping the pigs out
of the cabbage patch," he said, then gestured at the
food. "But the *sarmale* proves they have a real affinity for each other, doesn't it?"

*   *   *

When Melanie got to the museum, Peter Drajan insisted that they have some tea, before returning to the archives. Since then, he hadn't said a word, so she didn't know if he wanted company or was reticent to look further. She decided to ask, "Why are you helping me? I mean, yesterday, you said it was difficult deciphering the script and translating the bastardized Latin and old Romanian."

He smiled sheepishly. "Not to mention manuscripts written in ancient Hungarian."

"Now you've made me feel terrible."

"Please, no." He blushed and looked down. "Anyone related to Nicholae Razdy deserves special attention."

"Why? I'm not him. I haven't earned the right."

"Has it occurred to you that someone else may be interested in Nicholae Razdy?"

"You?" she asked, surprised.

He made a self-effacing shrug. "It is of no consequence." Out of his desk, he took a folder containing the data they had accumulated the day before. He started to rise, then hesitated and sighed. "Before—before we begin, Miss Ross, I must tell you that I have seen all of your films and I very much admire your performances."

It was her turn to blush. "Why, thank you," she said quietly. "And I don't want to take all your time. Shouldn't we get started?"

Drajan nodded, pushed his glasses up straight, then reviewed the information, his voice a monotone. Nicholae Razdy, the peasant revolutionary, died in 1405 at the age of forty-one; thus, he was born in 1364. Melanie circled the date and made a note for herself. The man was educated, successful, given to philosophic rumination, and . . . privileged? Why would he be privileged? There was a more fundamental question; why was he adopted?

"But isn't it a natural thing for someone to want to care for an orphaned infant?" Melanie asked.

"Not in the fourteenth century," Drajan replied. He explained how cheap human life was during that dark time, especially regarding children. Most women would have six or seven births, of which two might survive to adulthood. Infant mortality could not be blamed totally on famine or pestilence, either. Mothers treated their babies casually—almost with indifference—leaving them on the stone or dirt floors at night with little protection from the elements.

"I can't believe that," she said. "A mother's love for her child is instinctive, no matter what century she lives in."

"How much love would you give a child if you knew that it would probably die no matter what you did?"

Melanie was pensive for a moment. Then she nodded. "All right, I'll go along with that, but isn't it beside the point? Nicholae Razdy *was* adopted!"

"Which means that he was a special child," Drajan replied. "A child of some significance."

She stared at him. "Why didn't you just say so in the first place?"

Eyes twinkling, he spread his hands and smiled, then rose from behind the desk. "Shall we return to the archives?"

*　　*　　*

Not too many days after his seventh birthday, Nicholae Razdy was told by his mother to put away his little wooden knights and dragons; he wouldn't have time for toys any more; he was old enough to work. Then he went out with his father and toiled in the fields. He did so without question because that was the way things were.

Later the same week, he helped his father take a wagonload of corn to the marketplace in Vladimir. While the elder Razdy sold and traded, Nicholae went off to socialize with the other youngsters. He won a footrace and then a battle with wooden swords, yet suddenly found himself an object of derision. The others teased him, saying that he was a freak because he did not have real parents. His prowess meant nothing. He did not know what they meant and was confounded. When they threw stones at him and chanted things, he defended himself, taking down three boys bigger than himself and pushing their faces into the dust until they cried for mercy and he felt vindicated.

Once back home, his mother scolded him for soiling and tearing the only tunic he owned for a trip to town. Mortified, he went off by himself and sat by the forest until the stars came out. Right then, he vowed to spend his life pursuing truth and to help others so they would not feel as alone as he. Finally, he returned home and found his parents talking in front of the fire. After a hush, they welcomed him, his mother embracing him and his father tousling his hair. He apologized for fighting and ruining his clothes, and they forgave him, advising him to forget the incident.

But he didn't. And when he went to town with his father again, the same thing happened, only this time his parents said nothing. After cleaning up in the river and nursing his bruises, he boldly confronted them, insisting that they hear why he had been fighting again. They did, exchanging fearful looks, and he demanded to know why the other boys said he was different.

"It is because you have not learned humility," his father said. "Your very presence challenges others and frightens them. They taunt you and fight you because they are afraid of you."

Nicholae was not satisfied. "Father, they say that I am the son of a sorceress."

His mother gasped.

"Is that true?"

Eyes blazing, his father slapped him, and sent him sprawling. He got up and cowered, but did not weep. "No, that is not true!" his father roared, brandishing his fist. "Does this woman look like a sorceress to you?"

Nicholae wiped blood off his nose and lip. "I have never seen a sorceress, Father."

"Well, then?"

"They—they also say that you are not my real parents."

Startled, the elder Razdys glanced at each other, then turned back to the boy, innocently so.

"Is that true?" he asked again.

His father kneeled in front of him, took his son's small hands in his own and gazed into his eyes. "Nicholae, what has come over you?"

"They keep saying things!" Tears welled up in his eyes.

"You mustn't listen! We are your real parents, Nicholae, and we have always been your real parents, do you understand?"

"Yes." He nodded.

"You must never let anyone tell you differently or you will be eternally damned for spurning your mother and your father who gave you the gift of life."

*   *   *

Melanie and Peter Drajan spent most of the day buried in the *letopisete* and other manuscripts of the fourteenth century, but all they found were a few different versions of Nicholae Razdy's glorious, but brief peasant uprising. It appeared that the man's origins were going to remain a mystery. They climbed the stairs reluctantly, neither wanting to admit defeat.

"What's really sad," commented Melanie, "is that obviously he never knew he was adopted."

Drajan nodded. "It's as if no one wanted him to know."

They reached the ground floor, and Melanie was about to say good-bye when she got a sudden inspiration. "Wait a minute! How good is that computer of yours?"

"It can give you every statistic that's in the archives."

"What if we asked for the year Nicholae Razdy was born—thirteen sixty-four?"

"The director of the museum would probably accuse me of wasting paper."

"We could narrow the scope, though, couldn't we?"

He was listening intently now. "Yes."

"Couldn't we ask for births in thirteen sixty-four?"

"Except Nicholae Razdy's name would not appear."

"That doesn't matter, does it? I mean, since he was given the name later on."

"What you're saying is we might find out if anyone was adopted and then—by process of elimination—we would know who in fact was Nicholae Razdy."

"Yes!"

"It's worth a try."

They hurried upstairs and into the computer room. As Drajan turned on the equipment, Melanie's excitement grew. Her heart was pounding; she was almost breathless.

"Thirteen sixty-four, in the town of Vladimir," he said, working the keyboard. "Births."

He punched the button, the screen lit up, and the read-out component spewed paper. After a pause, he typed in "adoptions," then pushed the button again. The screen flashed several times, but eventually showed only "Xs" and "Os." Drajan frowned.

"Nothing."

"Damn."

He went over, picked up the read-outs and examined them. There were several thousand entries. He shrugged. "I suppose you could attempt to trace each name here, Miss Ross, but quite frankly, it could take years. I'm sure you have other commitments, no?"

Melanie remained staring at the computer screen as if she hadn't heard him. The room seemed to dissolve around her, and there was that symphony inside her head again. For a moment, she thought she was going to faint and then everything came clear.

"What about deaths?" she asked abruptly and did not know why she had said it.

"Deaths?" he replied, puzzled.

"Yes! Deaths in the year thirteen sixty-four."

He threw up his hands. "I dont see the point. Nicholae Razdy was born in thirteen sixty-four."

"Would you mind?" She gestured at the keyboard.

"But why?"

"I don't *know* why."

"All right, all right."

He shuffled to the machine, peered curiously at Melanie over his glasses, then worked the keyboard. "Thirteen sixty-four, in the town of Vladimir . . . deaths."

The computer produced another read-out. Without comment, Drajan handed it to Melanie, and her eyes quickly, intuitively, swept down the list. She did not consciously know what she was looking for. Suddenly, she felt a twinge in her belly and stopped. She pointed to a name.

"There."

Drajan leaned over her shoulder and studied the list. "Veronica Preda?"

"Yes."

He was astonished. "Do you know who Veronica Preda was?"

"She was a heroine who saved the town of Vladimir from a Szekler raid and then was burned at the stake for witchcraft."

He was surprised. "You do know."

"Yes."

"And you say that she was the real mother of Nicholae Razdy?"

"Possibly."

"I don't see the connection."

Melanie shrugged. "She was special, he was special."

"All right. Suppose what you say is true. Why wasn't Nicholae Razdy told about his famous mother?"

"Would you want to go through life, believing your mother was a witch?"

"Not particularly, but by the same logic, why would a witch's son have privileges and, ultimately, an education?"

"I don't know," she said.

He paced the room, pondering Melanie's suggestions, occasionally stopping to remove and clean his glasses. "Maybe ... maybe the townspeople were grateful to Veronica Preda and saw no reason her son shouldn't profit from the one good thing she had done in her life."

"Yes!" she exclaimed. "That makes sense!"

"Except in the fourteenth century people weren't given to charity."

"Oh."

Drajan frowned and looked off, deliberating with himself. "Well, I suppose we could examine the documents we have regarding Veronica Preda." He blushed. "Although, I must say, Miss Ross, your logic escapes me."

Melanie laughed. "Don't tell anyone, but it escapes me, too."

Several hours later, they discovered an unpublished, unreproduced manuscript written by Thomas Adevarescu, a clergyman who had chronicled a sympathetic biography of Veronica Preda titled *Memoirs of a Dark Time.* (Shortly after his work was read by the authorities, he was seized, imprisoned, and asked to recant what he had written. When he refused, he was beheaded.) The manuscript chronicled Veronica Preda's celebrated trial for witchcraft leading to her execution. It reported that while she was in the dungeon of the Vladimir castle, she did in fact give birth to a child, but there was no mention of her infant after that. Finally, Peter Drajan looked up from the document, rubbing his eyes and complaining that the language was so obscure, he was going to need the help of the computer to construct a translation.

"It is getting late, too," he said apologetically.

"At least we have something to look forward to."

"Yes." He nodded and patted the old manuscript. "I must say, I find the fact that Veronica Preda had a child in 1364 remarkably coincidental."

"You don't believe she was Nicholae Razdy's real mother."

He sighed and smiled. "It is circumstantially possible, but I am skeptical. It would help if we knew who the father was."

"What does Thomas Adevarescu say?" She gestured at the manuscript. "Do you have time to look for that?"

Drajan skimmed the pages, mumbling. "I'll probably still need a translation, but maybe there's something here. . . ." Suddenly, he straightened up and frowned. "How strange."

"What's wrong?"

"The last page is missing."

*   *   *

Melanie drove along Highway 73, chasing the late afternoon sun. Intent on the sharp curves and steep grades, she did not notice the beauty of the mountains and forests, softened by a light pink haze. She did not notice Sergeant Ionescu in a cream-colored Fiat with a noisy engine a half-kilometer behind her, either.

She arrived at the town of Vladimir just after sunset and parked her car on the side street, where she and Mihail had eaten dinner on "Shepherd's Custom" day just two months ago. Now the town was much quieter. A few shopkeepers closed up and straggled toward a tavern. In the distance, she could hear an accordion, a guitar, gentle laughter, and then children playing on the steps of the People's Council building where a late meeting was in progress. No one paid attention to her as she crossed the square. Had they looked, they might have seen that her stride was controlled and reverent—more appropriate for a church than the cobblestones of Vladimir.

She removed her dark glasses, swept her hair out of her face and stood gazing at the statue of Veronica Preda. She didn't know why she had come; she hadn't bothered to analyze the feelings. All she could think was that she was staring at a long-lost heritage. True, she did not yet have hard evidence that Veronica Preda was an ancestor of hers, but she didn't need it. She *knew*.

"Hello, Veronica," she said softly, admiring the flowing lines of the black granite sculpture that evoked a timeless duality. Veronica Preda must have been a courageous, yet vulnerable person. Melanie shuddered. A witch too? It didn't seem to fit. Her instincts told her that Veronica had been unjustly accused.

The sculpture mesmerized her, and she felt warm despite a cold breeze. *What secrets do you hold, Veronica Preda? What do you know that spellbinds me six hundred years later?* She brushed away a tear. *Who was the father of your child?*

Melanie sighed and looked away. The street lights had come on, and the sky was a deep purple. She decided to leave, then looked at the statue again, wondering if there were a connection between Veronica's child and her witchcraft trial. Melanie's eyes narrowed. That was worth investigating.

She stepped over the small fence, carefully avoiding the flowers, and went to the statue. She touched the stone affectionately and smiled sadly. *I share your pain.*

*   *   *

His head splitting, Mihail Popescu picked up the telephone, asked the studio operator for an outside line, and dialed with a shaking hand. He was furious because he'd had to excuse himself from an important meeting with Martin Tetranovich, regarding the "look" and "style" of their film. Only he could not ignore the pain.

"Alo?"

"Doctor Schadt?" he whispered hoarsely.

"Yes?" came the melodious reply.

"This is Mihail Popescu. My head is *killing* me!"

There was a pause.

"You must take your pills if you want to be free of the migraines."

"I do take them!"

"Regularly?"

"They make me dizzy! I have blackouts!"

"You must take the pills regularly if you want the desired effect."

"Isn't there something else you can give me?"

"Not without further consultation."

"Can I make an appointment?"

"Of course. When would you like to come in?"

"Tomorrow."

"That is not possible."

"The day after then?"

"That is not possible either."

"Next week?" he asked desperately.

"Next month will be fine. Shall we say Tuesday the twenty-third at five o'clock?"

"Mei Doamne! Can't you see me any earlier?"

"If I have a cancellation, I'll telephone you," he said cheerfully. *"La revedere."*

Cursing, Mihail slammed down the telephone. He felt trapped inside his head. The pain radiated like a hot sun beating down, and he had left his pills at home. He rushed back to the conference room, offered his apologies to a clearly disappointed—perhaps offended—Martin Tetranovich, then left the studio.

When he got home, he ran up the stairs, burst inside and headed straight for the medicine chest. He swallowed a pill, then waited tensely until the throbbing subsided. Sighing with relief, he staggered into the kitchen, nodded at his wife Ioana, then slumped in a chair. She regarded him indifferently, her large, doelike eyes drifting to the melodrama that blared from the television.

"Did you have a bad day?"

"No, I had a good day."

She took a beer out of the refrigerator and handed it to him. "Martin Tetranovich is pleased with you, then?"

"He is *extremely* pleased with me," Mihail lied, then swigged the beer.

"Good." She sat down heavily, and continued staring at the television.

"How are the children?"

"They will be home soon."

"I said, how are they?"

"Fine."

"Good." He sipped his beer, regarded her objectively and tried not to be critical of her physical appearance. She really was not bad looking. In the past he had seen other men admire her. It was just that to him she was so uninspiring. After Melanie Ross, he couldn't bring himself to touch Ioana. He shuddered. What was he doing to himself? He had spit on Melanie Ross! Ever since, he could not believe what he had done, and he hated himself for it. The gesture was so cruel, so unnecessary, so unlike him. He had considered apologizing. Except, how could he ask forgiveness for such an insult? It was not possible. He felt as though he had turned off a light in his soul—extinguished love. He had settled for an average wife and a job shooting a film about the Hunedora steel mills. As the Americans say, terrific. He cursed under his breath. If only Melanie had said yes or nodded or given him a sign—something. Then he could be applying for a visa and getting his passport in order and collecting his things and making his plans and—He scowled abruptly. Perhaps she thought that he didn't really love her.

"No." He shook his head. "No, that's not possible."

Ioana turned. "What did you say?"

"Nothing."

"By the way, are you feeling any better?"

"Yes. Much."

She smiled. "That's something, I suppose." She looked at him as if he were an object rather than a person. "Your so-called sick leave didn't take you to Brasov, did it?"

"No," he snapped. "Should it have?"

She shrugged. "There have been rumors, that's all."

"Rumors about what?"

"Murder."

"What are you talking about?"

"In the market today I heard that three people in Brasov had been killed by some creature or ... who knows? ... There are plenty of insane human beings walking around these days, even in Romania."

"Well, I wasn't in Brasov and I know nothing about any murders."

"I thought you might have heard something," she said, her voice fading as she gave her full attention to the television again.

Mihail went into the bedroom, laid down and stared at the ceiling. Usually, he never gave a second thought to rumors, but his wife's comments about murders in Brasov had interested him.

Suddenly, he leaped up and began pacing. His mind raced. Although he liked to think that Melanie had come back to Romania to be with him, he knew that she had done so for other reasons. She said that she had been cursed. She said that she was a monster. At one point, she even blamed him for her problems! Then she went to Dr. Schadt to be treated for demonic possession. Next, she had gone off on a bizarre quest for her roots like an elderly lady in search of partners for canasta. In reality, wasn't that an alibi?

If there were murders in Brasov, he would not rule out Melanie as a suspect.

Yes, he nodded, if she were capable of becoming a psychological monster—if she were cursed—then she was capable of murder. And the more he considered the notion, the more convinced he became. He wondered if he should go to the police? Why? There was no good reason. Melanie Ross had never threatened him. All the police would do would be to ask embarrassing questions. Then Ioana would know for certain about the affair. They would find out at the studio. His career would be jeopardized. No. There was no reason he should become involved. No good could possibly come of it. He stopped pacing. Or could it?

If Melanie Ross had committed three murders, then that was the real reason she had returned to Romania. The fact that she hadn't left yet meant she was going to commit more. He shuddered. His lover wasn't possessed by a demon; she was possessed by a vendetta, and he doubted that Schadt could cure that. Vengeance didn't belong to the bizarre or the occult. It was a human trait, rooted in reality. Saying that she became a monster was just another alibi.

Suddenly, Mihail slapped his forehead. If she were a murderer, then he, too, was an alibi! Surely that would explain why she had telephoned him when she first got back, strung him along and then rejected him! He wasn't her lover! He was her *excuse!*

He sat down heavily on the bed and stared at the floor, feeling deceived and sorrowful. He had thought his charm was working; he had thought she was falling in love with him; he had thought she wanted him. None of that was true. He sighed and reddened. Humiliation built inside him, suffocating his dreams. Once again, he felt like a shell of a man— an ordinary Eastern European technician struggling to be an artist with a camera.

He stood and went to the window, a habit he had picked up from her. "My dear Melanie Ross, well, well," he muttered to himself. "You certainly have made a fool of me, haven't you? And I suppose there is nothing I can do." His mind idled along, reviewing his speculations.

She came back to Romania to kill. And she wasn't finished yet. He shuddered, wondering who was next. Then he got an idea. The magic, the enormity of it made him gasp. If Melanie Ross had used him as an excuse, then he would be more than happy to continue as one. Of course, he fully expected her to reciprocate by sponsoring his immigration to America. Wouldn't it be tragic if he were forced to ring the police and inform them than his former lover was a demented killer?

He must telephone her soon.

As he left the bedroom for another beer, he shook his head sadly, convinced she had used him; violated his trust. In such circumstances, how quickly love sours. How quickly it becomes a tool for personal gain.

Eight

When Melanie awakened the next morning she was in a good mood despite her problems. Since discovering that she could be related to Veronica Preda, she felt as if she had found an old friend. Her solitude, her murderous compulsions, seemed easier to endure. She almost phoned Dr. Schadt to tell him she had improved, then decided to wait until she had finished looking into the short and tragic life of her ancestor. She felt she was on the verge of learning something crucial. The good doctor could wait.

At the museum, Peter Drajan greeted her with a weary smile and handed her a large portion of the Adevarescu *letopiset*, now roughly translated into both modern Romanian and English, thanks to the computer. She was amazed and held the pages preciously.

"I—I'm honored."

We have become the talk of the staff."

"Oh?"

He blushed and averted his eyes. "Until they saw this manuscript, they thought that something funny was going on between you and me."

She did not laugh. "And still they allowed you to go forward on my behalf?"

"All due respect, but it is not on your behalf, Miss Ross. History is one of our national pastimes, especially when it involves the *Szeklers* and the *Vlahi*."

She didn't know what to say, but it didn't matter, for he had left his desk with the remainder of the manuscript and was heading toward the computer room. There was nothing to do except read.

She opened the folder with a trembling hand.

*   *   *

The church bells tolled noon, announcing that the time had come, but the crowd had already gathered in the town square of Vladimir and was waiting expectantly. Public witchcraft trials were a source of entertainment, sophisticated commoners and merchants seeing them as morality plays. Jugs of ale and spiced wine were passed around. A few minstrels were brave enough to sing hastily composed, sympathetic ballads about the young woman who would be judged, yet the songs always ended praising the church and the Lord. Suddenly, a hush came over the crowd. Then the murmurs grew, changing either to derisive jeers or shouts of support.

Veronica Preda was brought forward, still wearing the bright skirt, loose blouse and embroidered bandanna from the day before when she had been arrested, only now her arms and legs were shackled with chains. The bailiff's deputies led her through the crowd to the edge of the square facing the church. She was told to stand and pray for deliverance, but she held her head high and refused to act penitent. *It doesn't matter what they say*, she thought. *God will protect me. I have done nothing wrong. And if they say I have sinned, then I will tell them I am only guilty of love.* She smiled, her hands automatically resting on her belly swollen with child.

The elders filed solemnly out of the church, looking nervous and hesitant. Theirs was not an easy task. They had to judge a woman who had been a heroine.

When they were seated comfortably at a long table shaded by an awning, the charges were read. Simply stated, Veronica Preda was accused of being a witch, practicing witchcraft, and associating with a sorcerer. In a clear, strong voice, she denied the accusations. They ordered her to be silent.

The evidence was presented by a deputy who testified that when he had arrested Veronica Preda, he had found in her possession evil potions and powders. Then he dropped two small bags onto the table. The elders called Vladimir's most eminent physician to come forward and examine the contents, which he did, while the crowd murmured with excitement. One substance was a combination of ingredients he could not identify; he told the elders he had never seen it before. The other substance was ground coriander, which—as everyone knew—was a love potion.

Veronica Preda blushed crimson and the crowd roared with laughter.

"As if she needed that!" someone shouted, referring to her delicate condition.

"Silence!" ordered the bailiff.

How careless of me, she thought. *I should have hidden it. Now he'll know. He'll think that he started loving me again because of the powder, won't he? It doesn't matter, I suppose. The important thing is that he really does love me again, and I know that he will never let any harm come to me. Just as I will never let any harm come to him. No, they will never know who my lover is, for if they found out, he could get into trouble. I will protect him to the end, and may God have mercy on these misguided souls.*

Regarding the aphrodisiac, the prosecutor argued that love was a divine ordinance and to win it by means of black magic was a serious offense against God and nature. About the other substance she was carrying, he said that since it was not a known or accepted medicine, then she must've had it for purposes of evil.

The elders took these points into consideration.

Then the prosecutor approached Veronica, his eyes gleaming, and demanded to know where she had gotten the powders.

"From a shaman in the forest."

He whirled to the elders, his hands raised in mock surrender. "She admits to consorting with a sorcerer!"

"I have done nothing wrong unless you think that love is a sin!"

"Silence!"

"Gentlemen, she freely admits it!"

The elders took this point into consideration too, now casting frowns at Veronica. Normally, they would have heard enough to issue a guilty verdict, but Veronica Preda had saved the town. She could not be condemned without a full hearing.

The prosecutor was speaking again, this time explaining to the elders the nature of Veronica's "heroic act." In his educated, but humble opinion, while Veronica was in the forest, obtaining the love potion, she was also practicing sorcery and had allowed the sorcerer to cast a spell over her. Said spell enabled her to prophecize that the Szeklers were going to attack Vladimir. "After all, isn't that the way these evildoers work? At first they do something good in order to disguise their grand designs, their plans for the triumph of the anti-Christ!"

The elders paused to deliberate the prosecutor's theory, some frowning, some nodding approval. Indecision hung in the air, causing the crowd to grow restless. Suddenly, a young man wearing the brown cloak and black hat of a shepherd stepped forward and demanded to be heard. Despite the bailiff screaming at him to be quiet, the elders agreed to listen to the shepherd, hoping he could bring something new to the hearing. He introduced himself as Jack the Younger from the town of Bran. He had known Veronica Preda for some time and had never seen her do anything that resembled practicing sorcery. In his opinion, she was innocent and should be released. Moreover, the elders should be ashamed for bringing to trial someone who had saved their lives.

Disgusted, the elders waved the shepherd away. He could not disprove the charges. As the deputies forced him to leave, crowd members were heard speculating that he was the father of her child. Perhaps he, too, should be arrested and tried for witchcraft? No, protested others, he is a shepherd and, hence, too ignorant to practice sorcery.

The scene quieted. After more consultation, the elders agreed that a love potion and a zealous prosecutor's theory—while alarming in themselves—were not enough to brand Veronica Preda a witch. Did the prosecutor have more evidence he wished to bring forth?

Beaming, the man announced that he did, indeed. He signalled the bailiff.

Deputies led forward a small, hunched man with a long beard, thick white hair, and blue eyes that glowed. He wore a ragged tunic and was also shackled. Veronica was visibly shocked, for she recognized him as the old wise one she had seen in the forest.

The deputies rudely pushed him in front of the elders—treatment he accepted without protest; rather, it was a hazard that went with the trade.

"Are you a sorcerer?" the prosecutor demanded.

"No. I am a shaman."

"I wasn't aware there was any difference."

The crowd laughed, delighted.

"You will know the difference come the Day of Judgment."

"Silence, sorcerer!"

The prosecutor gestured at Veronica. "Did you see this woman in the forest?"

The shaman smiled placidly and nodded. "Yes."

"For what reason?"

"That is none of your business."

The crowd laughed again, this time at the expense of the prosecutor.

"You refuse to say why you saw Veronica Preda?" he shouted, hot with anger.

"I subscribe to the Hippocratic oath as faithfully as a doctor, young man."

"Listen to that!" The prosecutor turned to the elders. "Blasphemy!"

While the elders deliberated for the final time, Veronica and the shaman stood together, facing them. Her mouth trembling, she began crying. "I'm sorry! God, I'm sorry! I didn't know all this would happen!"

"There was no way you could have," the shaman replied calmly. "But you must remain steadfast. We are surrounded by evil. Pure evil."

Shortly thereafter, the elders decided that Veronica was guilty of practicing witchcraft and must be punished. Since the sorcerer *qua* shaman freely admitted his occupation, there was no need to try him. He, too, was guilty and must be punished.

Both were condemned to death.

Veronica gasped involuntarily. She was led away, while the crowd broke up, murmuring.

They took her and the shaman to the dungeon in the Vladimir castle, the elders magnanimously deciding that the executions would be postponed until Veronica had given birth to her child.

They put her into a dank stone cell with no light or ventilation, gave her a stool and blanket, put fresh straw on the floor, and then locked the door. She was left to her memories. And from beyond her claustrophobic walls sometimes she heard the agonized screams of prisoners being tortured. She withdrew into herself and tried to merge with her unborn child.

As the weeks passed, an aura of harmony grew around her, and the guard who fed her took to remarking that she might be a saint. He was replaced.

Occasionally, she thought of her lover, and the memories would bring on good feelings. She remained confident he would rescue her.

One day her cell door opened at an unscheduled time, but she did not see her lover standing there. Instead, it was the shepherd, Jack the Younger, now wearing the light mail of the turnkey. She was astonished.

"We must be quick," he whispered, helping her to her feet. "Extremely so."

She nodded and gulped, her eyes like those of a

frightened animal. Then she followed him out of her cell and along the tunneled corridors past hundreds of heavy, curved doors that muffled the cries but not the stench of the wretched. They came out of the catacombs into the cavernous front room and paused while Jack the Younger made sure it was safe. She saw a semi-conscious man left hanging limply on the great stretching wheel. His arms and legs had been elongated, their joints separated beyond repair. He gazed at Veronica, then smiled weakly as if to apologize for his appearance and to wish her good luck. She shivered; his pain must have been incredible.

Timid, she crept across the room behind the shepherd, hesitating at the door for one, final look at the man on the wheel, offering him solace and hope with her eyes. Then she went up the curving stairs and into the small courtyard, where the most privileged prisoners were allowed to exercise. Although indirect, the sunlight blinded her. Moaning, she shielded her eyes and huddled in the stone alcove. Jack had to pull her across the space, and then they were going up another flight of stairs. When he carefully pushed open the door at the top, a sudden gust of wind howled ominously, and he had to hold the door to keep it from banging into the stone wall.

They followed a narrow passageway, rushing now, sensing freedom. Finally, they entered a room, where Veronica had been given a cursory medical examination before she was taken to the dungeon. Now the room was empty. In the distance, she could hear shouts, cheers, and applause. She looked at the shepherd inquisitively.

"They're having a jousting tournament," he explained. "That is why the castle is deserted. We should be able to escape without trouble."

They crossed the room and cautiously started down the great, long corridor that led past the *donjon* to the outside. Suddenly, they heard voices. Jack grabbed Veronica and pulled her into a room, but she lost her balance and fell, overturning a bench that banged on the stone. She scrambled up. They dashed into a small cloister and hid. Flattened against the wall, Veronica gasped for breath, her heart pounding.

"Who's there?" someone called.

Jack slowly withdrew his sword from its sheath and raised it high.

Veronica heard someone coming into the room, then nothing. The silence was excruciating.

A cat meowed.

The person laughed with relief. "You ought to be more careful, cat, knocking over the furniture and all."

The cat meowed again, this time insistently.

"What is it? You want your head scratched? Come here, then."

Another meow.

Cold sweat ran down Veronica's sides. She looked up at Jack. He was trembling, yet remained poised, his eyes locked on the opening to the cloister.

"Don't run from me, cat!"

Suddenly, the cat sauntered into the cloister and looked up at Veronica and Jack, tail switching, eyes malevolent. Puffing up, it hissed at them and backed away.

"What is it? What have you found?"

All is lost.

Bursting out of the cloister, Jack swung at the man, but missed.

"Guards!" the man screamed. *"Guards!"*

Then Jack ran him through, grabbed Veronica and sprinted away, but guards materialized so quickly that they had no chance to escape. Jack fought them off for a while, but was no match for their skill and numbers. They killed him. Veronica was seized, scolded, and returned to her hole in the dungeon.

When the corridor was quiet again, the cat meandered forth, pausing occasionally to rub against the walls as if the castle were his.

In a sense it was.

*   *   *

Constantin Goga's telephone buzzed. Without looking up from a report he was studying, he answered "*Da?*"

"Sergeant Ionescu is calling, sir. Line one."

With a grunt, Goga punched the telephone, his thick eyebrows raising automatically. "It's about time you phoned, Sergeant. What do you have for me?"

"She did not leave her hotel last night, *Locotenent.*"

"There was no murder last night, either." He leaned back in his swivel chair. "And today, Sergeant? Where has she gone today?"

"To the museum again. I have spoken to the director, and he says that she is engaged in some harmless research."

"Which the state is paying for, undoubtedly."

"I did not have the courage to ask, *Locotenent.*"

"What is this research about?"

"She is looking into her past. According to the director, it is a passion with Americans. And that would come from a collective lack of identity, would it not?"

"Save the patronizing remarks, Ionescu! You are more enamored of the Americans than you admit! It doesn't become a Romanian cop."

"Yes, sir."

"You should listen to Tchaikovsky instead of that country-western nonsense."

"Country *and* western, sir."

"Don't bore me with capitalist trivia, Ionescu, unless it has to do with our suspect."

"Sir, she is leaving the building!"

"Stay close to her, Sergeant."

"I will shadow her like a Carpathian druid."

Goga scowled and rolled his eyes. "You go from one form of decadence to another, don't you, Ionescu?"

"I like to think of myself as a Renaissance man, sir."

*   *   *

Melanie left the museum at sunset. As she drove back to the hotel, she pondered what she had read, troubled by questions arising from the missing page of the manuscript. She could not believe that Veronica Preda's story was a simple case of injustice and stupidity. There must be something more.

A secret that Veronica had taken to her grave.

Why, for example, had she been accused of witchcraft in the first place? She was a heroine! The chronicle by Thomas Adevarescu didn't offer an explanation. It also didn't say why Veronica Preda had visited a shaman. Melanie frowned. Obviously, Veronica had seen the shaman to get an aphrodisiac. Still, she was not a naïve woman—she would not have advertised her trip. Someone must have found out and told the authorities. Except, why would she need a love potion at all? She was young and pretty and bright and unmarried and—pregnant! Since the child was a product of love—as opposed to marriage—Veronica's visit to the shaman made no sense. The chronicler, Adevarescu, hadn't been able to figure out the logic, either, so he remained silent. Unless, of course, the explanation was on the missing last page.

Perhaps the shepherd, Jack the Younger (assumed to be the father of the child), had balked when he learned she was pregnant, and Veronica had gotten the potion to renew his desire. Melanie shook her head, no. Jack the Younger had spoken in Veronica's defense; he sacrificed his life trying to save her. There was no lack of love on his part. Therefore,

Veronica had gotten the love potion for someone else.

But who? she wondered, crossing the hotel lobby and riding up the elevator. Then it came to her. *The real father of the child.* A man she had slept with and fallen in love with who was not interested in sharing her life. And he could have been the one who betrayed her to the town elders.

A chill ran through Melanie. As she entered her room, she nodded fiercely, deciding that somehow she would find out who that man was, even though the news would come six hundred years too late for Veronica Preda.

Somehow, it mattered. *I'll write the missing page to Thomas Adevarescu's letopiset myself.*

Suddenly, she realized she should call Dr. Schadt and tell him what she had learned. Hoping he'd still be at his institute, she turned and started for the telephone.

She never made it.

A cramp seized her stomach, and she grunted as the breath whooshed out of her. Hunched over, she staggered forward, then had to drop to her hands and knees. The retching started. Gradually, it became rhythmic as the change took control of her mind.

She smiled hideously.

* * *

Constantin Goga sipped the fine Russian vodka and enjoyed the bittersweet taste. He liked to savor it, a habit not shared by his peers who threw the stuff down in the same crude way as the Soviets. *It takes all kinds, even,* he supposed, *the Yankees.*

His wife came out of the kitchen, carrying a plat-

ter of roast pork. His mouth watered. Right behind
her was his mother (visiting from Wallachia) who
held a dish of steaming corn. Children followed
with potatoes, gravy, cabbage, and salad. Beaming,
Goga got to his feet and hurried to the table. He
started to sit down, but his mother stopped him and
insisted that they all remain standing while she
delivered a traditional grace. Goga closed his eyes
and went along with the ritual. It was the longest
prayer of thanks in his recent memory.

Finally, they were all seated. Grinning politely,
he waited patiently while his mother was served
and then his wife. The aroma of the gravy seemed to
dance up his nose. He reached for the meat.

The telephone rang.

Muttering, he left the table, went into the living
room and answered. Sergeant Ionescu was on the
line, talking so urgently that Goga did not have a
chance to respond. There really wasn't much he
could have said anyway. Pale and shaken, he hung
up and slowly went back to the table even though
his appetite was ruined.

"I warned him! I told him a long time ago!"

"What's the matter, darling?" asked his wife.

"Sergeant Ionescu's car has broken down."

*   *   *

Stoic, Dr. Schadt sat on his receptionist's desk in
the foyer of the institute, the telephone to his ear. A
curious frown on his face, he listened and nodded
silently, then hung up and pushed off the desk. He
had been on his way out the door for the first time
in three days. Now his plans had abruptly changed.
With a reluctant sigh, he glanced up, then mounted
the staircase, heading for the sanctuary of his office.

Somewhere in the distance, bells tolled, reminding the city of Timisoara that it was eight o'clock in the morning.

Melanie Ross had just phoned, desperate with the news that several hours ago she had found herself in the presence of a freshly-mutilated body.

Once again.

Schadt kicked open his office door, mumbling to himself. Just an hour before, he had finally given up researching her strange illness. The solution seemed beyond his comprehension. Meanwhile, she continued to change. And to kill.

He tried to drive that overwhelming news from his mind so he could ponder what else she had said. Ironically, he supposed it helped not to think of one's star patient as a murderer. He dropped into the chair behind his desk and rubbed his tired eyes, recalling the conversation. She had said that she was a descendant from the notorious peasant revolutionary, Nicholae Razdy. Furthermore, she believed that he was the son of the legendary Transylvanian heroine, Veronica Preda, who had been burned at the stake. Really, that was all Schadt needed to know, and as far as he was concerned, his research was all for naught at this point. Very possibly, Veronica Preda was an ancestor of Melanie Ross. So, he had not been wrong. As a matter of fact, he had been waiting for her discoveries to confirm his suspicions. Suddenly, he frowned. If they were true, then Melanie Ross might be in serious trouble. He opened her file again and anxiously checked the dates, nodding soberly. Melanie Ross was twenty-six years old. Veronica Preda had lived from 1338 to 1364; she was twenty-six when she died.

He went further into the file, eventually uncovering the missing page to the Thomas Adevarescu *letopiset* he had spirited out of the Brasov museum some time ago. He reread it carefully, closed his eyes and moaned, "Stay calm, Schadt, stay calm. Nothing is certain until it occurs, especially prophecy of an implicit nature."

He got up, grabbed his bag, and began stuffing items into it. His mind raced, and he mumbled involuntarily, "The supernatural is way ahead of you this time, isn't it? Bah, Schadt! You're researching the pharmaceutics of psychological transference, while the other side rolls along, gathering momentum, moving toward an iniquitous conclusion. You must *do* something!" He heard the door open and close downstairs and knew that Tanya had arrived, so he rushed out into the corridor and—uncharacteristically—shouted.

"Tanya!"

"Are you all right, Doctor?"

"I'm fine! Book me a compartment on the next train to Brasov!"

"Yes, sir."

At the head of the stairs, he leaned over the railing and saw her going through a schedule she'd taken out of the receptionist's desk.

"The Orient Express stops in Brasov, doesn't it?" she asked innocently.

"Tanya, I don't care what train goes to Brasov! I just want to be there as soon as possible!"

*　　*　　*

Melanie stared at the telephone, both devastated and amazed by her conversation with Dr. Schadt. In effect, he said he didn't want to hear about another murder. Of course he was relieved that she was unharmed and safe, but he only seemed interested in the research she had done at the museum of history. What did that mean? She shook her head. Schadt had said nothing about being closer to a cure or an explanation. That left her with alternatives she had already rejected: either going to the police or committing suicide. She bit her lip, determined. Schadt may still be stymied, but she was one step away from solving the riddle of Veronica Preda, which was related to her own enigmatic compulsions.

She remained seated on the bed, obsessively wringing her hands, her haunted eyes downcast. If only she didn't feel so empty, so naked, so alone. She grimaced and nodded. No matter how she felt, she must unlock the mystery of Veronica Preda.

So resolved, she went to the table by the window and studied her notes. She discovered nothing, and she already knew that additional trips to the Brasov museum would be fruitless. What she needed was another approach. *Another museum? There are dozens of museums in Romania.* She closed her eyes and drifted out of herself.

In her mind, she saw a massive gray fist and dwelled on it. Gradually, the image dissolved into a *donjon*, and suddenly she knew what she would do. She opened her eyes.

The Vladimir castle.

It, too, was a museum, and since Veronica Preda had been an unfortunate part of its history, Melanie believed she might find something there. Like another ancient document or even an *objet d'art*. It was worth a chance; it was definitely better than languishing in her hotel room, dreading she would be seized by another compulsion. Yes, she should make the trip; she had nothing to lose.

Except she needed someone to help with the research, should there be such an opportunity. Although hesitant, she telephoned Peter Drajan, explained what she wanted to do and asked if he would like to go with her.

"What a charming idea."

"You'll come?" she asked in disbelief.

"I'll have to ask." He placed her on hold for five minutes. When he came back on the line, though, he sounded deflated; someone had pinpricked his fantasies. He declined wistfully, saying that he had a full day's work piled high on his desk. "Perhaps another time, Miss Ross. After you, ah, have contacted the authorities and made the proper arrangements?"

"Yes," she whispered. *"La revedere."* Frowning sadly, she hung up. *I don't have time to make the proper arrangements!*

Suddenly, she sat up straight. *What about Mihail Popescu? He would know where to find things there, wouldn't he? If he can show me a dungeon that's been hidden for centuries, surely he must know every nook and cranny and relic and artifact in the entire complex! Not only that, he*—She frowned and blushed. The last time she saw him, they didn't exactly part as friends. She felt a surge of humiliation. *He spit on me.* Her jaw muscles worked furiously. If she called and asked him, she would not be able to live with herself. Besides, why give him the satisfaction of knowing that she needed his—help? Her ears burned. *God, after what's happened, does that man still have a hold on me?*

She stood and went to the window, shaking her head vehemently. *No,* she thought, *I don't need his help or anything else.* She automatically went back to her notes, rummaged through them and came up with her blanket letter of permission, signed by the Brasov senior official, Octavian Bogdanovici.

I'll go to the Vladimir castle by myself.

She showered, dressed in jeans, boots, and a summer blouse, then gave her face and hair a dismal, hasty once-over at the vanity. She sighed woefully, wondering if she would ever feel pretty again. Then she left the mirror and packed an overnight case with her notes, dictionary, maps, and guide book.

Before she left, she tried phoning John, but there was no answer. He was on his way to Romania. She was disturbed because he hadn't called to say when he was arriving. Maybe he'd sent a telegram, which hadn't been delivered yet. Or—maybe he was angry and had just climbed on a plane.

That was more likely.

Downstairs, she summoned the desk clerk and did not notice his eyes flitting back and forth as he approached her.

"Are there any messages or mail for me?"

"Not this morning, Miss Ross."

She hesitated, preoccupied and worried, fiddling with her hat and dark glasses.

"Is there something I can do for you, *doamna*?"

"Yes, you can. If my husband happens to arrive, would you please tell him that I have gone to the Vladimir castle?"

"Certainly." He wrote it down. "And if you are not there?"

"Then . . . well, I don't know. I suppose you should tell him to just wait for me here."

"Very good, Miss Ross."

Then she hurried out of the hotel, hopeful that this would be her last journey into uncertainty.

*　　*　　*

Because the man lived alone, his body wasn't discovered until an intimate coworker went to his flat to find out why he hadn't come to work and wouldn't answer his telephone. This fact did not comfort Constantin Goga as he made his meticulous (but unnecessary) review of the scene. The victim was a secretary for the regional Ministry of Interior office (the local political police), and it was rumored that he had been a homosexual. Normally, Goga would have suspected a lover, but in this case, he didn't bother. Throat and belly slashed.

Again.

When the lieutenant left the flat, he noticed neighbors buzzing to each other and was annoyed. In a few more days—given a few more victims—his gag order on the press would be irrelevant; everyone would know about the Brasov murders, including the hungry yellow journalists of the West. They would hound him.

He climbed into his car, started it, turned and saw Sergeant Ionescu standing forlornly on the steps. Rolling down the window, he yelled, "For the sake of Christ, get in, Sergeant! We don't have all day!"

Ionescu obediently moved to the car, opened the door and reluctantly slid in opposite his superior. His voice quavering, he profusely apologized for his blunder the evening before, while Goga pulled out into heavy traffic without looking.

"It does not matter," stated the lieutenant.

"Sir?"

"From now on, I will be following her personally."

"Still, I am sorry that I let you down, *locotenent*."

"It wasn't you, Ionescu, it was your car! Although you should know by now that a Fiat is a piece of shit! Of all the Western manufacturers, the Italians make the worst garbage of all! How many times have I told you that?"

"Many times, sir."

He patted the steering wheel of his unmarked police sedan. "Next time, buy a Dacia."

"Yes, sir."

"That is, if you can afford one after the board reviews your conduct and decides if you are still worthy of sergeant stripes."

*   *   *

Dissatisfied, Mihail Popescu poured himself a fourth cup of tea, then went back into his studio office and stared at the morning edition of *Romania libera*, but saw only words. He could not get Melanie Ross out of his mind. Her green eyes, full mouth, exotic face, dark hair, and alabaster flesh danced before him: lush visions of paradise. Unwillingly, he had allowed her to become his image of an adventuresome future in the West. Ever since they had parted, the idea had grown stronger. And now he sat waiting for a director to review a script with him, where the most dramatic event was the "marriage of nuts and bolts." He grinned ruefully, tossed away the newspaper, picked up the script, flipped through it, then tossed it away, too. He got up and walked around the room, feeling trapped. Yes, he was more convinced than ever that Melanie Ross was his passport to a new life, but he could do nothing about it. He was working! If only he had known what was really going on when he had been with her in Brasov! If only he hadn't left in favor of his recent promotion!

The dowdy secretary stuck her head into the room.

"Martin Tetranovich just called. He isn't coming in today, so you're on your own, Mihail."

"Oh. Thank you." He stood there motionless, methodically thinking of other preproduction matters he could address himself to. He could have lunch, then check out the complement of new Angenieux lenses the camera department had purchased. Except he'd already looked at them, and he wasn't hungry, either. He shrugged and relaxed, realizing he was free for the day. He might as well—Suddenly, he chastised himself for standing there like an oaf. If there was nothing for him to do, it meant that God had given him another chance! He could see her again; make amends. She was almost his before when he had told her that he loved her. Only this time he would have the advantage. He knew what was going on. He went to the telephone, dialed the operator and asked for an outside line. Then he rang the Carpati Hotel in Brasov.

"Melanie Ross, please," he asked in English, automatically disguising both his nationality and identity. Drumming his fingers on the table, he rehearsed his profuse apologies, figuring he would cite the pressures of his new job, his wife, and his recent migraine attacks as excuses for his behavior. One way or another he would get back into her good graces. He had to get to America and no longer cared if she were a murderer. When she was with him she was a woman. The thought of her as a killer—and a lover—made his loins stir, and he smiled. It was going to be an interesting reunion.

"I'm sorry, sir, but she is not in."

"What?" he said, shocked.

"She is not in, sir. Would you care to leave a message?"

"Well, yes. I mean, no. Can you tell me where she has gone to?"

"One moment."

He was placed on hold. Then a deeper, more masculine voice came on the line. "Is this the husband of *Doamna* Ross?"

Husband? Why in God's name was he asking him that? Unless, her husband—

"*Alo?*" Is someone there?"

"Yes," he nodded furtively and tried to keep his voice steady. "This is her husband."

"Welcome to Romania, Mr. Ross! I'm sorry, but your wife is not here. She said to tell you that she has gone to the Vladimir castle for the day."

"Thank you," he said, slowly hanging up and staring off. Why on earth, he wondered, had she gone back there? Unless . . . her next victim had gone to the castle, too. He couldn't imagine she would have any other reason! He exhaled in a hiss and leaned back in the chair. That news was almost as astonishing as the information that her husband was coming to Romania! Suddenly, he straightened up, realizing that if he didn't act quickly, he would miss his opportunity of a lifetime. Once her husband arrived, Mihail wouldn't have a chance to even get close to her. And he needed to see her one more time, offer his love, and propose his business.

He checked his watch. It was noon. If he left immediately, taking Highway 1 and then the 73A cut-off around Brasov, he could get to the Vladimir castle in under four hours. Since they didn't close until five, that should give him plenty of time.

He borrowed a studio car, telling the transportation department, in Hollywood jargon, that he was going "location scouting." Then he left the city, ominously heading north along a wide *bulevardul* through the flickering shade of the lime trees.

*   *   *

When Constantin Goga learned that Melanie Ross had already left the Carpati Hotel, he was unconcerned because the desk clerk also told him where she was going and how long ago she had left. The lieutenant started for the restaurant on the mezzanine to have lunch just as Sergeant Ionescu came hurrying into the lobby.

"Sir, the *Viciu-Primar* has just called for you on the radio. He wants to see you immediately."

Goga sighed, realizing his plans for an excellent meal were not going to materialize. He knew the *Viciu-Primar* wanted a suspect. If he could not tell the *Viciu-Primar* they had one, then the *Viciu-Primar* would threaten him with the loss of his job and pension. Goga smiled cynically. At times, that was reality—even in socialist Romania's second city. To him, the horror of the Brasov murders was that they were a sign of decadence. He doubted that the *Viciu-Primar*, or any other politician, saw the crimes in such moral terms. To them, the murders were merely a political embarrassment.

Only he wasn't worried because he could tell the *Viciu-Primar* about Melanie Ross. He knew that the politicians would be shocked and confused that the alien killer was an American film actress of some renown. They would worry about an international incident; they might even opt for a diplomatic exchange of some sort. Goga nodded. Except this time he couldn't lose. If they did not punish Melanie Ross to his satisfaction, then he would complain at the next meeting of the National Party Congress and call for reform. He would emerge as a new leader with a new rallying cry: *Death to all criminals for they are irresponsible free-thinkers.*

He picked up the telephone on the hotel desk, dialed the *sectie de politie* and asked for the dispatcher to send a car for him. Afer hanging up, he turned to Ionescu and placed his hand on the man's shoulder.

"Melanie Ross has gone to the Vladimir castle, Sergeant. Do you know where that is?"

"Of course, sir."

"I want you to take my car. . . ."

"Yes, sir."

"Go there. . . ."

"Yes, sir."

"And effect surveillance."

"Yes, sir."

"In the event the unexpected occurs, I know that I can rely on you to take appropriate action."

"I won't fail you, *Locotenent*."

"This is a chance for you to redeem yourself, Ionescu." He smiled warmly, but his eyes were black. "Your last chance."

*   *   *

Melanie parked in the gravel lot next to a line of buses, walked to the keep and went inside. In the rotunda, she was greeted by the same guide as before, although he did not appear to recognize her. The heavy flow of tourists was a constant distraction. Handing her a brochure, he gave her his brief spiel, gazed at her breasts, and wished her a pleasant afternoon. She nodded politely, then asked if she could speak with the O.N.T. director for the castle. Fear came into the guide's eyes—of course she could speak to the director, he said in broken English, but had he done something to offend her?

She assured him that he had not. Grateful, he led her through a side door, spoke crisply to a secretary and had Melanie wait.

Once in the director's office, she asked him if she could visit the archives, then showed him her letter of permission. After reading the letter, the director said that while her request was unusual, he could see no harm in it, only she would have to wait for their assistant curator to return from lunch, probably in an hour or two. He hoped she would not be too terribly inconvenienced.

Melanie replied that she wouldn't mind coming back later at all. There was plenty to see in the Vladimir castle. So, as she left the office, she checked her watch, figuring she'd return around three-thirty or four, and if she needed more than an hour in the archives, she'd spend the night at one of the nearby ski lodges and return in the morning.

She started down the great, long corridor toward the crown room, suddenly anxious to see the afternoon sunlight shining through the stained-glass windows again. In a hurry, she didn't bother to look at the large oil painting, which hung in the entranceway.

If she had, she would have seen the likeness of a smug countess holding and stroking a white cat with a gray tail.

*   *   *

Dr. Schadt alighted from the train at the Brasov station and was extremely impressed. He did not take readily to contemporary architecture, but as he hurried toward the main terminal with the help of speed walkways and escalators, he couldn't help admiring the sweeping lines, the flowing curves of preformed concrete and steel, obviously made with great care and skill. The station was clean, too, and well lit from recessed sources not discernible to the naked eye. He hadn't seen such an ultramodern facility since traveling to Montreal some time ago and never one as appealing. He smiled indulgently. Perhaps the beauty of the Brasov station was an omen that good was on the horizon. Was destiny finally in his sway? One never knew, but his stride was buoyant and his spirit invigorated as he angled for the ACR booth to rent a car.

He surprised the girl behind the counter by producing a driver's license that did not have an expiration date.

"How did you get this?" she asked in awe.

"My dear young lady, the explanation is simple," he replied, his eyes twinkling. "Some of my skills have never gone out of date."

*   *   *

Highway 73A intersected with Highway 73 just south of the village of Risnov. Mihail waited at the junction impatiently as a horse-drawn wagon loaded with hay turned in front of him. Ignoring the driver's forbidding, impassive stare, he revved his engine, then snaked left onto 73 and sped away. Soon, he was skirting the vast, pear-shaped valley that once belonged to his family. In the distance, the small farms looked serene and prosperous. Their fields were ripe—ready for an early harvest. A flock of game birds lifted from a grove of trees and drifted toward a stream, where livestock grazed. Mihail breathed deeply, enjoying the fresh scent of pines mixed with just-cut hay, then felt a twinge of sadness. He wished he had lived here long ago. The land would have been his then—the crops, the animals, the ladies even. His. In reality, he was no longer welcome here. This valley was not his; he did not belong; he could not deceive himself any longer. Frowning, he lit a cigarette, clenched the wheel tightly and accelerated hard, trying to outrun the pastoral beauty, the sweet smells, the air, heavy with life. Never before had the valley affected him so; it was like leaving an ample woman behind. He brushed away angry tears, then flipped his cigarette butt out the window. "Control yourself, Mihail," he told himself. "The best is yet to come. Your princess awaits you. And your paradise." He relaxed a little. His mind wandered, and he imagined returning to the Vladimir castle as a long-lost heir. He would demand his title and his crown, then leave this land for the sweeter clime of the West where such grandeur was appreciated. Suddenly, his eyes widened, and he straightened up in the seat. Wasn't that exactly what he was doing? He leaned back, once again satisfied with himself.

A short while later, he saw the sign for the turn-off, slowed down, then swung left onto the access road. He down-shifted to first, and the car crawled up the mountain, engine whining. At the summit, he glimpsed the castle below squatting on its rock shelf overlooking the gorge. The late afternoon sun was behind the massive *donjon*, making its shadow aim toward Mihail.

There it was.

His heartbeat quickened, and he descended into the forest. After winding down the grade and crossing the plain, he drove up to the electric gate and waited for the caretaker to shuffle out and take his money. If the old man were surprised that a visitor had come so late in the day, he showed no reaction. Instead, he opened the gate, humming along with the Mozart that blared from the gatehouse, and waved Mihail through. Accelerating off, Mihail automatically glanced in his rearview mirror. The caretaker went back inside, presumably to continue sitting in front of his radio, alone with his lost dreams.

Except Mihail had not seen Sergeant Ionescu there. Nor did he realize that the detective had recognized him as Melanie Ross's companion and now was on the phone to his superior in Brasov.

*   *   *

After visiting the crown room, Melanie went up three spiral staircases, then down another long corridor and into the living quarters for the nobility. She meandered there for a good hour, becoming so absorbed that time escaped her. She seemed to merge with the relics of the centuries.

In a turret at the far end was the bedroom suite for the men who had once ruled this castle—the counts. She slowly strolled through the main room, pausing to inspect the armor, the embroidered tapestries, and the *objets d'art*, most of them gifts from foreign lands. Clothes were there, too, each display showing the favorite garb (for all occasions) of each count who had slept there. Melanie admired the brocades and silks and wools, all surprisingly well preserved.

She wandered into an antechamber that was sparsely furnished with a bed, chair, valet, and toilet—the timeless rudiments of human existence. The tiny room faced west, and orange sunlight streamed in through a window, giving the walls a warm glow.

She was drawn to a locked glass case that displayed the jewelry of Count Vladimir I. There were many precious stones, bracelets, gold medallions, inlaid buckles and the like, but what captivated her was a silver band with a black stone on which was carved the Vladimir crest. Her heart pounding, she swept her hair back with a trembling hand, and leaned closer to the case.

It was a signet ring.

Below it was a card that had an explanation in five languages, one of them English. It read:

THE SIGNET RING OF COUNT VLADIMIR I

The Count had his jewelers make many of these, for he was fond of giving them away as a token of his esteem and generosity. This particular ring was taken from the body of Nicholae Razdy, killed leading a peasant revolt against Vladimir II, the Count's son, in the year 1405.

Her mouth fell open, and she gazed at the ring. The black stone glittered. She was surprised that she hadn't made the connection before. She sighed, realizing that now she didn't have to look into the castle archives.

Historians had always assumed that Count Vladimir I had shown Nicholae Razdy favor and given him a signet ring because he had done well at a church school in Brasov. Of course they hadn't known that Veronica Preda was Nicholae Razdy's mother. No, the count hadn't arbitrarily bestowed the ring on the young peasant just because the lad had gotten an education.

The count had done so because Nicholae Razdy was his son!

Slowly, Melanie straightened up, folded her arms across her chest, and stared off. The history she'd crammed into her head over the past few days finally began to make sense. She closed her eyes, thinking of Veronica Preda.

I wonder if he gave her a signet ring too?

Nine

Veronica shivered and moved closer to the small fire inside the mud hut with the thatched roof deep in the forest. Huddled there, she watched the old wise one as he worked cheerfully at a long table, seemingly not bothered by the damp cold. There were dozens of urns and jars on the table along with the precise tools and measures of the apothecary. Occasionally, he would take small amounts of herbs from the urns and mash them into a powder with a grinding stone. Then he mixed the powders together, tasted them, giggled devilishly, carefully sifted the stuff into a bag. He repeated the process with several ounces of seeds; bagged that, too, and turned to Veronica, smiling.

"Add a spoonful to whatever he drinks and he will be yours forever."

She took the bags and nodded reverently.

"If he seems to tire of you again, try the other bag, so alternating each until he grows weary of being tired of you."

"Thank you."

"I doubt that you will need all of the medicine, so when you are finished with it—"

"I can give it to my cousin Grendia, whose husband seeks a divorce."

He frowned. "No, no, no! You must dispose of it discreetly! You know how the clergymen feel about me!" Shaking his head, he straightened up, a determined look in his eyes. "And for once I am tired of running from them. I only wish to do my work in peace and worship God."

She automatically crossed herself.

"Come, come, Veronica. I am not a priest."

Blushing, she stood, then gave him a bottle of wine, a shoulder of pork, and a loaf of bread as payment.

He nodded. "Now—leave me so that I may rest and think." He smiled. "And if your cousin truly needs help, you may tell her where to find me."

Veronica started home, moving quietly through the dense pines so if anyone was nearby she would pass unseen and unheard. Although she didn't quite fathom it, she respected the shaman's desire for privacy. Suddenly, she blushed with embarrassment. She dared not tell him that she'd already told Grendia of his magic.

As she traipsed along the twisting paths through the forest, the love potions in her skirt pocket seemed hot against her leg, and she thought about how she had come to need them. She'd always known that nothing could ever come of her affair with Vladimir. He was a noble, pledged and married to another since birth. Veronica was a common lass, a *taran*. By tacit agreement, their rendezvous were secret—she smiled—and sweet. She adored Vladimir; she could never get her fill of him, yet being patient and passive, she would happily take whatever he was willing to give. Mostly, it had been a quick coupling while he was supposed to be meditating alone in the crown room, and usually she found those liaisons gratifying. Sometimes, it was a casual stroll and quiet conversation in the gardens of his private courtyard. Such was the character of their last meeting, the one when she had told him he was going to be the father of her child. Since he had no children by his legitimate wife then, she made her announcement eagerly, hoping he would respond enthusiastically. Maybe they could go abroad and start a new life together, she suggested. No longer would she have to hide part of her life. Throwing her arms around him, she prayed that it would be so and told him she loved him.

Except he pushed her away and turned his back on her. Cold and angry, he called her a wanton slut, saying her child was not his. Astonished, she endured his jealous tirade and waited for him to come to his senses. He did not. Instead, he insisted that she leave and never return. She protested quietly, saying that he was the only man she had ever lain with and thus her child must be his. He would not listen. Rather, he mentioned rumors of her and a shepherd together. How could she even think he'd want to run away with her when she would stoop to intimacies with a shepherd? Then he left her alone with her tears, the emptiness of furtive memories, and a child growing in her belly.

Logically, her first thoughts were about his accusations. Even though there was no truth to them, she saw how they had come about and was horrified. Several months previously, Jack the Younger, a shepherd from Bran, had met her in the marketplace and was attracted to her despite her reputation as a barren, frigid old maid. The same age as she, he had never been married, either, and he wore that badge proudly. She found him charming, and didn't think it wrong or harmful to be seen with him in public. He was pleasing to the eyes; he was a friend.

Except he fell in love with her.

When he asked her to marry him, she cried and said no. Never. He was confused. She said she loved him as a brother. Her feelings went no further. She could not deny her heart; she was pledged to Vladimir. The count? Jack asked, amazed. She nodded and then swore him to secrecy. Typical of the unrequited lover, he declared that he would remain faithful to her regardless, and if she ever tired of her affair with the count, he would be waiting. They said good-bye.

Yet the winds of rumor had it that she and the shepherd were lovers. Even her family asked her about marriage plans and approved of the handsome shepherd from Bran. They were disappointed when she told them that he was not for her. *As long as I can have Vladimir*, she thought, *I will never marry.* But Vladimir did not believe her story, and she realized how powerful rumors could be. She needed something just as strong to get her man back, so she went to the shaman and told him her problems. He listened stoically, refused to judge anyone involved (except to say that Jack the Younger was foolish), then agreed to help her. Now she was on her way back to the village, fervently hopeful.

In the middle of the forest, she smelled smoke and the odors of roasting venison. She came to a clearing, peered through some underbrush and saw horses tethered. Around cooking fires were some fifty Szeklers, weary from traveling. Veronica gasped and sank down to the ground. All her life she had heard about the ruthless outlaws, notorious for plundering villages, murdering men, and raping women. Now they were right in front of her. She dared not move.

For hours, she lay still, trying to breathe quietly and ignore the insects flitting around her eyes and ears. After sunset, the Szeklers passed wineskins around and relaxed. The sentries became casual, gravitating toward the warmth of the fires and companionship. The liquor loosened their tongues, too, and Veronica heard a smattering of lewd jokes, followed by various accounts of past exploits, one brigand attempting to top the other. Finally, arguments ensued. One small and scrawny Szekler, so far the object of cruel humor, shouted drunkenly to an antagonist that he would show them all who was the bravest and the best when they raided the town of Vladimir the next day! They laughed and hooted at him.

White with fear, Veronica crawled around the clearing, careful to make no sound. She knew she should wait until they were all sleeping, but after hearing their plans, she had to warn the townspeople as soon as possible. Once out of earshot, she ran through the forest and across the fields, her lungs hurting, her legs feeling dead. Instead of going home, she went straight to the church, got the priest out of bed, and told him what she had overheard. They went to the bailiff who sounded the alarm. Before dawn, a detachment of knights, foot soldiers, and deputies had mobilized the citizens and built defenses. When the Szeklers attacked that morning, they were routed, and Veronica was a heroine.

She went around constantly embarrassed because she was not used to the accolades. After several days, she even moved out of her parents' house, preferring the solitude of the barn, where she dreamed of her lover and wondered how she could give him the love potion. For lack of a better idea, she took to sending Vladimir anonymous but amorous verse through the post, which went to the castle and then on to Brasov everyday.

Soon, Vladimir's squire brought her a message, which said the count wanted to see her again. Delighted, she kept the rendezvous, bringing her lover a jug of hot spiced wine, which contained the love potion. Vladimir was cold toward her at first and demanded that she stop sending him the verse because someone might find out about them. Namely, his wife. Then he seemed to warm to her presence and congratulated her on saving the town. She modestly accepted his acknowledgments and demurely offered him the spiced wine. He drank without suspicion and asked her how she had found out about the Szeklers. She explained that she had been walking in the forest and had stumbled upon their camp. He nodded astutely and said nothing. She poured him more wine. He drank.

He became gentle and loving, then restless and lustful. Eyes slitted, he embraced her, saying he missed her and wanted her. She almost swooned. He made love to her right there on the floor of the crown room with unusual passion. She was convinced that the shaman's potion had worked. When she left the castle that evening, she was certain that Vladimir would leave his wife. They would go off somewhere, raise a family and live happily ever after. Thank God.

What Veronica did not know was that the wine had left a lingering taste in the count's mouth. At first he thought she had poisoned him, then found himself desiring another woman, which seemed strange so soon after having her. Since he himself had given unwilling damsels love potions, he was familiar with their effect, although he was both surprised and amused that someone would use one on him. Veronica should be congratulated on her shrewdness. Just to be certain, he tried the wine on the daughter of an adviser and when she practically raped him, he was positive what Veronica had done. He smiled. Why else would she have been in the forest?

Veronica also never knew that Vladimir considered her troublesome and wanted to be rid of her. She had no idea that he had discreetly asked his advisers to find out how she, of all people, had known about the pending Szekler attack. Obviously, no one could answer the question, least of all Veronica, who could not say why she had been in the forest. Gossip spread through the castle and the town. Did Veronica Preda have magical powers? Could she see into the future? What had she been doing, wandering alone in the forest, dangerous even for experienced hunters? Everyone knew that evil lurked there; the forest was a place for ghosts and creatures and witches and—Witches?

Deputies seized her immediately.

After the birth of her child in the dungeon, she was allowed to nurse and love the baby boy for a month. As new mothers often are, she was calm and serene, comforted by knowing that through him, her flesh and blood would live on. Her mind and spirit? —they belonged to another place and time. To God, perhaps.

She knew then that she wanted to die. Except for a clandestine love, her life had been mundane or miserable. Surely something better awaited her soul, even if it were an eternal sleep.

They took her to the town square and tied her to a

stake. The shaman was bound right beside her. While the obligatory crowd gathered, men stacked wood around her and complained that the logs were partially green, which meant the fire wouldn't be hot enough. They continued building the pyre anyway, their conversation drifting to women and crusades. Meanwhile, the shaman grew restless, pulling against his bonds and grunting, his eyes rolling. Some onlookers jeered him and threw rocks at him. Sweating, he twisted and muttered, and Veronica could see a faint aura around him. She was amazed and forgot where she was.

After an elder read the sentence and the priest damned their souls, a man called Gheorghe poured pitch over the pyre, then set it ablaze, a vacuous grin on his face. Enveloped by smoke, Veronica coughed and gasped for breath; her eyes stung with tears. When the smoke cleared, she felt heat from below. It was mildly pleasant at first, then became intense and painful. Flames seared her feet. She jumped, bit her lip, finally screamed. The sensation was awful! It wouldn't stop! She writhed and pulled against her bonds, grinding her teeth. *God, Vladimir*, she thought desperately, *please save me before it's too late! Please! I have suffered too much!* She smelled her feet burning and vomited. Her head reeled. Still conscious, she forced herself to hold it high. She looked down on the crowd, now a sea of upturned faces, some pleased, some sickened, some indifferent, some entranced. While others urged him on, Gheorghe stirred up the fire, then doused it with pitch. A flash.

Flames billowed high. Veronica's clothes caught fire and burned off. She screamed again. The fire died down for a moment, and she could hear the shaman chanting in a high, fierce voice. He called upon the power of the good to vindicate him someday. People laughed, so he solemnly, angrily cursed them for an eternity. Those were his last words.

There was an explosion of flames.

Veronica's hair caught fire. She managed one final look skyward, then slumped and with a great shudder, died.

*   *   *

Melanie stood in the antechamber silhouetted by the orange light coming in the window. Eyes closed, she hugged herself and swayed back and forth, her face tense and twisted with grief. She tried to hold back the inevitable tears, not wanting to lose control here and call attention to herself. *Veronica Preda was betrayed! She lived in a world of deceit and treachery, yet was guided by love. And they mocked the passion inside her by burning her to death! Damn them!* She burst into sobs, covered her face and sank to her knees, overcome by the tragedy of her ancestor.

She had often wondered why Dr. Schadt had insisted that she do the research. He had echoed the priest, saying she must find her soul. Well, if she descended from a used and spurned maiden who became a pile of ashes, then she didn't see the point. If her spirit was also rooted in an idealistic peasant revolutionary who was betrayed by his principles—well, she didn't see the point of that discovery, either. What was Schadt driving at? That she had tragedy in her blood? That her life was a predestined horror story?

She looked up and spread her hands in supplication. *I accept that then! I accept I accept! Now please, God, let me forget! Let me be normal again!*

She placed her hands and face against the case, the glass felt cool against her flesh. Her jaw went slack, and—slowly—she slid to the floor. She made no effort to stop herself. Utterly heartbroken, she was burnt out inside and wished that she could die. *Except for the pain.* It was still there, haunting her. She wanted to understand. She wanted release. Re-

demption. And then let the gods do what they want
with her.

* * *

Mihail came softly into the bedroom suite, paused
and looked around, appreciating the quiet. For hours
now he had been distracted—even buffeted—by tourists who made the task of searching for someone
almost impossible. But up here there was no one.
Heavy with anticipation, he peeked into the various
sleeping quarters, looking for Melanie Ross.

Or one of her victims.

His hands grew clammy and his throat dry. He
heard weeping and smiled. So she *was* here, high in
a turret of the Vladimir castle. Fitting. The drama of
the future staged on the bulwark of the past, he
thought, then grimaced at his pretentiousness. Nevertheless, is not history a never-ending death?

He went to the antechamber and looked inside.
She was crumpled on the floor, heaving with sobs.
He glanced around quickly, but saw nothing—no
one—which would explain her sorrow. He felt a
pang of sympathy, but resisting the urge to comfort
her, not wanting to startle her. So he stood in the
shadows and watched her.

When her grief subsided, she slowly got to her
feet, went to the window and looked out. A pink
glow edged her head and shoulders, and a slight
breeze wafted through her hair. The beauty of the
light and the composition amazed Mihail. He longed
for a camera. Failing that, he closed his eyes and
tried to etch the scene onto his brain so that he
might be able to imitate it someday.

When he opened his eyes, he almost gasped, for
the light had changed. Melanie was lost in a shaft as

if surrounded by mist from a waterfall. Frowning, Mihail forced himself to shake off the reverie. Right now their reality was not the stuff of dreams; it must be dealt with. He cocked his ear for noises behind him, but heard nothing. Good. No tourists, no staff members were in the area. He stepped inside the room and closed the door behind him.

"Yes, it is a beautiful view, isn't it?"

She spun around, eyes wide with fear, put her hand to her mouth and backed against the wall.

He raised his hands. "*Scuzati.* I didn't mean to frighten you."

"What are you doing here?" she whispered harshly.

"Remember?" He smiled. "I come here all the time. Perhaps a more appropriate question is: what are you doing here?"

"Is there a law against touring the Vladimir castle?"

"Not that I know of."

"How did you find me?"

"You are assuming I was looking for you."

Her mouth formed a brief, brittle smile, and she nodded. "All right, I'll assume nothing." She paused. "What do you want then?"

He half-shrugged and glanced down. "To apologize."

She did not respond and he could feel her eyes searching his face, looking for a sign, a clue to his intent.

"I had no right to treat you like I did when I saw you last. I had no right to demand a commitment of you." He sat on the bed and leaned against the wall. "For that, I am sorry."

Bewildered, she came forward and perched on the edge of the very same bed, still studying him. "You came all the way here to tell me that?"

"It's not as if you don't hold a certain fascination for me."

She looked away nervously and swept her hair back with a trembling hand. "That's over now," she said without conviction.

He gazed at her. "You know, if you had confided in me, I might have been able to help."

"I don't know what you mean."

He shrugged again. "It is of no consequence now."

"Mihail! What are you talking about?"

"You have committed murder."

She stiffened, turned and stared at him, panic in her eyes.

"You were so clever, as a matter of fact, that I didn't even realize you were using me as an alibi."

"I—I wasn't!"

He grinned. "Come, come, Melanie. Usually when two people have an affair, there are no secrets between them."

"I *wasn't!*"

"Perhaps not, but if the police ever had reason to suspect you, you could have told them you were with me."

"That was *not* my intention! I wanted you around because I *wanted* you!"

"How flattering," he said lightly, then got up and went to the window.

"It's true."

She sounded sincere. Perhaps she hadn't used him. He could have been wrong. She could have been just confused because her mind said one thing, her heart another. She deserved one last chance. And please, God, he prayed, let her choose him. He turned and asked eagerly, "Do you love me then?"

"No, I'm sorry."

He sagged. "Are you quite sure?"

She nodded slowly.

"In that case," he said flatly, "we still have some unfinished business."

She looked sick. "Please. Just leave me alone now."

"Tomorrow you are going to accompany me to the American embassy in Bucuresti to sponsor my immigration."

"No," she whispered. "I have given you too much of myself already."

"Then I have no choice but to contact the police and tell them you are responsible for the murders in Brasov."

"No!"

He turned beseechingly. "You must understand that I don't like being in this position!" He came back to the bed and sat next to her. She shrank away from him. "Only you haven't given me any alternative!"

"Won't you leave me alone?" she cried, moving away from him.

"You could have followed your heart! I gave you every opportunity! Believe me, I did not want to use you as you have used me!"

"Damn you," she hissed. "God *damn* you!"

He went after her, speaking gently. "I don't even want to know why you killed those people. I'll close my eyes and assume they deserved their fate. And I'm even willing to act as your alibi again!"

"What?"

He nodded and smiled, his eyes glowing. "Melanie Ross, I love you with all my heart, but if I have to, I will go to the police."

"No."

"Then you will sponsor my immigration?"

For a long time, she looked into his eyes, and he could see the helpless despair in them. Then she nodded weakly and slumped against the wall. "Yes."

*   *   *

Melanie pressed her face into the stone and wept silently. She had always feared her life would come to this—where she would be forced to make a choice between principle and survival. So she had. She would go to Bucharest with Mihail and take him to the United States and try to explain what she had done, although she knew that no matter what she said, others would see it in a different light. She would emerge as a tired and tainted woman. Her life would never be the same. Maybe that's what the inner voices—that bittersweet theme—had been cautioning her about all along. *John will listen, though. I'm sure of it. After all, we didn't marry each other because we were impatient people. He will give me a chance to explain.* She felt Mihail's hand patting her shoulder and then caressing her back. The very same hand that would dial the number of the police if she did not do what he wanted. Yet, she did not recoil; she let him run his hand in light circles over her back. Gradually, her breathing relaxed and her tears subsided. Her flesh began tingling where his hand touched it through the blouse.

She heard him whispering to her in a low, singsong voice. She frowned curiously, for she couldn't understand what he was saying. Then she realized he was murmuring in Romanian. His voice was so calming, so . . . paralyzing. She felt outside of herself—an invisible observer of a scene both lyrical and ominous. This was a prelude.

He led her to the bed, pushed her down, and lay

beside her. Then he put his hands in her hair and lifted her face to his. "*Mei amori.*"

She went limp and he kissed her. Sighing, she closed her eyes and drifted into him, totally submissive. It seemed easier. She felt his hands plucking at her body as if playing an instrument, and she was mildly surprised. *Why does he want me? I'm no longer beautiful or unattainable. I'm not even here.*

He began unbuttoning her blouse.

No matter what he says, this man is going to betray me. I will be deceived the same way my ancestor, Veronica, was deceived because it is in my blood—as it is in his. History goes in cycles. So does tragedy. Must it be this way? Am I predestined to suffer as she did? What have I done to deserve this?

Suddenly, she opened her eyes and stared up at the ceiling now gray in twilight. *What am I doing?* She rolled into a ball, then quickly sat up, breathing hard. "No."

"What's the matter?"

"My husband's coming."

He snorted. "He isn't here now."

"I can't get involved," she said, anguished. "Not any longer."

"But we are going to America together."

"That's one thing. This is another."

He smiled expansively. "We are not new to each other, are we?"

"No." *Something is terribly wrong!*

"I thought it would be nice if we made love here on this ancient bed amidst the relics of counts and countesses. It will seal our partnership, don't you think?"

She stared at him and gulped, her eyes wide and fearful. *That's how he found me! He called the hotel and got the message I left for John!* She got up and backed across the room, fastening her blouse. "You're planning to betray him, too!"

"What are you talking about?"

"You know!"

"Come here, *mei amori*." He went after her.

"Leave me alone!" She moved away from him.

He cornered her, grabbed both her wrists and pulled her to him, embracing her, trying to kiss her. *He is cold and bestial.* She pushed away and slapped him hard. Eyes blinking, he stepped backward and regarded her with surprised anger. Then he grunted and charged her. She swung a fist and to her amazement, hit him in the head. The blow was light but it caused him to stumble. Arms flailing, he careened into the display case, smashing it and landing on the floor, buried in shards of glass.

"Don't you ever touch me again! Ever!"

Dumbfounded, he sat up, not immediately realizing what had happened. His face and arms were cut badly; blood soaked through his shirt and dripped onto stone.

Hysterical, Melanie ran away. She went down the spiral staircase, two steps at a time, one thought foremost in her head. *I must not let John come to this place! He is in danger!* Yet she did not know why the premonition was so sudden or urgent.

When she reached the ground floor, she dashed blindly toward the rotunda, unmindful that no one was in the corridor. Her footfalls echoed harsh and flat off the walls.

*   *   *

After a long, onerous flight, John Ross arrived at the Otopeni International Airport only to encounter a zealous customs official looking for cocaine smugglers. Then he had to endure the frustration of arranging for a flight to Brasov. (Had he known he was only three hours away by car, he would have driven.) Since his plane didn't leave for an hour, he escaped to the bar, an oasis in any land, so he thought. The waitress spoke no English. In desperation, he tried to communicate with hand signals, but to no avail. Finally, he managed to order a beer by pointing to an empty bottle on an adjacent table and smiling. When the brew came, he drank slowly, enjoying the rich taste and a sense of accomplishment. Then he observed the people around him and recorded his first impressions of this strange land. He detected a national lethargy not unlike his sense of Mexico or Asia. Only here the malaise seemed touched by mysticism, which in turn had been painted over by the reality of everyday communism. He laughed quietly. Already the paint had cracked and the layers of the past were showing through. Some things couldn't be hidden behind a veil of socialism. He listened to a couple talking intimately in a corner, fascinated by the lilting quality of their voices. How could anyone march to that language? Or drive a tank? It was ludicrous. Some people just didn't belong in the twentieth century; their cultural heritage didn't fit. The Romanians were one of them. Making hand signals at the waitress, he ordered another beer and wondered what Melanie's lover looked like. Count Dracula wearing a hero's medal and carrying an AK-47?

He frowned, scolding himself for yukking it up. There was something here that had turned his beloved Melanie into a killer. Something that could also transform a confession into a premonition. Something elusive, yet timeless. Wasn't that why he had come to Romania? He scowled, quickly finished his second beer, then left the bar. No, he had come here to save her.

Except as he crossed the terminal and headed for the *Tarom* section, he saw Melanie as a monster in his mind's eye—the unfinished painting. His monument to the darkness in the soul. Like a camera, his brain focused on the eyes and mouth: three naked patches of white canvas.

An announcement came over the loudspeaker and a flight attendant with a toothy smile waved at him. He collected his boarding pass and walked through the gate toward the idling turbo-jet. Under a fat moon, its silhouette resembled a giant mosquito ready to sortie forth in search of blood.

* * *

Cursing, Mihail cleaned the glass out of his wounds as best he could, then took a sheet off the bed, tore it into strips and awkwardly bandaged the cuts on his arms with fumbling hands. He couldn't get the cloth tight enough to stop the bleeding.

Pale and shaken, he hurried for the stairs. His primary concern was to get away from the castle as unobtrusively as possible. All his life he'd had a great fear of being noticed (and thus condemned), but especially here and now. He would deal with Melanie Ross later—after he'd seen a doctor and gone back to Bucharest.

Once on the first floor, he walked normally and hoped no one would see the trail of blood he was leaving. When he came into the rotunda he was bewildered because it was deserted and he saw her there, screaming and pounding on the front door.

"God, let me out of here! Please! I must save my husband, please!"

Horrified, he thought that surely the O.N.T. security guards would—his head snapped around. There were no guards. Of course. The Vladimir castle was closed for the day.

While he had been upstairs with Melanie, the bureaucrats had shooed the tourists out, set the alarm systems, locked up and gone home to *tuica* and television. *Mei doamne!* What was he going to do? He considered breaking into the O.N.T. office and using the telephone there. He would call the gate and ask the caretaker to let him out. He frowned and shook his head. No matter what he did, there would be questions. Many questions. They would want to know why he was in the castle after hours with a hysterical American woman, not to mention why he was cut and bleeding. They would find the smashed display case and God knows *what* they would accuse him of! Better to find a way out of the castle or failing that, wait and sneak out after they opened in the morning. Except he must find a first-aid kit and dress his wounds or he was going to be in serious trouble long before morning.

He found one on the second floor of the *donjon*, took it out of the wall cabinet and started back for the rotunda, intending to ask Melanie to help him. Then he hesitated because he didn't hear her anymore. The silence was eerie. Before, there had always been sounds of some kind.

Suddenly, it occurred to him that he didn't really know why Melanie Ross had come to the castle. In the heat of the moment upstairs, his questions had gone unanswered. He remembered assuming she had

come here to murder someone, only he had found
no sign of a victim. He frowned.

And now they were here alone.

He ran back into the *donjon* and hid in an alcove.
Was she waiting to kill him? He felt a surge of
panic, then suppressed it, and shook his head. No,
he was being paranoid. Probably she had come to
the castle for the same reasons she had gone to the
museum in Brasov—to look into her geneology.
Besides, if she wanted to kill him she'd already had
many golden opportunities. How could he think of
such a thing! They had been lovers!

Still, he considered not going back to the rotunda.
He could search for a way out elsewhere. Except he
might as well save himself the effort. He knew the
castle well. Unless one wanted to climb the wall
and jump to his death, there was no way out other
than the front door. Just as the medieval fortress
was built to keep people out, ironically it also kept
people in. Likewise, he knew that O.N.T. had in-
stalled a modern security system while making the
place into a tourist attraction. If he could open the
front door (which he doubted since it was bolted
from the outside), he would set off the alarm. Local
guards and police would quickly materialize. He
sighed. As before, he decided to wait until morning.
Meanwhile, he had no intention of bleeding to
death.

Scowling, he straightened his shoulders and
marched out of the *donjon*, ignoring the terrible silence, the early darkness. He crossed the open courtyard, hurried along the arcade and into the castle
entranceway, grateful that there was light there.

"Melanie, I've hurt myself upstairs and I need
to—"

He stopped short. His eyes swept the rotunda. He

gasped involuntarily, and the back of his neck tingled. He spun around.

She wasn't there.

He tried to calm himself but failed. Where had she gone? His heart pounded. Sweat beaded up on his forehead; it ran cold down his sides. He thought he heard something behind him and whirled around again, but nothing was there. Trembling, he swallowed hard, breathed deeply and nodded. He could protect himself. The Brasov murders didn't matter—he could defend himself against the likes of Melanie Ross. But how? With his bare hands? His wounds were throbbing now, and he had trouble closing his fist. If anything, he felt dissipated and weak. He needed something to protect himself with.

A short distance away, across the rotunda, was a resplendent display of a knight's armor. Mihail grinned.

The sword. He could use the sword. He hurried to the display. As quietly as possible, he stepped over the velvet rope barrier and reached for the weapon.

It wasn't there.

*   *   *

Dr. Schadt sped along Highway 73 in his rented car, thinking about having sex with Tanya in order to control his anxieties. He was so involved in his reverie that he missed the road to the Vladimir castle and had to cautiously turn around and go back the way he came. Frowning, he drove up the mountain, then down the other side, straining to see through patches of thick fog that loomed in front of him without warning. Soon, he came to the gate, stopped and tapped his horn lightly.

The elderly caretaker quickly shuffled out of the gatehouse, propelled by excitement. Habitually rubbing his face, he peered at the car, but couldn't see past the headlights. He came alongside for a better view and shielded his eyes.

"Da?"

"My good man," Schadt replied, "a patient of mine visited the castle earlier today and has not yet returned. I can only assume that somehow she had been inadvertently locked inside. Would you be so kind as to open the gate and escort me?"

The caretaker shook his head, mumbled something and jerked his thumb over his shoulder. Schadt looked past him and saw a small wiry man whose face fell into an apologetic smile without effort. From underneath his trenchcoat, he produced a badge.

"I am Sergeant Ionescu from the Brasov *sectie de politie*. Would you please get out of the car?"

Schadt obeyed. Having spent his childhood in South Africa, he knew better than to argue with the authorities. The policeman searched him for weapons and seemed relieved to find none. He straightened up, holding out his hand.

"Your papers, please."

Schadt gave him his identification. The sergeant read it quickly, frowned at Schadt and pocketed the card.

"If you don't mind me asking, Doctor Schadt, how is it that a man of your stature has come all the way from Timisoara to the Vladimir castle at this particular hour? Surely you know that all of the O.N.T. centers close at five o'clock."

"I didn't know that, Sergeant!"

He shrugged. "It doesn't matter. No one gets in or out until Lieutenant Goga arrives."

"But I have reason to believe a patient of mine is inside!"

He smiled grimly. "And who would that be? Melanie Ross or Mihail Popescu?"

Schadt stiffened. He went to the gate, clutched the wire helplessly and stared at the black outline of the castle, mumbling, "My God, she's in there with him? Why didn't I warn her of the man's treachery?"

* * *

Mihail was huddled by the display, shaking with fear, trying to figure out some way to escape.

A clacking noise.

He lurched back and tried to turn simultaneously, but got tangled up in the rope barrier. He fell heavily to the floor and his head bounced on the stone. Screaming in pain, he thrashed until the sensation passed, then scrambled to his feet. Slowly, he turned, alert and watchful. He backed against the wall and edged along it toward the dark corridor. If he hid, he'd be safe. She wouldn't know where to find him—he hoped to God! When he was in the corridor and out of the light, he did not feel so vulnerable. With a sigh, he started forward, intending to conceal himself in the first cloister he could find. Suddenly, he stopped and stared, mouth agape, eyes wide with surprise.

She stood before him, her lips curled in a hideous sneer, the sword hanging loosely, easily in her gnarled hand. Her yellow eyes glowed malevolently. *Mei Doamne!* they were the eyes of a predator! She came toward him, her twisted hulk moving gracefully.

"Melanie," he whispered hoarsely, holding up his hands and shaking his head. "My God, Melanie, please!"

She growled low, the sound inhuman and out of

time. The utterance cut through him, making him cold to the bone, and he could control himself no longer.

With a terrified scream, he bolted and ran.

*   *   *

Melanie was right behind him, running easily, feeling strong yet giddy and light. Briefly, she imagined her feet were winged and she was flying. Then she concentrated on her prey, staying a consistent ten yards behind him. They went to the end of the corridor, up the stairs, and along another corridor. She could see him convulse, heaving for breath. She laughed and enjoyed his pain and fear. *He is from a distant past, and we are at the end of a long, dark road. He deserves to die. He must die!* The urge became compelling. She had to kill him now! She couldn't wait! With a giant roar, she sprinted alongside him, raised the sword, hesitated—trying to decide where to cut him first. She could smell his fear; she could hear his terrified whimpers. She was so close. *So close.* With a growl of triumph, she aimed for his neck and brought the blade down with all her strength.

At the last moment, her prey darted down a flight of stairs. The sword hit the floor, and the shock jarred through her body. She slipped and went down, losing her grip on the weapon. It fell onto the stairs and clattered down to the first floor.

Moments later, she got back up to her feet, but by that time, her prey was nowhere in sight, and the castle was awesomely quiet. She frowned and cursed herself for becoming so overly eager. Now she would have to hunt the man, and she didn't have her sword any more. *I don't need it. I'll tear him apart with my bare hands.*

Cautious now, she went down the stairs, looking

for him—smelling him out. He was here somewhere. He could not have gone far. She would find him.

She reached the ground floor, paused, sniffed, then trotted down the corridor to the first doorway. With a grunt, she sprang lightly into the room, ready to attack. He was not there. She went on to the next room, then hesitated. *Is that a noise? Somewhere farther down the corridor?*

*   *   *

Mihail stood in the cloister behind the crown room, bent over, trying to catch his breath and wondering if he were going to be sick. At least he'd had the presence of mind to pick up her dropped sword. Gradually, his panting subsided. He straightened up and listened, hoping for silence, hoping she'd killed herself up there on the second floor.

No such luck.

There were faint, muffled sounds up the corridor, coming closer. Resisting the urge to scream, he entered the sequestered passageway and hurried to the door and stairs. Going down quickly, he remembered the dungeon. He would be safe there. She wasn't in her right mind now. She had become a monster. She would not remember that he had taken her down to the dungeon a long time ago. He hurried across the small courtyard to the alcove and the hidden door, removed the crucial stone, pulled the latch, and the door sprang open. He started to dash down the final steps, then stopped and frowned. If she did happen to find her way here and she saw the loose stone, she would know. Nodding, he picked it up and pitched it into the black hole in front of him. He heard it bounce and slap against the moss-covered walls, then crash against the heavy wooden door far below. Satisfied, he took one last, long look behind him, stepped into the hole, and closed the door behind him. By touch, he slowly descended the steps and was gratified when he could see the faint cast of moonlight coming up from the ventilation slots in the outer dungeon wall.

At the bottom of the steps, he took up his final position, bracing himself against the wall and pointing the sword upwards. Huddled there, he rested, too, and after a while, became calm. He hadn't heard any sounds above him for quite sometime. His confidence grew, and he planned how he would leave the castle undetected in the morning. Grinning, he was comforted by the darkness. Of course he would survive! She would never find him down here! And if she did, she would be greeted by cold steel.

Suddenly, he felt a stiffness come over him, not related to the damp cold. He slumped, had to drop to his hands and knees, and gag. This time he was going to be sick, he just knew it, he—Moaning, clutching at his stomach, he rose and burst through the door to the dungeon, unaware what he was doing. He turned and looked in all directions, panting heavily now, half-crazed. Berserk.

*   *   *

Scowling, Melanie checked all the rooms, but found no trace of her prey. She paced restlessly along the corridor, angry at herself. How could she have miscalculated and missed him up there on the second floor? Such an error was beneath her; she was shamefaced; her pride was hurt. *No human being has ever outsmarted me. It is a disgrace! When I find him, he will pay. I will kill him slowly and relish his agony.*

Wait a moment!

She stood motionless and listened. Sure enough, she heard a faint thud far beneath her. Then another. Her teeth chattered involuntarily; her hands flexed; her saliva dripped onto the floor.

She tracked the sounds into the crown room, then noticed that the walls were unusually thick for no apparent reason. She grinned shrewdly. Unless some clever artisan of those dark, medieval days had used the wall to disguise a staircase. A thorough inspection did not reveal a hidden door, but then again, who said it had to be *inside* the crown room?

She went into the adjacent room. As she suspected, behind the cloister at one end was a narrow passageway. She nodded with satisfaction, then suddenly stepped back and looked at the floor. Yes, she *had* smelled blood. There were stains, black against the stone, almost dry now. So her prey was injured. Good. Let him writhe in pain while she stalked him.

She loped down the passageway to the door, went through it carefully, descended the stairs and came out on a small, barren courtyard, bright in the moonlight. At first she thought she had come to a dead-end; except his blood stains were here, too, and they led to a stone wall in an alcove. What then? Her prey couldn't fly, could he? Not if he were human. She inspected the spot where the blood stains ended and saw a missing stone from the alcove's side wall. Without hesitation, she stuck her hand inside and touched something wooden.

A latch.

She pulled it. The wall sprang open. Grinning, she straightened up and peered into the blackness. Although she heard nothing, she knew he was down there. She could *feel* it. Nodding, she started down the steps, her hands guiding the way. Shivering with pleasure, she anticipated the violence just ahead.

At the base of the steps was a door with an iron grate, now ajar. She pushed it open and crept into a large, cavernous room lit by dim moonlight. *A dungeon? How fitting, how apropos.* Suddenly she heard a rumble, spun around, then stepped back and gasped with astonishment. She blinked, rubbed her eyes and looked again.

Her prey stood by a great stretching wheel, only he wasn't a simpering, frightened human being any more. He was just as grotesque as she!

She shook her head, not believing what she saw. *Am I looking at a reflection of myself? Has the moonlight made some weird, magical effect?* No, the horrible creature was moving, slowly coming toward her, feinting with a sword, his jagged teeth gnashing.

There was no time for thought.

He lunged at her, thrusting with the sword. She leaned out of the way, but lost her balance and fell. Quickly, he was over her—poised—the weapon raised high, now coming down swiftly toward her face. At the last instant, she rolled, and the blade missed, plunging into the ground. She scrambled up and backed away, snarling defensively. She was nervous, yet alert for an opening, a weakness. He pursued, moving confidently, the weapon waving in front of him.

She touched something with her foot. It was a large stone. She reached down, picked it up, and as he charged, hurled it with all her strength. The stone smacked into his head, right between the eyes. He dropped the sword and staggered back, bleeding profusely, his hands clawing at his smashed nose and forehead. Then he fell heavily to the ground and twitched, making gurgling noises.

She approached him slowly, paused to study him, then coiled and sprang for his throat.

He vanished.

*   *   *

Melanie found herself sitting on the dusty floor of the dungeon near fresh pools of blood but there was no body. Shaking with fear, she looked around wildly, but saw nothing unusual except—

She heard a high-pitched shriek.

She glanced up and saw—or thought she saw—a large bat circle once, then disappear into the catacombs. She shuddered, remembering her first visit to this place. What had happened this time? She knew she'd changed again, but was very relieved she wasn't staring at another corpse. *Except where did the blood come from? Mihail. I left him lying on the floor in a pile of shattered glass, only that was high in a turret. He isn't here, too, is he? In this— this dungeon. How did I get here? And if the blood isn't mine, is it his? Except that's impossible because there is no sign of him!* She glanced up where the bat had been, then quickly looked down, not wanting to entertain that thought. She got to her feet, intending to leave the dungeon, but was distracted. Several yards away, she saw the moonlight glinting off something metallic. She went there, discovered a sword, and picked it up without knowing why. She paused, looked off, and reflected. Inner voices swelled to a crescendo, and she was compelled to go deeper into the dungeon. She walked through the catacombs and entered a particular cell, although it appeared no different from the others.

The melody became sweet.

Tears streamed down her face. She dropped to her knees and crawled through the dust of ancient straw to the wall. With a trembling hand, she felt a precise distance along the base, then patted a particular stone the way a blind woman would touch a lover. With the sword, she pried the stone loose, then dropped the blade, flattened out and reached into the hole with both hands. She found an object and pulled it out. It glowed silver in the dim light, and she was stupified.

It was a signet ring.

In awe, she slipped the ring onto her finger. Suddenly, she fainted, her head smashing into the wall.

Ten

I am Veronica Preda.

Like everyone else, I was born into this world, not knowing myself except for memories of my current life. Now I realize that I had no choice in the matter. I was given this life to fulfill a legacy, a destiny. Six hundred years ago, I was betrayed by a man who spawned rumor and innuendo. Six hundred years ago I was tried and found guilty of witchcraft, but the only sin I ever committed was love. Six hundred years ago I was imprisoned and then burned at the stake. I still feel the awful heat, that terrible, searing pain, and I can remember when I was a child waking up in the middle of the night screaming, convinced that our house was in flames. My parents were good, loving souls, and they saw me through those awkward years, but they never understood. How could they possibly have known? This realization—this proof—is not the stuff of textbook reality. Rather, it is dreams transformed into experience. It is me understanding that I am a permanent part of the cosmos, and that I will see the wonders of the future for many times to come.

Except what has eternity in store for me? Am I to

know who I am only to face death again and again, undeservedly so?

* * *

Melanie opened her eyes, blinked, tried to raise her head, but groaned and could not. It throbbed. She glanced at the ancient signet ring still on her hand, astounded by the discovery and what it meant. Tentatively, she rolled her head back and forth and realized that she was lying on a cot with her feet elevated. She groaned again. *Where am I?*

"Aha," said someone in a heavy accent. "You are finally awake?"

She turned toward the voice. *And who is that large man over there with the black eyes and the face like a rough brick?*

"Please allow me to introduce myself," he said, his English choppy but precise. "I am Lieutenant Contantin Goga of the Brasov police."

"Police?"

"Yes," he nodded. "The police."

With deliberate slowness, he folded the newspaper he had been reading, relit a half-smoked cigar, then got up from a swivel chair and approached her.

"Is that where I am?"

"No, no, no, *Domnisoara* Ross. At least not yet." He allowed himself a chunky smile. "We are in the O.N.T. office at the Vladimir castle. I found you quite some time ago down below in an obscure dungeon. It appears that you received a nasty blow on the head, and—for your own safety and comfort—I did not want you moved until you regained consciousness, although we did take the liberty of bringing you upstairs."

"I—I don't recall what happened to me."

"You don't recall?"

"No," she said, her voice tiny and weak.

"Obviously." He looked away, then spoke ironically. "But I would not worry if I were you. The member of my staff experienced in dealing with such emergencies has examined you and found nothing seriously wrong. A slight concussion is the extent of it. And incredible as it seems, we do have a doctor waiting. Your doctor."

*   *   *

For hours, Schadt had been in the rotunda, but so far no one had told him anything. Long ago he had given up questioning the inscrutable Sergeant Ionescu who was both his guard and deaf ear. Ultimately, the police wouldn't let him see her, but they wouldn't let him leave either. That didn't matter. He would not have gone anywhere, even if he could have. He was determined to make sure she was all right and see her safely out of this place. Castles made him nervous.

He felt responsible and was angry at himself, for he had not expected the police to become involved. Yet, in hindsight, he realized that a fool with the brains of a lizard would have predicted their arrival sooner or later. He sighed. If murders are committed, one should not anticipate the police to slovenly look the other way. One should at least consider them! After all, investigating murder is the acme of their profession!

Unfortunately, Dr. Schadt was not a practical man. And that, he considered to be his most annoying fault. He looked skyward, quietly praying, Lord, if you are awake at this ungodly hour, you have some improvements to make when it comes to my mental processes. Might I have an injection of common sense? Or must I discover how to manufacture its chemical equivalent on my own?

At least she was alive though. That much he knew. But he didn't understand why they were making him wait. Despite his innate fear of the authorities, he grew more and more annoyed. Nowadays, the police acted as if guided by divine ordinancy. No one was allowed to question their manners or methods. Not even they themselves! "Humph," he muttered. "It was bad enough when the priests used to act like that!"

Someone knocked lightly on the O.N.T. office door from the inside. Sergeant Ionescu opened it, stuck his head inside, and exchanged a brusque remark with the lieutenant, Constantin Goga. Then he looked at Schadt impassively and motioned with his head. "You may see her now."

"So soon?" Schadt muttered sarcastically as he strode into the room. When he saw her on the cot, though, he lost his composure, rushed to her side and took her hand. *"Mei Doamne!* Are you all right?"

"I think so," she whispered.

He turned and glared at Goga who stood like a dead tree, his hands behind his back. "If you are responsible for this, Lieutenant, I will file a complaint with the people's council and ask that you be reprimanded!" Then he quickly averted his eyes, becoming timid. Never before had he spoken so sharply to a policeman.

Goga advanced, checking his watch expectantly. "It is almost morning, and there is much to be done, Doctor Schadt, so if you don't mind, please save me the histrionics. *Domnisoara* Ross is a patient of yours, and I am allowing you the courtesy of a brief physical examination. Nothing more."

Grimly, Schadt turned to Melanie, embarrassed

and frightened. This Goga was cool, experienced, and professional. There would be no bluffing here. If he were going to save Melanie Ross from the police, then he would need more than righteous indignation. This was a different, unusual *mise en scène*. Something was out of kilter with the indomitable Lieutenant Goga. Did he owe his allegiance to the city of Brasov and the Socialist Republic of Romania? Or did he serve a more distant and murky authority? Schadt frowned and his skin tingled, a sign that he was in the presence of another reality. He forced himself to remain calm.

Then he felt the signet ring on Melanie's hand and stared at it curiously, wondering why he had not noticed the heirloom the first time they had met. He remembered: *she hadn't been wearing it then.* He inspected the ring and her discovery suddenly dawned on him; he gazed into her eyes, nodding sympathetically. His suspicions had finally been confirmed.

"We have been together before."

"I don't know," she whispered. "So much is happening I don't understand."

Nervously, he patted her hand, his eyes darting to and fro. "Everything is as it was, as near as I can detect," he said softly.

"Are you sure?"

"We are surrounded by evil. Pure evil."

And then Goga was standing over him impatiently. "Are you quite satisfied, Doctor Schadt?"

He straightened up, turned to Goga, and gestured at the bump on her head. "This is a serious injury, Lieutenant! I must take her to the hospital immediately!"

Goga was unimpressed. "If she needs hospitalization, that decision will be made at the *sectie de politie* in Brasov."

"What do you mean?"

"We have some questions for her." He smiled crisply.

"Regarding what?"

"The brutal murders of five respected citizens."

"But surely you cannot suspect Melanie Ross! She is a renowned film actress! She is an American tourist! Yours is the most audacious accusation I've ever heard!"

Goga grinned smugly. "I have made no such accusation."

Schadt blushed at the obvious finesse. "You didn't have to!"

"Dr. Schadt, we do not question people indiscriminately," the lieutenant said patiently. "We have been following Melanie Ross for quite some time. Furthermore, we have reason to believe that another serious crime may have been committed tonight."

"Where?"

"Here, my good man. Right here."

"Bah!" said Schadt disgustedly. "How can you have a murder without a body? There is no corpse!"

"Don't worry. We shall discover one."

Hesitant, Schadt looked away, unsure of himself because he did not know what the lieutenant was up to. Then he asked defensively: "Just who do you expect to find?"

Goga looked at Melanie, his black eyes reading her face, then replied, "Mihail Popescu."

*   *   *

Shocked, Melanie sat up and returned Goga's stare. "No!" she whispered. "No, that's not possible!"

"You two were locked inside this castle last night,"

Goga said, almost gently. "Simply put, now you are alive and he is missing."

"That proves nothing!" Schadt interrupted.

Groping for words, Melanie said, "Then he . . . he must have left somehow!"

"For your sake, *Domnisoara* Ross, I certainly hope so, because we have found bloodstains all over the castle."

Just then, a technician entered the room from an inner door, carrying a stone and a knight's sword, both labeled and sealed in clear plastic bags. He spoke to Goga confidentially. The lieutenant hefted the stone and sword, glanced at Melanie, then gave them back to the technician who left via the outer door.

"Popescu's bloodstains, *Domnisoara* Ross. And your fingerprints." He smiled, bowed, and graciously offered her his hand. "Shall we go?"

Melanie nodded dumbly, her face ashen. She took the rotund detective's hand because she wasn't sure she had the strength to stand. He led her out of the office, across the rotunda and through the mammoth wooden doors she had pounded on so futilely the evening before. The air outside was much cooler, and she shivered as they went down the steps and across the parking lot, their footsteps crunching on the gravel. They had ahold of her arms now, Goga on one side, Sergeant Ionescu on the other. Schadt walked behind them, muttering incomprehensively, occasionally asking the lieutenant questions, which were ignored.

As they walked through the misty, predawn gray, she thought of John and wondered if he were still alive. Nodding quickly, she was still hopeful since he hadn't come to the castle. Maybe his plane had been delayed or maybe he hadn't gotten her message and was waiting at the hotel. There was no way of knowing. Still, it would help if she had a clear idea what had happened to Mihail Popescu. She remembered the large bat in the dungeon and was filled with fear and revulsion. The image was too bizarre and evil; she was unwilling to accept it. Ironically, if that were the only explanation of Mihail Popescu's disappearance, then John was probably safe, and Lieutenant Goga would have an open-and-shut murder case against her.

What if history really is repeating itself? If that's the case, then John is still in grave danger! God, please don't let him become an innocent victim! He doesn't deserve any of this! I don't care if it's too late for me! She closed her eyes and could see Veronica Preda being led to the stake. She could feel them bind her arms and legs. She could smell the smoke, the burning flesh. She could feel the fierce heat. *John, I love you no matter what.*

She looked over her shoulder at the diminutive Dutchman, tears welling up in her eyes. "Doctor Schadt, please—will you find my husband and tell him what has happened to me?"

"Of course, my dear." He trotted alongside. "And you can rest assured that after I have lodged a complaint with the People's Council, I will also tell the American Consul-General about this ... this pig of a policeman!"

*　　*　　*

Goga stopped in his tracks, spun around, and faced the doctor. He was enraged. "I don't give a damn about the American Consul-General or any other diplomats, Schadt! In my opinion, Melanie Ross is guilty of the Brasov murders! She will be tried, convicted, and condemned!" He sneered, his lips curling. "As your decadent French colleagues would say, *fait accompli*."

"You should have the class of a Frenchman, you pompous oaf!" Schadt replied.

Goga pointed at the doctor with his cigar butt. "One more word, Schadt, one more impudent remark, and I will arrest you for insulting an *ofiter de politie*, which, as you may not know, is a crime against the state!"

The doctor backed away.

Goga continued gesticulating at Schadt, wondering if he could get away with slapping the little man silly. He could not recall ever becoming emotional in the line of duty. Why did he hate this doctor so much? He turned away and shrugged in spite of himself. Maybe he was upset because Schadt had questioned his authority. Yes, of course. That had to be it. No one had ever done that before; it was an unsettling, unpleasant experience. He hoped it was not indicative of a new defiant influence creeping in from the West. Then he felt a calming hand on his massive shoulder and glanced behind him. It was Sergeant Ionescu.

"How are we to proceed, sir?"

"You—you go on ahead."

Ionescu nodded, saluted, then went to the Dacia borrowed from his superior, got in and drove off.

Goga led Melanie to a black Zil sedan and ushered her into the back seat. Meanwhile, the technician put his equipment and the evidence into the trunk, then climbed into the front seat.

His hand on the door, Goga glared at Schadt who was hurrying toward a battered Renault at the other end of the parking lot. Schadt had not seen the last of him. Goga would not forget the abuse that had come out of his mouth! He nodded shrewdly. Perhaps now that he had solved the Brasov murders, the *Viciu-Primar* would do him a favor and ask the Ministry of Interior in Timisoara to investigate the political sympathies of a monger in pharmaceutics, one Dr. Fritz G. Schadt. Then Goga slid behind the wheel, but had to hunt for the ignition, since he was still unfamiliar with the Russian automobile and couldn't make any sense out of the soviet symbols. Eventually, he started the car and drove off, tires spitting gravel.

He was anxious to get back to Brasov and the imagined triumphs that awaited him, so he sped up the access road, annoyed that the Zil squealed on the sharp turns. The damned mechanics hadn't put enough air pressure in the tires! Then he glanced in the rearview mirror and admired his prize catch, the beautiful Melanie Ross. How the mighty of the West do fall. She had assumed that she could do whatever she pleased here in the new Romania. Now—too late—she understood that no one gets away with violating Romanian social order.

Soon, they came to Highway 73 and Goga turned right. The sun was rising in front of them, steam rose and curled like smoke off the wet macadam. He eased back in the driver's seat, lit a fresh cigar, then punched the gas pedal, one thick hand on the steering wheel. The Zil cruised like a juggernaut, gathering momentum.

"Would you please slow down?" Melanie asked.

"What for?" he said, irritated. "I thought you Americans were accustomed to speed. They say you go through life like Roman candles, so what is the difference?"

She did not respond.

Goga forgot her and thought of his wife and children. He tried to recall the last time they had been together as a family aside from the vicissitudes of daily life. He frowned. Was it Christmas? Was it that long ago? Although his family never complained, maybe he had been working too much. Maybe his job was so all-consuming that he didn't realize it. Perhaps now that this, his most sensational case, was finished, he should reassess his priorities. He nodded. That would be a wise and prudent thing to do. He hadn't had a vacation since his promotion some seven years ago, had he? Maybe he should take a week off with the family. He smiled. Not a bad thought. They could take the train down to Sulina, where the Danube met the Black Sea. The kids could enjoy the beach, while he and the wife shared wine and fresh black caviar! What a grand idea! He exhaled in a sigh, and his breath fogged the windshield. He leaned forward and wiped it clear with his handkerchief.

They climbed into the mountains, the Zil taking the steep grades effortlessly. The valley dropped away from them, and soon the road was bordered by low stone walls. Beyond were cliffs, jagged rock outcroppings, and occasionally a stunted bush that defied nature. Goga was lost in the dreams of his wife and black caviar. His cigar smoldered in the ashtray, but neither the technician nor Melanie had the courage to complain about the smoke.

They crested a summit and started down the other side. Sunlight glanced off the hood and shone in Goga's eyes. Flinching, he groped for the visor. When he heard a horrified gasp from the back seat, he looked back at the road. The highway curved, and he was speeding straight for the edge! He jerked hard on the wheel, slid into the turn, and accelerated to avoid fishtailing.

Just around the curve a shepherd was leading his sheep up the road!

"Look out, for God's sake!"

"*Dracie!*" Goga instinctively went for the brake, but his foot missed the pedal. Weaving back and forth, he frantically hunted for the brake, finally found it, jammed the pedal to the floor.

Tires smoking, the Zil went into a slide, out of control.

*   *   *

Melanie saw the world in front of her careen and seesaw: the sheep, the shepherd, the mountains, the rocks, the highway, the wall, the sky. Her last conscious act was to grasp the door handle.

The car tipped, then rolled.

The force slammed her against the seat; her breath whooshed out. Then the door popped open, and she tumbled out hard onto the road, arms and legs akimbo. The car smashed through the wall, teetered, then went over the edge of the cliff, bounced off a rock shelf, hurtled through the air, end over end, landed far below and exploded.

Unaware of her cuts and bruises, Melanie crawled through the stone rubble to the edge and stared down into the gorge. Constantin Goga, his technician, and the Zil sedan now were a ball of flames and soon would be a twisted black spot on the rugged Transylvanian landscape. Trembling violently, she backed away from the edge of the cliff and looked behind her, still on her hands and knees.

The shepherd had led the sheep off the road and back up the mountain slope! In brown cloak and wide-brimmed black hat, he leaned on his staff and stared at her, his eyes wide and unblinking. The sun filtered through the pines silhouetting the shepherd. He became an apparition. Melanie thought she saw an aura, a faint glow around his figure, but couldn't be sure because the effect of the sun was so magical. Suddenly, the sky clouded over, and she saw the shepherd's face. She gasped and put her hand to her mouth.

It was John!

She tried to rise but her vision blurred. She pitched forward onto the highway, unconscious.

The next thing she knew, someone was dabbing her face with a wet cloth and pulling up and down on the waistband of her jeans. She opened her eyes, recognized Dr. Schadt and was relieved. Then she felt the stinging pain of her abrasions. Wincing, she sat up and started crying.

"Come, come, my dear! The middle of a mountain road through Transylvania is no place for either you or me."

She nodded, and he helped her up, then led her toward the Renault parked where the sheep had turned off the road. Remembering John, she pulled away from Schadt, ran to the slope and scrambled up it. She ignored the doctor's protests from below and zigzagged through the sheep, curiously docile and silent.

"John, wait!" she cried. "John! It's me! Melanie!"

The shepherd stepped out from behind a tree and regarded her impassively. *"Da?"* he said.

She stopped abruptly and just stared, not believing her eyes.

He was not John.

Rather, he was an old man with a face which was a mystery of wrinkles. *"N-am vedet nimic,"* he said. *"Absolut nimic."*

She wanted to speak, but there was nothing to say. She raised her arm, then let it fall loosely to her side. His eyes twinkling, the shepherd smiled, nodded, then resumed climbing the mountain with his flock. The sky cleared, and when Melanie looked again, the sunlight was in her face and she could no longer see him.

Disconsolate and confused, she turned and went back down the mountain to where Schadt waited patiently alongside the road. "What happened, Doctor Schadt? What happened?"

He took her hand, led her to his car and helped her inside. Then he climbed in the driver's seat, started the car and cautiously pulled out onto the road.

"Will you please tell me what's going on before I go crazy?" she whispered urgently.

"Calm down, my dear, calm down! You must not question destiny or automobile accidents."

"But—"

"Just be thankful that you are alive."

"I am, believe me! But if that wasn't my husband John back there, then who was it?"

"I am not certain of anything," he stated, "but let me remind you of one fact."

"What?"

"In the past, neither Veronica Preda nor the shaman nor the shepherd lad survived, did they?"

"How did you know that?" she asked, astonished.

He smiled. "For one thing, I, too, have read the Adevarescu *letopiset*."

"You were the one who took the last page!"

"Yes."

"But why?"

"Because it postulated that Count Vladimir betrayed his lover, Veronica Preda."

"And you didn't want anyone else to know that?"

"I had to prove a theory of mine, regarding the

personal collective unconscious, a sphere of the mind I discovered while searching for pharmaceutics that could be applied to Jungian psychology," he said evasively.

"Oh." She frowned, dissatisfied.

Then he shrugged. "But right now it is of no consequence."

"What do you mean?"

"We are alive, are we not?"

"Yes." She nodded dumbly, suddenly mesmerized by the signet ring on her finger. It flashed in the sunlight, and she fell back on the seat. She wore the wisdom of the centuries, and she was overwhelmed.

"You are the shaman, aren't you?"

"Exactly " Schadt laughed and nodded

"And Mihail Popescu?" she asked hesitantly "What of him?"

Schadt scowled She would ask the mystery of mysteries, wouldn't she? "I'm not certain " He paused, drumming his fingers on the steering wheel "There are some things I haven't worked out yet "

"Oh."

A long pause. Schadt concentrated hard. There was something he didn't know—something that had eluded him all along. "When   when were you first attracted to Mihail Popescu?"

"In the castle. Last spring. As we left the dungeon. I couldn't let go of his hand."

"What happened in the dungeon?"

"I—I fainted."

"Why?" he asked sharply, his heartbeat quickening.

"Because . . ." She hesitated, then nodded slowly. "A bat was caught in my hair. I can remember his wings beating against my face. I must have panicked."

"Is that all?"

"I don't know."

"Did the creature bite you?"

"I don't recall. Except . . ."

"Go on."

"Last night," she whispered softly, "last night after the change when I woke up in the dungeon, I thought I saw one circling."

Schadt nodded vehemently and sighed. *Bats. They've been in that dungeon ever since it was built. I cursed them six hundred years ago. I should have known. Christ, I should have known! How could I have overlooked the damned bats?*

At least it's beginning to make sense now. Yes, at least it's coming clear. And it's about time, too, Schadt! If your thinking becomes any more methodical, soon you'll be nominated for a Nobel Prize.

"Are you going to tell me what all that means?"

He nodded. "There is nothing left to be done."

They drove along in silence for a while. To the north were the majestic Fagaras, their peaks bathed in sunlight. Suddenly, he quietly told her what he himself had been unsure of until just now.

The story began a long time ago.

When he was a student, Schadt's teachers preached the absurdity of the human condition and the finite nature of the human mind. If someone asked "Why?" the response was always "Why not?" The pedants said that there was no key to life; the eternal questions would go eternally unanswered. Schadt had never been able to accept their views because permanent death made no sense to him. Of course, there was infinite wisdom and logic in the cycles of nature, but why have a being as complex and intelligent as man, if ultimately there were no future for the individual? Such questions led the young Schadt to study reincarnation, which he found fascinating, yet eventually disappointing because no one had ever shown that reincarnation was anything more than wishful thinking. True, there were numerous religious explanations, but all of these invited him to accept their precepts on faith and not worry about the rest.

Well, Fritz G. Schadt was an inquisitive man, a hopeless romantic, an exacting scientist, a sympathetic doctor, and an ambitious intellectual. He did not want to be considered a fool because of his personal views. So he set out to prove that reincarnation was not just idle fantasy. He became so engrossed in his research that after a while, he was convinced that reincarnation was the monolith behind existence, the key to the cosmos.

Naturally, Schadt developed admiration for Nietzsche and Hegel, and finally became a devout apostle of Carl Gustav Jung, eminent psychologist and thinker.

Meanwhile, he established a practice as a physician specializing in psychopharmaceuticology; soon, his amazing research (not to mention a steady clientele from the West) more than paid the bills.

Gradually, though, his work in one field influenced his endeavors in the other. After years of demonstrating that thoughts and feelings were soluble and could be synthesized into chemicals, he finally discovered the *personal collective unconscious*, which he proudly announced was a major step forward, not just in Jungian psychology, but as a way to explain all things.

Simply put, when a person experienced *déjà vu* that was an example of the personal collective unconscious in action. Jung's basic notion was that culture, behavior, even morality were passed on from generation to generation as psychic genes. Chemicals, perhaps. That storehouse of knowledge along with repressed personal events became the province of man's unconscious mind.

Schadt took the theory one step further: if an individual carried the archetypes of civilization inside his head, did that not suggest that he might

have been there? And if that individual could demonstrate he had lived a past life, then Schadt was
correct about everyone possessing a personal collective unconscious. In turn, that explained reincarnation.

For conclusive proof, all he had to do was document the personal collective unconscious at work;
or show evidence of someone recalling a specific
incident from a previous life.

That was why he had removed the last page of the
Adevarescu *letopiset*. If he had left the manuscript
intact, then she would have known that Count Vladimir I was Veronica Preda's lover, without visiting
the castle.

"And I never would've found the signet ring," she
said, in awe.

"Precisely," he replied. "In thirteen sixty-four,
you hid the ring in your cell to protect your lover, a
noble gesture that was betrayed. Last night you un-
covered it and put that betrayal behind you forever."

"I don't understand."

"My apologies. I am getting ahead of myself. Let
me go back, my dear. Let me go back."

And so he continued his story.

As a natural off-shoot of his reincarnation studies,
Schadt delved into his own past and became convinced that he had been a shaman in the fourteenth
century who was burned at the stake along with a
heroine named Veronica Preda. Still, he could never
prove that he was the shaman and became morose
over the unjust sufferings of those innocents so long
ago. For years, he was blocked; his research stymied.

Then Mihail Popescu came to him for treatment
of migraine headaches.

After looking into his patient's background, Schadt
found out that Popescu descended from royalty,

which piqued his curiosity. Guided by his intuition, he traced Popescu's lineage to the fourteenth century and the Vladimir castle, then grew suspicious. Could it be?

Meanwhile, Popescu was in therapy and Schadt knew that his condition was psychic in nature. So he entertained a radical hypothesis: Mihail Popescu's headaches were punishment (by destiny, God, whatever) for past sins. After further investigation, he finally concluded that Popescu was the reincarnation of Count Vladimir I and that the hour of retribution was at hand. After all, hadn't Popescu come to him? To prove his theory, Schadt concocted a pharmaceutic, which on occasion would make Mihail Popescu see himself as the worst of his collective fantasies. The doctor reasoned that if he were right about reincarnation, then Mihail Popescu would know unconsciously those evil souls (himself included) responsible for the wickedness of 1364. (If Schadt were wrong, then nothing would happen and no one would be the wiser.) The drug was also laced with a painkiller for relief of headaches and a memory dysfunction, which produced blackouts and amnesia. Obviously, Schadt wanted his patient to think he was being cured and not to remember what actually occurred. Having a penchant for irony, the doctor called his powerful new synthetic "the powdered horn of the unicorn."

With the drug, Mihail Popescu underwent a psychological transmutation. He became a raving maniac with a mission: guided by his personal collective unconscious, he murdered other souls responsible for those fourteenth-century atrocities.

Melanie gasped. "You mean *I* didn't kill those people?"

"No, my dear, although I must admit that for a

while there you gave me quite a scare." He chuckled. "As a matter of fact, the only reason I didn't go to the police—aside from inherently disliking them—was there were no innocent victims. They all deserved to die, including Constantin Goga, who I assume is doomed to be an authority figure in some future life, too."

"But how can you be sure?" she asked, horrified.

"Your personal collective unconscious led you to the scenes of those crimes, did it not?"

"Yes."

He smiled. "Your psychic totality wanted revenge too."

"So then I had the same—the same disease as he did."

"Yes."

"The same compulsions."

"Yes."

"Then how do you know I *didn't* murder those people?"

"You remembered being at the scenes. He remembered nothing."

Puzzled, she shook her head. "Well, then, why did the seizures happen when they did?"

"In Mihail Popescu's case, they occurred when he took the pills."

"In mine?"

"I'm not sure. Although if I had to guess, I'd say that your transmutations came about when you thought the worst of yourself."

"But if you knew what was wrong with me," she cried, "why didn't you just cure me!"

"There is no cure."

She gasped with horror.

He chuckled. "Don't worry, my dear, don't worry. I doubt that you will be having any more attacks."

"What makes you so sure?" she asked hollowly, her face gaunt and pale now.

"Mihail Popescu won't be taking any more pills." He smiled.

A pause.

"What baffled me," he went on ebulliently, "was how you could have possibly become infected with a synthetic I had personally mixed and given to Mihail Popescu."

"How did I?"

"Bats," he said lightly.

"*Bats?*"

"Yes. I underestimated the power of evil. I hadn't the slightest idea Mihail Popescu could dematerialize as a person and emerge as a bat. Not until you told me what had happened to you in the dungeon."

"But how—"

"Look at your forehead in the mirror."

She frowned at him and started to protest.

"Go on!"

Confused, she obeyed, inspecting herself in the Renault's rearview mirror. After careful scrutiny, she fell back in the seat, her eyes wide with surprise.

"Well?"

"There are tiny marks," she whispered. "Scars. Whether you recall or not, you were bitten by a bat. Repeatedly."

Shivering, she hugged herself and stared out the window, absorbing the revelations. Her fingers dug into her sides.

Schadt glanced at her sympathetically and speculated about her thoughts. The poor woman had been through so much. She had emerged just as much a heroine now as she had in the fourteenth century. But to be under the spell of a man for six hundred years and then to find out he wasn't necessarily human! He shuddered. He couldn't blame her if she was filled with self-loathing. He couldn't blame her if she were angry at him for keeping so much from her. There was really nothing he could say that would have done any good. There wasn't anything he could have done to lessen her ordeal or change the outcome. Destiny held the cards and played the trumps. He was not a principal in this particular drama. He could only thank God and the Fates that they had seen fit to let them have their day in court, so to speak. And he fervently hoped they didn't see him as a philosophic parvenu and decide to deal one more hand. He rather liked having a door to the supernatural.

And beyond.

*   *   *

Melanie gazed out the window at the mountains and trees, feeling flat and detached. The occasional stands of beech and alder amidst the evergreen forests still impressed her. Then she saw a patch of white and scarlet wildflowers. The shock of color startled her, and as they drove past, she looked back wistfully. Finally, she turned forward and reflected. After all that had happened, she was amazed she could see beauty. The trees, the mountains, the fields, the sky, the road even. Beauty was all around her. She smiled. *Is the human spirit so resilient?* She closed her eyes so she could visualize the flowers again.

She saw bats.

Velvet wings brushing her body. Minuscule teeth slicing her flesh. Tiny claws scratching her urgently. She could smell the ancient dust of the dungeon floor. *Am I to remain a prisoner of darkness? Doomed to dream of horrors? God, set me free! Give me release! There is nothing left for me to know!* Tears rolled down her face. *I do not want nor need largess. I will be infinitely happy with the touch of a soft breeze, the sound of laughter, the simplicity of a flower.* She felt Dr. Schadt pat her leg and glanced at him.

"Your ordeal is over."

"Yes."

"But there are moments of terror ahead. Nothing changes instantly. Your nightmares will fade away gradually just as your dreams will become reality slowly."

He nodded. "Such is the work of destiny."

She relaxed, her head lolling back on the seat. She felt empty and giddy and—she frowned. Not yet free. Something restrained her, enveloped her—something implacable.

Schadt turned off the highway, and Melanie realized suddenly that he had not taken her back to Brasov. The battered Renault was chugging down the narrow, cobblestoned streets of Vladimir, the doctor peering over the steering wheel, intent, trying to hide a half-smile and a twinkle in his eye.

Surprised, she asked, "Why are we coming here?"

"Don't you want to find your husband?"

"He's in Vladimir?"

"If I were him and it were my first trip to Romania, I certainly wouldn't want to spend my time lollygagging about in a hotel lobby."

"But how do you know he's here?"

The enigmatic Schadt shrugged expansively. "I don't."

*   *   *

John Ross had been gazing at the statue of Veronica Preda ever since arriving in this quaint, but unfamiliar town square early in the morning.

After his flight had been inexplicably diverted to another city, then allowed to proceed, he'd finally made it to Brasov around two A.M. only to learn that Melanie had gone to a castle named Vladimir and hadn't yet returned. Concerned, he telephoned the castle, but got no answer. Then he quizzed the recalcitrant night clerk who told him in halting English that frequently tourists stayed at nearby mountain chalets when they visited castles to avoid the long round-trip from the city. Since he had no desire to wait in Brasov, John figured he'd do likewise. Despite the clerk's astonishment, John insisted that he telephone the resident ACR agent. No, he didn't care how late it was. When the man sleepily came downstairs, John said he wanted to rent a car immediately. No, he could not wait until the office opened at nine. Instead of arguing, the agent complied with that timeless, acquiescent laze common to native Transylvanians.

After tracing out his route on a map, John set out for the castle, driving carefully along the twisting, precarious Highway 73. Worried, he hoped that Melanie was all right, then wondered why he hadn't come to Romania sooner. Was he motivated purely by Melanie's affair? He frowned and hoped he was a bigger person than that. Then he shrugged. Reasons weren't important. He loved her, he was here, and he wanted to be with her.

Suddenly, he got tired. His head nodded and his eyes kept closing. Sleep was coming over him like a drug; he was powerless to stop it. He had the good sense to pull off the road and doze, although curiously, he didn't consciously remember doing it. When he finally got to the castle, it was dawn, and the caretaker steadfastly refused to open the gate until normal visiting hours. John asked him about nearby chalets, but the old man just mumbled sententiously in Romanian. There was nothing John could do but wait. Rather than go back to Brasov, he drove to the closest town, intending to phone the Carpati Hotel, leave a message for Melanie and then eat some breakfast.

Except he saw the statue first.

Saving his own unfinished painting at home, he could not recall having ever been so captivated by a work of art. That included his exposure to the great masterpieces while in art school. He guessed it was because the statue resembled an abstract likeness of Melanie, except it did not have the alienation of Surrealism. Rather, there was just enough Impressionism and emotion to give the work a mystical quality. John concluded that it could be any exotically beautiful woman.

He read the artist's name off the plaque on the pedestal, but it was no one of fortune or fame. An obscure sculptor had done this piece and yet it had to be the most perfect work of art John Ross had ever seen.

The church bells rang. Disturbed, cuckoo birds flew out of the belfry. John was not distracted; for him, Veronica seemed to smile.

* * *

"There he is!" Melanie cried, turning to Schadt, amazed. "You were right! He's in the square, looking at the statue!"

Schadt parked on the side street next to the People's Council offices. Melanie started to get out of the car, but the doctor restrained her.

"My dear, you must remember that he probably

knows nothing about the astonishing chain of events you and I have been caught up in."

She nodded. "Yes."

"You must be gentle with him."

"I understand."

"Explain things to him slowly so that he might appreciate and savor your courage as well as his own."

She looked down and blushed, thinking that she didn't deserve his praise.

"I do not mean to imply, however, that you should dally here in Romania. At this particular time, a sojourn in another place might be more prudent."

"What do you mean?'

He brushed off the sleeves of his coat for no apparent reason. "There is no way of knowing how long it will take the Brasov police to sift through the wreckage of Lieutenant Goga's automobile and discover that you weren't killed in the unfortunate accident."

She gulped and nodded, then got out of the car and started across the square. Suddenly, she stopped and turned back to Schadt, who was standing on the sidewalk now. "Thanks," she said softly.

He waved at her impatiently and did not bother to look up. An orange alley cat had found him and was rubbing against his legs. Preoccupied, the doctor scratched the cat's head and stroked its sides, mouthing sweet nothings. Ecstatic, the cat rolled on the cobblestones, and Schadt went to one knee. Soon, man and cat were nuzzling each other, and from a distance, the pair appeared inseparable and quite delighted they'd crossed paths.

Melanie went to John. He saw her and gasped with surprise, but before he could speak, she was embracing him tightly. They swayed together in front of the statue, whispering endearments.

"I'm glad I came. I mean, I don't want to get in the way, but it's great to see that you're all right. I've been worried about you."

She nodded, her eyes downcast. Suddenly, she was embarrassed and didn't know what to say; guilt surged through her, making her knees weak. Then she shook her head and forced herself to look at him. "John, I'm sorry."

"Okay."

"It's over. All of it."

"You don't have to say anything, Melanie. Really."

She sighed and fell against him, her hands flat on his chest. Still, something was wrong. This closeness, this mutual tenderness seemed forced, and she was confused. Had too much damage been done to their relationship? One couldn't help but wonder. Only now wasn't the time to think of that. She pushed away from him, then took his hand.

"I want you to meet Doctor Schadt." She led him to the edge of the square.

Dr. Schadt and the orange cat had vanished in the Renault.

Melanie was crestfallen. "He left! He didn't even give me a chance to say good-bye!"

"Maybe you can call him when we get back to the hotel," John suggested.

Except she hadn't heard. Moaning, she hurried away from him, shocked and terrified.

She felt those stirrings again.

Nausea churned in her belly; she became dizzy. Panicked, she fought the impulse to retch, but could not control herself.

"Melanie? Melanie, what are you doing?"

She shook her head, then tried to warn him to

stay away from her, to run, to get out of her life before she ruined him, for she was doomed. Condemned by the fates. Dr. Schadt was gone and she couldn't stop the seizure! Her hands flexed like claws. Her teeth chattered and clacked. *My God, the horror! I feel awful!*

She dropped to her hands and knees in front of the statue of Veronica Preda, her stomach heaving. Soon she would be riding the crest. Soon she would be that disgusting creature from the depths of her psyche. Soon she would have amazing prowess and strength. Soon she would lust to kill.

John.

Please, no! Don't let this happen! Don't let me do this!

Suddenly she saw the signet ring on her finger, the black stone glittering. She crawled through the flowers to the statue, got up, took the ring off her hand and slipped it onto one graceful, delicate finger of black granite.

The compulsion passed.

Gasping, she fell back and collapsed in the flowers. *Take my melancholy, Veronica, take my sorrow. Take my darkness. Sprinkle those ashes in the winds of remembrance and let them mingle with the ancient dust of the centuries. I have fulfilled you and now we are both free. Sweet release, Veronica. We have sweet release.*

"Good-bye, Veronica," she whispered.

"Are you all right?" said John anxiously, kneeling beside her.

She nodded, her eyes brimming with tears, her lips trembling.

"What happened?"

"I—I don't know."

He gave her a strange look, then helped her up.

They walked slowly toward his rented car. He held her hand tightly.

"You sure you're feeling all right?"

"Yes."

"Good. I'll try not to worry. I'll try to believe you."

They walked in silence.

He gestured over his shoulder. "You know, I think that statue is one of the most beautiful works of art I've ever seen."

Her heart sang. She swept her hair out of her face and smiled devilishly. "You mean I've got competition now?"

Epilogue

At the edge of the square, John half-turned for one last glance at the statue. Astonished, he stopped, shook his head, then looked again. *No,* he thought, *that can't be! That's not possible!*

But it was.

In his eyes, Veronica Preda now resembled the painting of Melanie as a psychological demon. He nodded slowly, continuing to stare at it, etching the vision into his brain He saw the eyes and mouth. Finally. They were there in complete, awful detail. Now he could finish his own work. He knew instantly what colors to mix and even what brushes to use

He started to ask why but inner voices told him not to question the amazing sight. Wisely, he nodded and just accepted it as a unique, albeit strange manifestation of the creative process.

Mind spinning, he turned to the car and held the passenger door for her. Then he walked around, got in the driver's side and slid behind the wheel. She was smiling at him radiantly.

A smile of his own crept across his face. Maybe there were two masterpieces in his soul. Maybe when he finished the one at home, he'd paint a portrait of the most beautiful woman in the world.

What would he title them?

He had already decided to call the first one *Veronica*, given the inspiration just received from her statue. The second masterpiece he would name *Melanie*.

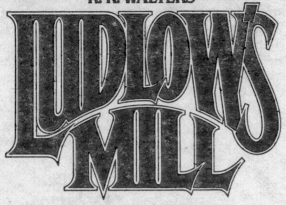

A KISS ON EACH CHEEK

Donald De Simone

Not since *The Godfather* has there been such an explosive novel of passion and betrayal, terror and suspense—written by an insider. Driven by fear to live under a new identity in an undisclosed U.S. city, Donald De Simone has written an explosive novel of life with the Mob—the sweet-savage world where loyalty is sealed in blood...where revenge is swift and merciless...where *A Kiss on Each Cheek* is the kiss of death.

☐ 40-469-7   A KISS ON EACH CHEEK $2.95